THE DECISION TREE

Elisa,
Who decides what really matters and creates the path to feeling appreciated for opening through conscious decisions? Nancy imagine knowing all you do is lovingly supported and the clearest way to— well, whatever you choose choose well!
Ken Friedman

A Novel by Ken Friedman

Published by Heart Publishing
Distributed By Adams Publishing Company,
Rainier, Washington

Published by
Heart Publishing
Distributed By Adams Publishing Company
PO Box 993
Rainier, WA 98576

Printed in the United States of America

First edition, 1996

"Library of Congress Catalog Card Number:" 96-94593
Friedman, Ken
The Decision Tree
I. Title

ISBN 0-9615868-6-9

"Love thy neighbor as thyself"
- Leviticus

"Know thyself"

"We are such stuff as dreams are made."
- Shakespeare, The Tempest

"Eternal energy is born out of infinity and is omnipresent."
- Eastern philosophy

Dedicated to all my neighbors.
When you wish upon a star, may all your dreams come true!
Love,
"ma mi"

Chapter One

The room was empty when I arrived, but the light through the windows brightened the small banquet room. I sat in the last row of chairs reviewing my notes while waiting for a woman who looked like she was looking for me.

I was certain my co-leader would arrive early so we could decide basic details like which one of us would start, and whether to take questions during our talks or at the end. Our only interaction had been through a friend of mine, Tanya, who had been a student and research assistant where I taught. She had relayed "where and when" information for our presentation, but instructed that essentially we should each prepare twenty minutes on our own topics and smile.

* * *

One Sunday Tanya and her friend co-worker came for brunch and to see my jazz trio perform at the popular restaurant/club Zanzibar Blue.

I had just finished a set and stopped at the bar for a freshly squeezed orange juice.

After a quick "thanks" to an appreciative couple and my usual invitation to come again sometime, I saw Tanya waving to me. I made my way through the room and borrowed a free chair from the people adjacent to her table. She introduced me to Rose, who was with her, and then we began catching up on each other's highlights from the past year.

After about five minutes she switched to the business

reason she was there. "Phil, the public relations firm we're working for is promoting a weekend Expo at a hotel here in center city Philadelphia called Quality of Life."

"I'm getting the impression you dreamed up some part for me."

"Yes, I guess I was too obvious?"

"A little, but what do you have in mind?"

"The workshop we created for you is called Life's Vibrations Through Colors and Sounds. The idea is to combine a presentation about music, led by you, with one about colors, led by a professional artist/artists' agent."

I had hesitated as though I was considering. "Sounds interesting. Okay, first I'll agree to do it, since you're a friend, but now, give me some details."

"Oh, thanks, that's really great. I knew you'd be willing to help."

She started explaining enthusiastically. "Our job is to invite speakers who will offer programs on topics related to the theme. The plan is to advertise the 'education and entertainment' lectures to draw attendance for the products being sold in large auditoriums adjoining the presentation rooms. With hundreds of booths crammed in like a Middle Eastern bazaar, people will sell their wares offering everything from vitamins and foods for giving people more healthy energy to water purification systems for protecting against the evils of public water. There will be chiropractors, acupuncturists, massage therapists, people with contraptions to help correct the postural alignment, yoga teachers, T'ai Chi trainers, Alexander Technique instructors as well as Reiki masters, Indian Shamans and other preventative health booths. Each one of them is pretty interesting, although I must admit together it gets to be a little overwhelming."

In a mock skeptical voice I asked, "So, why invite two artists to this thing and who is the other person?"

"We haven't confirmed the woman who will do it with you

yet, but the idea is that creativity is just as much a key to our quality of life as any of the others. At least it is to me. Your background in music and an artist's perspective tie together, and have a role at least as significant as any of the others. Anyway, I thought this topic would add a light diversion to the schedule."

I chided her, "You really just want an experienced performer to entertain one of the groups. I assume you came up with the name first to draw attendance and figured we'd fill in the corresponding information."

"I'd only admit to it if forced," she replied smiling. "It's the second Sunday in September, eight weeks from today sometime in the late afternoon. Do you think you can do it then?

"I'll check my schedule, but I'm willing to help out if I'm available."

"Actually, the title piques my curiosity a little anyway," I admitted to her, "but how long do you want me to talk? How will colors be tied to my research on sound? And, from what you know about my research, do you have a particular area you want me to discuss?"

"I'll have to call you with the details and arrangements, but, I think the essence of the subjects will turn out to be similar. Basically explain in layman's terms your ideas about how singing can change stress levels and moods by measurable physiological improvements in the mind and body. Give a few examples with your usual flare showing the connection between vibrations in music and the brain. The co-leader will do the equivalent with how colors in our homes and lives create moods and feelings. Each of your talks will be independent of the other, but I'm sure the symmetry will come through.

"The most important thing is to approach the day with the perspective of having some fun. After all, as you've said before, 'Speaking or teaching is mostly just a form of entertainment.' Besides the workshop is just one in a wide range of topics covering everything from "The Effects of Organic Farming on the Environment" to "Explaining Ourselves to Aliens if They Were Ever to Ask." I'm certain whatever you do will be fine."

Aaron, my drummer, came to get me and I hurried a goodbye as I needed to return to the stage for the next set. The next time I saw Tanya was for a minute the day of the expo when she directed me to the correct room and ran off to find another speaker who had not checked in yet.

* * *

I closed my eyes and pictured a room full of attentive people enjoying my talk. It was a technique I used to prepare every time I gave a presentation.

As my eyes opened, my attention was drawn to a ball of energy walking in the door. I knew any questions about my partner in the program and how we would coordinate the presentation were about to be answered. She moved quickly, but gracefully across the room toward me.

I was momentarily transfixed, and found myself somewhere between staring and not staring while noting her appearance and style. Her shoulder length black hair framed a simple beauty in her face showing her heritage as partly Asian and partly European. Her soft brown eyes showed patience, but also a mischievous sparkle.

She carried an air of confidence and poise that must have come from an inner strength, and told me not to take her lightly. She was dressed in a business suit, but almost immediately threw the jacket over a chair, revealing an exquisite hand painted silk blouse cut low enough to reveal a small sapphire stone in the necklace resting above her breasts. She had panache and beauty combined with elegance and dignity.

I stood as she approached and introduced myself.

"Greetings, I'm professor Philip Andrews, but please call me Phil. I assume you're my partner in this presentation?"

"Yes," she replied. "I'm Sam, but I'm trying to figure out

what I'm doing here. Do you know? I was walking though the maze of booths trying to find this room. Do you realize some of those people are crazy? Are you one of the crazy ones? Someone asked me what planet I was from. Have you ever been to anything like this before? And just in case no one has asked you yet, let me be the first, what planet are you from?"

I was caught completely off guard. Was I supposed to respond by answering, or were her questions rhetorical? From her appearance I expected her demeanor would be a touch more reserved. Compared with the elegance in her manner her response was more like a college kid in a bar room. Then, before I could answer, she flipped to what I might have expected, but with an air of overdone dignity.

"Oh, excuse me, you must prefer the stiff, proper approach. Greetings professor. I am Samantha LeFleur. Shall we get to work?"

She had said practically nothing, and whether deliberate or not, had me off balance. I was tongue-tied and feeling slightly foolish. I thought it was impossible that my serious, formal scientist side showed through to her that quickly. However, if she did perceive that side, I knew she would also soon pick up the creative musician in me who could be the witty life of a party. The key was to avoid over analyzing, and open my mouth before the moment was too far gone.

"You have an exceptional way of saying hello. Actually I came right to the room, but I peeked into the packed auditorium and it did look like another world."

I smiled confidently, "The last time I checked I was from Earth, unless we walked into a worm hole. Should I assume you had a similar response, or were you able to think of something more clever?"

Sam broke into a wide smile and laughed. "You're all right. No, your response was actually quicker than mine. I told him, 'I'll get back to you on it,' and made an exit back into the crowd.

"I must be caught in the clamor of this expo thing," she said explaining her initial remarks. "You seem like you know how to roll with the punches. Maybe you can explain to me why the two of us were invited to give a presentation at a holistic health fair. Who came up with the idea for this event, and why invite us?"

"Didn't you talk with Tanya? She set up some of the speakers and asked me to help her out."

Sam responded, "Oh, I get it. She arranged this with Jean Pierre, who is the dean of the art school where I graduated. The rest of the world calls him by his given name, John Gilbert; do you know him?"

I shook my head. "No, but I do recall she knows someone who is associated with an art school and also prominent in the city."

"I haven't figured out yet if this is filling a favor for him, or if he thinks he is doing me a favor." Sam continued, "We work on a business together and sometimes he sets up meetings for me while I'm traveling, but usually with more prep info than this one."

"Well, I have a philosophy. Although it has gotten me into a few predicaments, I've adopted the approach that when a door opens in front of me, I go through it. Who knows? There may be a present waiting on the other side."

I felt I was on firmer ground once I espoused one of my life philosophies. Sam seemed to shift also.

"This is one of the more unusual surprises I've had, but it's starting to seem like it could have an unexpectedly positive side. Maybe I'll give some thought to your philosophy."

I thought she meant that as a compliment, but before I was able to respond, our introduction took a surprising change of direction. Sam took my arm, gestured with her other hand toward a table in the front corner of the room and escorted me there while saying, "All right, I guess we should really get started on this presentation."

I willingly followed her lead, but while my mouth was saying, "I'm right with you." my mind was processing various thoughts and sensations in rapid succession.

Sam was holding my arm close to her side, and I could feel her warmth. Her presence was sensuously alluring. With the surprise, my hormones had my body's sensations competing for attention with my mind's various thoughts.

I remembered how much I enjoyed the touch of a woman. After a series of relationships, I had sworn off any more. During this period of abstinence, I had become more secure within myself. I had realized my priority was to wait until I found a woman who, like me, was secure enough to be alone, but still open to finding an equal, loving partner.

Until that moment I would have said I was still in my solitary period and not really looking to jump into anything. On the other hand, my body's response to her touch and being next to her opened my imagination, and in that moment I remembered what I had been missing. I wasn't overwhelmed, although she felt perfect next to me, but I was intrigued and open to see where this would lead.

I suddenly realized I was thinking about Sam as to whether, and how, she would be compatible in a relationship. A woman friend once told me, "Women consider that possibility when they first meet someone, but men don't think that way." In a way I agreed because I felt my thoughts were way ahead of what I considered normal for these first minutes. However, my mind was on a roll, and kept going on to more thoughts.

I was curious whether her questions were an indication of her sense of humor. A sense of humor was one of the most important attributes I looked for in a person. Whatever was going on in her mind, she already had me smiling. She also had me scrambling to ascertain where we were going next; clearly a sharp mind. I thought, "Two key attributes plus her beauty."

Although my serious side was telling me to get started

working on the presentation, some other part of me just wanted to find out more about her.

The spell and my inward thoughts were broken when I heard Sam's voice.

"Have you given any thought as to how to approach talking to a group as diverse as this Expo is? And, what tack you would like to take?"

"What?"

She looked at me funny. "We'd better decide how we want to do this. Are you sure you're from earth?"

This was certainly someone to get to know better. However, for the moment I needed to focus on the matter at hand.

"Yes." I recovered, "I get the sense you're an experienced speaker. Let's introduce our ideas for only fifteen minutes and then open it up so we can get everyone involved. Why don't you go first, and then after I've spoken we can ask for questions and wing it."

Sam agreed, "That sounds like a plan," in unison with my, "Sound like a plan?" and we both laughed.

"We'll just have to be flexible. I'm pretty skilled in flexible. How about you?" Sam asked.

"Sure. It's like meeting a musician and trading improvisations the first time. It's really only a matter of not stepping on each other's toes while smoothly bringing each other into the dance."

Sam nodded, "I've got it. We each have our specialties, or instruments, ready and take turns following and leading. You know, I'd wondered if I'd be matched with an inexperienced speaker, but you seem to know what you're doing."

"Thanks. I decided I'd just show up prepared and have faith you'd have your act together."

"That sounds like one of my Uncle's sayings: 'Balance yourself and the universe will align.'

We looked up and I saw Rose, the woman I had met with

Tanya, walking toward us. I also realized a few dozen people had already found seats and were watching us expectantly.

"Nice to see you again, Phil." And introducing herself to Sam, "Hi, I'm Rose. I'm here to introduce you, but first I want your okay on the biographical statements, Tanya wrote, before I read them."

We each skimmed the sketches for a minute and gave our approval. She waited for everyone to find a seat and walked over to the podium to begin.

"Welcome to the "Quality of Life" Expo and the workshop "Life's Vibrations Through Colors and Sounds." I have the pleasure of introducing your speakers today.

"Samantha LeFleur was raised in the state of Washington and attended the Pennsylvania Academy for the Fine Arts here in Philadelphia. She is a partner in Present Works of Art, a firm she created to represent her work and the work of other artists to galleries and interior designers. Her business has expanded to include international artists, and she is also organizing sales for charities. Sam will present her ideas on how the colors which surround us, including how we dress, affect our moods and our behavior."

She turned to Sam, who waved her hand to a small round of applause. Turning back to her notes, she introduced me.

"Professor Philip Andrews is from New Jersey originally. He is a graduate of Philadelphia's highly regarded Curtis Institute of Music, and received his doctorate at the University of Pennsylvania. His research combines the disciplines of music and science to explore the effects of sound vibrations on human physiology. He is currently a professor at Temple University where he is teaching and continuing his research. Phil, as many of you may know him, is also a local jazz musician who performs regularly in the area."

"I'll turn the program over to them. Please give them both a warm welcome."

Sam stepped to the front of the small room and looked over the forty or fifty people who had filled it. She began, "Everyone close your eyes for a minute, and see if you can remember what color the walls are in this room. Next, after a moment, focus on what color clothes you are wearing."

It was easy as an observer to notice how Sam proceeded with the group and how, as with me, she had a flair for catching people off guard. But, somehow she simultaneously put people at ease. She took control and immediately commanded a respect which seemed to come so naturally that she took it for granted.

As she told everyone to open their eyes, people looked around at the walls of the hotel room which were lavender with a rose border. Then, as if no one wanted to admit that they had to look at their own clothes, they sheepishly glanced down at what they were wearing.

Sam stole back their attention, "Many people are oblivious to colors in a room, and, although more aware of the clothes they are wearing, few consider what meaning is being telegraphed by either." She continued to explain and her real point quickly became apparent, "It is not only noticing the colors, but realizing they are purposely chosen to have a certain effect. For instance, the color of this room was intended to give people the feeling of warmth and friendliness.

"There are other examples of how subtly, or not so subtly, our surroundings are designed for the purpose of creating specific feelings.

"For example," she offered as evidence, "green is considered a healing color and is often found in hospitals. Red is meant to be racy when used in clothes and cars. Orange in restaurants can increase a patron's appetite. Blue is a cool calming color, and is used in airplanes to give people a sense of stability and calm. The color purple is used to give a sense of royalty or a noble feeling."

Sensing that people understood her point, Sam switched

to clothing.

"Will someone volunteer to be an example of how personality traits are perceptible from colors of clothes?"

A man in front raised his hand.

"Great, please stand up. Can everyone see he is wearing black pants and a white sweater with pink shirt collar?"

Sam offered a general assessment of his personality based on her observations of his attire.

"I would surmise from the pink shirt that you are sensitive to how others feel about you. The combination of the black and white suggests you have a strong belief system regarding what behaviors are right or wrong for yourself and others. Based on the combination of pink with the black and white, you are sensitive to people's emotional reaction in discussions, but there is a tendency for you to challenge yourself to see both sides of a situation before making a judgment. Also, white gives the suggestion of purity, while the black actually suggests a process of change."

The man acknowledged that these general attributes described him reasonably well and the point was made. The group and I began to understand that whether consciously or subconsciously, everyone's clothing offers clues regarding the nature of a person.

Sam segued from these examples to emphasize her main point, "By understanding the meaning of colors surrounding you and how someone designed the mood, you will be freed from reacting to your environment. A world of insights is waiting to open if you simply pay attention. The key is being aware of what colors are in your life, and realizing what meaning the colors offer and why.

"Observe your image as when you look in a mirror. Self-awareness opens a door to understanding why you act in particular ways. While looking at your clothes, questions may jump out at you, such as, 'Am I dressing to attract or keep a lover, a business client, or someone else whose approval matters enough to dictate my attire?'

"Any answer without introducing judgment is really fine. Identifying the 'why' is a first step toward recognizing what matters in your life. For me the essence of consciously creating my world is to be true to myself through my words and actions."

"Take proactive steps to support the components you value in relationships and life. I find expressing through words or paintings contains the essence of being naked before the world or whoever is appraising my work. All the love and passion instilled in my art reveals my inner self, and in a moment an observer says, "Yes, I like it." or "I don't like this one." and moves on to the next. But, what really mattered is the meaning I find through my expressions.

"A better question, though, is, 'Did you feel anything?' The one measure of art, or life, is its ability to elicit emotions."

I thought, "The passion infused in Sam's life was evident just from listening her. I admired Sam's confident presentation of her thoughts and opinions. There was a natural feeling about her; nothing fake or contrived. I considered the way she was forthright and spoke her mind without inhibition was forged from the courage required to be an artist. Having exhibited her creations, she required the self-confidence to transcend opinions regarding self-expression."

I made a note of the ideas that were new to me, and a couple that corroborated thoughts I had explored myself. I committed to be more aware of the impact of colors and to pay more attention to their meaning in my surroundings. I considered how an artist would require objectivity for observing everyday interactions.

Confirming my thought, Sam ended with the point, "By training your eye, you can begin to apply the skill. In life will take on a vibrancy of all the shades of green on a Scottish dale, rather than being just a field. The real trick, though, is to go even beyond the awareness of colors, and appreciate how the feelings evoked resonate within you."

Sam smiled toward me, while saying to everyone, "I'll answer any questions with Professor Andrews after he mesmerizes you with his thoughts and handsome looks."

As I stood, my cheeks warmed with a grin and I am sure my face showed her comment produced a rose color. She may have been teasing, but I chose to take her compliment as another promising sign. As I walked to the podium with a boom box, tape recorder in my hand, my composure returned as my blush faded.

My presentation started with an example in the same manner as Sam's. I pressed the button to play. Everyone in the room, including Sam, "came to" at the shock of suddenly hearing a loud rock song. After about five seconds and having grabbed everyone's attention, I lowered the volume and let the subsequent silence sink in.

"I believe you will see an immediate parallel to the points that Sam just made. The choice of music offers a glimpse at the personality of the one choosing the music just as the examples of color. Listen and imagine what personality characteristics you would associate, or what type of person you identify with each type of music. Also pay attention to any change or any physical aspect such as facial expressions, sighs, emotions, or even pictures that evoke a physical memory like dancing."

I next played a jazz ballad, and asked, "Can you feel the difference, either positively or negatively, and notice how the change in music effects your physiology?"

People nodded in agreement although the answer was meant to be obvious.

I continued, "This simple example is intended to show how emotions and physical states clearly change depending on the musical environment. Now pay attention to your physical and emotional reactions as I play some other examples, and note the associations between the feelings and the music."

I played parts of a love ballad that was often associated with a wedding ceremony, followed by the middle of the traditional wedding march, and prompted, "Can you remember or picture yourself, or someone, crying at a wedding when the music begins?"

Next I played a couple of dance tunes that were readily recognizable and pointed to the shift in the nature of people's expressions. I asked, "Do these songs make you want to jump up to dance, or can you remember songs that do?"

"In fact, the thought alone of a certain piece or type of music can produce identifiable, although sometimes subtle, changes in a person's state of mind. A more definable change takes place when a person is singing or playing an instrument. That is what I consider the ultimate example, when a musician actually feels the music within and truly becomes the vibration.

"Being the instrument produces physiological changes beyond the readily observable changes. Deep diaphragmatic breathing during singing or humming involves a deep breath into the belly, and a slow, drawn out exhalation while making a vibrating sound. The physical process required in singing adds rich oxygen to the blood and can make the singer feel light headed. One way to show this, and introduce the main theme of my research is through humming. Everyone please join me, and hum along with me for a minute or so."

I began to hum "America the Beautiful" and, after everyone overcame the first moments of embarrassment, they joined in with me.

"This sensation is a quick example how singing, or in this case humming, no matter what style of music, creates vibrations in the instruments we call our bodies. While singing, the physical and emotional states can be measured to show a relatively moderate blood pressure and a generally calm demeanor. Also, the brain wave activity can be measured to show a positive change in the vibrational balance of the right and left hemispheres of the brain.

I wrapped up my presentation by mentioning, "The next phase of my ever expanding research is going to explore how the state of consciousness during singing compares with the brain frequencies and physiological states during meditation. Of course, exploration is never ending, but that's also the fun."

After I finished, we opened the floor to questions. A bunch of hands went up immediately. People's responses showed enthusiasm and almost everyone asked questions.

One person commented, "I feel like I been living in black and white. I realize now just how much I previously took music and colors for granted even though I've been immersed in them."

Another person agreed, " I'm certain that consciously noticing details will help me appreciate and understand messages surrounding me."

A couple thanked us, "Now we better understand why our child always wears black and listens to loud music."

I could tell people really got the main point of our presentations because many made a similar comment: "It's fun to learn a new game where we can be more aware of our surroundings and understand ourselves more clearly."

While responding to questions we each explained more about our backgrounds and our careers, and a few people stayed to talk with us on their way out.

The last person to leave wanted to know more about my research. He pointed to his own experience saying, "I sing in a choir and really appreciate what you mean about music influencing my body's physiology, but I never before heard anyone described what I felt."

After everyone was gone, I said, "I feel a high from seeing our interests and livelihoods have meaning to others."

"Indeed," Sam agreed. "Knowing others appreciate what we've accomplished in life gives me a sense of validation. We were able to touch their lives and have fun too."

Sharing the process of creating this feeling made me feel connected to Sam and kindled my desire to find out more about her. Our talks inferred compatibility, and of all the possible people, places and ways it could have all come together, I sensed we would find more to our meeting than two speakers sharing the same room.

* * *

I suggested we continue our talk over a bite to eat and Sam agreed. We went around the corner to a small cafe and dessert shop where people often lingered to talk or read. It was the ideal place for a relaxed conversation. The idea of a snack was also appealing since I had made a point to have an early dinner before the presentation. Our appetites were whetted from the smells of the desserts, but we decided to order some food first.

The waiter was casual, and left us menus so we could peruse the choices of salads and sandwiches. Neither of us really needed the menus, though, since we had each been to the cafe often enough to know what we wanted.

Sam put aside the menu and said, "There are a few things here that are my favorites and I get them almost every time I eat here. They have the best Caesar salad, excellent salsa and guacamole with chips and for desert I love their special deep dish apple pie with chocolate ice cream, topped with freshly whipped cream."

She had picked my favorites for this cafe also. I looked at her and suggested, "You know the portions are big enough for two. How would you feel about sharing? We could be formal, but I sense you're willing to break from decorum."

She agreed but insisted, "As long as we have separate plates. We don't know each other that well yet."

We were not in a hurry even though we were both hungry after thinking about our choices. When the waiter eventually found us to take our order, we were wrapped up again in reviewing the talks we had given, and sharing more ideas and questions on each other's topic. The enthusiasm from our presentation carried over, and ranged through all sorts of related subjects. Over dessert and cups of herbal tea we were still discussing our ideas, and very little about each other. I was thrilled to meet someone so excited about what she did, who was also curious about my areas of interest.

"I'm enjoying all we've been talking about, but I'd like to know about you too," I finally said.

"Let's each share a recent story about something outrageous we've done," Sam interjected to take the conversation in the new direction. "People are basically story-tellers, and it gives insights in a way that is more fun than the resume' information people usually exchange."

I agreed to the challenge but suggested, "Just to make sure I know what kind of story you mean, I'll let you go first."

Sam agreed readily. As her face lit up, I knew a happy memory had entered her mind.

"My last vacation was a small group tour on a boat off the coast of the Baja in Mexico," she began. "The trip was designed to be an escape for me, and also to get to know Alex away from the distractions of everyday life. Alexia is my sixteen-year-old daughter."

I could tell she noted that my face did not change when she mentioned that she had a daughter.

She continued, "After flying into Las Paz and walking around to see the villas and bazaars, we spent the night in a simple hotel. Early the next morning we set out for the boat that would be home for the following eight days. There were eighteen people in our group plus the crew and tour guides."

Sam became animated as she described how she and Alex left the small ship most days in Zodiac boats to snorkel through the crystal waters, and to get closer to the sea life.

"The most amazing thing happened while we were

snorkeling. A mother sea lion swam directly toward me. She would veer-off and then repeat, but come increasingly closer each time until she was within arm's reach.

"Once the sea lion realized the group posed no threat to her pups, the mother and the pups began to play games. It was as though they were pleased we came to visit them on their own surf, and wanted to greet and entertain us."

"The animals were equally inquisitive about how humans moved in the water, and teased us for our awkwardness. They were clearly the masters of a world that people could only visit. Even when they went to sun themselves on the rocks, the scooting movement up the rocks was effortless compared to how humans move.

"When we swam back to the Zodiac, we were right next to another sea lion that had its flippers on the boat, and was playing with a ball held on a string by the leader of the tour.

"The best part, though, was sharing it with Alex. I felt as though we went through a rite of passage. In case you haven't had the pleasure of experiencing children through the ages of thirteen to sixteen, even the best ones can exhibit a monstrous side. Even though I think Alex was a little embarrassed about being with her mom, some of her adolescent demons were tamed. Alex has always been independent, but we connected for parts of each day. She seemed to mature into a young woman and I saw her in a new light.

"When I thought about it, I could even understand what my mother must have gone through with me. I realized a parent's love and respect is often hidden while the parent maintains a role of authority. By its very nature, showing respect to an authority figure creates a closeness, and at the same time, a separateness. Perhaps like a mother cat and her kitten, they can play in the same room, but with an unspoken deference that defines the love and respect relationship. The mother might show her love by defending the kit, but if the kit steps out of line the mother's discipline both unites them and defines a boundary."

"Exploring the natural environment with the sea lions and sharing the experience with Alex, created a level playing field where we were equal. On top of that, Alex, who was already very respectful of nature, felt the experience changed her life forever. Being immersed in all the sea life which also included blue whales, seals, otters and gray whales, seemed to awaken a new depth of life and open a new realm of possibilities."

I was impressed. I could picture everything Sam said as if she had sketched a picture right in front of me. The thought occurred to mc to call and make a reservation that minute, but only if I could convince Sam to go with me.

It was my turn next. Before I started my story, I told Sam, "I also have a daughter, Anna, who is thirteen years old. The story I've decided to tell does not include her, but I promise I'll tell you about Anna in another one."

Sam had an inquisitive look at my mention of Anna. I sensed a curiosity in Sam which paralleled my questions about who she was and what was going on in her life. On the other hand I was enjoying the process of learning slowly for now and leaving mysteries about each other for another time.

I began wistfully, "Well, the most outrageous, magic night of my life was really playing music."

"For all the jazz piano I've performed, I never reached the level of being nationally known or even playing with musicians who were recording artists. One night, though, I received a call from the owner of Zanzibar Blue, the jazz club on 11th street, where I play regularly.

"He told me that Art Farmer, a master Flugel-horn musician, was in town that night, and needed a piano player because his regular one missed a flight into Philadelphia. I agreed, and headed over to the club immediately to meet and practice with him and the rest of his quintet.

"The stage at Zanzibar is almost fully occupied by a grand

piano, and looks out over small tables and a bar that snugly fits about eighty people.

"I had played there a hundred times, but before the performance started that evening, my adrenaline was barely able to keep up with my excitement. I sat at the piano where I normally feel right at home, but in that moment I felt unsure of myself. I looked out toward the room full of people, but saw only the bright lights in my eyes. I heard a surprising silence that made me wonder if anyone was really there at all.

"I looked over at the other musicians. We were all ready and waiting for the count to set the beat. I could feel perspiration on my forehead and also down my back. The stage lights weren't hotter or brighter than usual, it was more like a beginner's nervous-energy. Perhaps it was compounded because the string bass and I started the first tune.

"I took a slow deep breath, and felt the keys and foot pedals to give me a sense of familiarity and comfort. I also heard a laugh from a waitress I knew, and in that moment the tension was broken. The sax player began the count and I began to play.

"At first, I was being overly conscious to play accurately. Then, I heard Art begin his first solo. The sound captured me, drew me in, and left me enthralled. I stared at him like a fan might, but keep right on playing. Right then I knew the difference between local players and the top acts. The depth shone through with a brilliant polish.

"This was a new realm for me. Practicing earlier in the day was only 'playing the notes' compared to the way I felt that evening. During the performance I entered the music and experienced a universe beyond. The music really got tight after the first couple of tunes and began to flow as sweetly as a breeze on a sunny day. Magic was in the air, and filled my being as if sorcerer's incense was tempting me to let go of my body and meld with the songs. I entered freely.

"Playing with master musicians raised my level of playing

above anything I had ever known. I could not have chosen or pushed myself to reach their level; I could only surrender to the music and play. The music poured out of me without even consciously trying. The feeling was like in a perfect dream where everything happens exactly as you desire.

"I stayed on a high from the music and the Zen state I had reached for days afterward. Even the words of praise from Art Farmer and the other musicians, not to mention the audience and friends who raved over the sound we produced, could compare with the internal feeling and sense of other worldliness I had finally reached through my music."

Sam's face showed she understood the deep meaning of my experience. In that moment I realized what Sam meant about how relating an experience would open an understanding of a person that hours of talking could miss. Now, though, I was ready to ask her at least a dozen questions about her life, and what brought her to this exact point in time with me.

Apparently my questions would wait.

Sam said, "That is an amazing story. You've opened dozens of questions I'd like to ask, but not now. I promised I'd meet Alex and visit with her and Randi, who is my best friend and business partner. Alex takes care of herself anymore, but always loves to stays at Randi's. I know part of her reason is to be in the 'cool' part of the city since we live in a quiet neighborhood near twenty-forth and Spruce.

"Randi is really a second mother to Alex, but they're also like sisters in a way a mother and daughter sometimes never reach."

"Sounds like a story for another time. I should get home also. Anna is visiting a friend of her's and will be home soon."

I asked if it was okay if I treated and reached to pick up the check. Sam agreed, but then really surprised me by asking if she could treat me to dinner on Friday evening.

I was thrilled and frustrated in the same moment. I explained, "I would love to, but I'm scheduled to perform with my trio at another club that night from nine-thirty until one-thirty in the morning."

Sam didn't waver, "The offer still stands. We can have an early dinner, and still have plenty of time to get you to your job."

"All right, I accept, but how about coming to see me play afterward?"

Sam contemplated a moment, "Dinner is set, but I'll have to hear you play another time. I need to be in New York for a couple of days, and prefer to get home early when I travel during the week."

"Okay, dinner this time and music another."

In a moment we had set date and a promise for a second as well. We walked out of the cafe and Sam hailed a cab while we were saying goodbye. A cab arrived within a minute and made our parting feel abrupt. She jumped in the cab and waved out the back as it pulled away. I waved back, but she was gone,and I was standing on the city street waving at thin air.

We had met only hours before, but I felt like there was a magnetic attraction between us. As I walked toward my car and Sam sped across town, I could picture her face and feel her energy as though she was still next to me. I had a feeling of lightness and a smile I desired to keep forever. I wondered if it was possible to hold the memory of a feeling, or if it was necessary to keep renewing the feeling each day. For the rest of the evening the sense of Sam's presence was easy to remember and I did hold the feeling. Even when I awoke the next morning, the feeling was so clear I almost expected to see Sam next to me.

It was the best Monday morning I could remember. My body was on the day at hand, but my mind was alternating between thinking about seeing Sam on Friday, and still being caught up in the night we met. I seemed to float as Anna and I prepared for school. Anna smiled at me. Without knowing exactly what was going on, it seemed as if she knew something was different and sensed my lightness.

Interlogue

The most volatile chemistry imaginable in this universe is that of a relationship. The awakening of one's ability to feel passion and also express it to another is, to me, the greatest adventure life can ever present. The shift from one-dimensional awareness to making decisions that involve others, creates a multi-dimensional proccss which is magnified by each additional person.

While I was in school the concept of a decision tree was defined for me. The explanation was that a decision tree started with a question, and that each possible answer branches to other questions. This process starts anew with each decision, and every question opens an infinite number of possible outcomes. In reality there will be only one result, but the key to the process is relating each choice to one's primary intention in life. Then an awareness is created in each step, and from the beginning question, the focus can be kept on achieving the desired result.

Understanding the idea conceptually is a first step, but applying the knowledge is fundamental to enjoying the life created from that point forward. By entering this process consciously, a person is also better prepared to make adjustments.

The ground work begins mostly by the trials and errors of life's experiences. As progress occurs, though, each learning experience begins to relate to a bigger picture. Each step, even the smallest ones, begin to take on clarity and focus toward a new dream. Asking different questions can open doors and conscious choices invariably take life in a new direction while breaking through previous barriers.

By observing ourselves in the light of a relationship, the past and present come together and give a fresh understanding of life. Writing down those thoughts, and the life questions of how, why and what was being presented, can give a tangible perspective. Each memory explored provides lessons from the branches of the path already chosen. Whatever one decides, though, questioning opens messages and interactions create mirrors so, in each moment, we can choose life

Being excited about life and what each new day brings, takes life to new heights. By accepting and being comfortable with ourselves, we can allow a partner to join in the journey toward a fuller life. This awakening will raise the standards of the journey so others are treated with respect. In that way every person and every event is enriched.

Each chapter shows how the characters progressively become capable of appreciating the meaning in their lives. Some show one aspect of life, while others open a flood of understanding. As you walk through their minds with me; as philosophies develop; as perceptions come to the light of day; as disjointed experiences connect; as stories offer up meaning; as intuitions are hearteningly shared; as sleeping volcanoes blow tops; as insights materialize; as footholds give way; as solid ground melts; as nature talks; as imbalance is balanced; as wants dissolve; and, as imagination is illumined, I will relate the process of how the characters lives were being reassembled. As they bring that knowledge to the present, journey forward with them and observe as they become proactive participants.

To visualize the moment Phil and Sam met, picture all the branches of their separate decision trees coming together to overlay for one instant, and then see all the branches emanating from that point. In the fresh light of recognition, all of the choices and infinite possible outcomes ever made, brought them separately to an identical place. The decision tree they create now will truly unfold as each decision contains the clarity of the whole.

Chapter 2

It was the middle of September, and Anna and I had just started the new school year. I felt content with my life which revolved around my teaching and performing. I taught or did school work all day on Tuesdays and Thursdays, and performed every other Friday night and some Sundays. Anna often met with friends after school and stayed with them on the nights I played.

Anna and I had committed to always reserve at least one weekend a month to take a day trip into the country side or visit my mother at the sea shore. We also planned a special night of each week to do something fun together. Usually the best evening for us was Wednesday and we often went to events in the city. One of our favorite activities was the student recitals at The Curtis Institute, but the Wednesday after meeting Sam, we walked to the Philadelphia Art Museum. But, rather than participate in the programs or tours, we toured the Degas retrospective visiting at the time. Then, over a great meal at the restaurant on the first floor, we discussed the periods in Degas's life from portraits, ballerinas and horses to the bathing scenes. Anna was especially drawn to the sculpture of the dancer, and as much as we lost our sense of time in the pictures, our hearts were stolen by imagining what the girl life was like who modeled for the bronze.

Throughout the evening my thoughts had drifted to Sam, but as we headed home I was filled with anticipation just to hear her voice and confirm our date. Sam and I had exchanged phone numbers the first night, and she promised to call from New York to make arrangements for Friday's dinner. It was as though I needed reassurance the night we met was real, and not just a dream. The realness was evident though from the lightness in my step and an added joy in everything.

When we arrived, I checked the messages on the answering machine. I was excited when I heard Sam's voice, "Hey handsome, are you there?"

There was a couple of seconds pause, "Ok, well, I guess you're out playing music or something fun I hope. I'm in New York. Actually, I think I'm having fun, but it's all mixed in with work stuff."

"I met with three artists I know, two gallery owners, and now I'm heading out to a friend's studio near the village for a small get-together thing. I'm staying near there at another friend's loft apartment in Chelsea. She lets me use it while she's out traveling with Broadway road shows."

I smiled as I pictured Sam talking to my machine. The tape was probably scrambling to keep up with her the way I had when we first met.

I grabbed a pen to jot down her friend's number, but my enthusiasm dropped as she said she would be back late, and not to bother calling. However, my spirits picked up again quickly as she gave instructions, "Meet me at six o'clock on Friday at Tang's, on South Street, it's my favorite Chinese restaurant."

I needed to be at a club called The Borgia Cafe by nine that night to be ready to play at nine thirty, and it was only five blocks away. That would give us three hours together to learn more about each other.

I almost felt like she was there talking to me. But, with her, "Well, gotta run, I'll see you Friday," I looked up.

Anna was in the next room and could easily hear the

message, but I wanted to hear Sam's voice again. I rewound and played the tape again twice.

* * *

The night we met at Tang's, we each wanted to hear the other's story of growing up, and understand part of the foundations that created our lives and personalities. Sam linked the process of learning to telling and listening to stories.

Sam requested my story first this time saying, "Embellish or make it on the poetic side for fun."

I began telling my childhood story. I even surprised myself at how much fun most of it was to remember. In a moment I had stepped back into my childhood and began painting a picture as the back drop for my childhood memories. I could easily see myself walking home from the beach in Sea Side Park, the small seashore resort town in New Jersey, where I grew up.

I waxed dreamily, "The wide sandy beach welcomed the white foam spreading before each greenish blue wave that crashed, and stretched to the tall sand dunes, with green and golden dune grass waving from behind the surrounding snow fences. Everything else for miles was sky and ocean. I loved to watch the sea gulls dip and fly through colors that varied with the moods and seasons of nature. The same spectrum of red to rose, violet to lavender and all imaginable colors of the sunrises and sunsets bled equally into the grays of the winter sky, as it did into the small white whiffs of clouds that disappeared into the clear blue of summer. Even now I can imagine an artist spilling a colorful palette into the sky to paint the bookends of daylight, and bathe the bay and ocean in the reflections. There were, and still are, endlessly blue and sun worshiped summer days, interrupted only by the beauty of a violent thunder and lightening storm. But to equally love the mist, wind or cold dark winters, meant that you lived there twelve months of the year."

Sam smiled, "It sounds beautiful. I'll need to get a peek at your beach sometime. Your romantic expressions about the place show your heart must open to a special part of you there."

"Yes. I know it does. You'll see as I describe it."

My elaborate details switched to more basic information, "Most of the year there were only a few families living within the blocks near my home and a bunch of retirees. There was barely a soul to be seen, and I often needed to be content alone with my imagination to guide me and with nature as my best friend. But, I did have a couple friends, Rob and Jeff, who were a couple of years older than I. They were the only ones around from September through May other than my family. Now we rarely see each other, but as kids, we explored the beach with a curiosity that expected to uncover a treasure under every seashell.

"We were surrounded by a world with plenty to do. We could always find some new discovery in the coves of each little sand bar island where we sailed. We came to understand the tides, currents and seasons from the old fishermen, who taught us between their casts into the surf for the stripped bass and blues so we could learn to catch the fish ourselves. Also, whenever possible, we would coerce a neighbor on the bay to take us sailing, water skiing or anything that involved boats, including watching work on the engines we were certain we would someday own.

"In addition to our busy fall and spring schedule, whole summer days were lost to swimming and surfing, beach volleyball, or anything else a kid could want."

"It sounds like you did everything a kid could want."

"Yes, but sometimes it was too much. Half the world came in the summer vacation with the hot weather, or at least half of New Jersey. People descended on the strip of barrier island. It was funny, all the retiree's families remembered they were alive, and filled every bed, sofa and even the floors when they came to visit, and still do. All the little towns swelled from summer renters or day trippers. The south end of the island, where I lived, was between Island Beach State Park and the boardwalk, with carnival rides, arcades, and food stands just a mile to the north. Combining the two attractions brought in every kid and adult from many more miles around. The state park preserved over ten miles of sand dunes as a wildlife sanctuary, and all the families who could not build there, built on every other square foot allowable. It was so crowded in the summer, the only sensible way to get around was to walk or ride a bike because the cars often crawled along, taking ten minutes to cover a mile. But, clearly the best place to be was either on the beach or on the water."

"I see what you mean. It sounds great, but sometimes it was too much of a good thing."

"Yes. Actually that's more of my adult view of it, as a kid I loved it all. The crowds were a unique education to have growing up. If you could believe someone would do something, they would. I think within the summer crowds any and every human trait imaginable, and many unimaginable, could be found. Now I prefer the spring and fall when it's quieter, and even the winter."

"Then," I resumed, "when it was biting cold in the middle of winter, life was a different story, everyone would magically disappear. We would still venture out to play in that amazing world cloaked in its winter suits, but we would match winter with layers of clothes to stay warm. Outdoor play was reserved for the weekends. On school days my life moved indoors, since by the time I made it home, it was already too dark to play outside. During this annual hibernation my family was the center of my life.

"I'm the youngest child of four, and my brothers and sister are between six and ten years older. There were the occasional storms between siblings, but my memory does not include hearing my parents yell at us or each other. With perspective I realize my parents created a nurturing environment for me to grow up in that made me trusting and open. I learned to get along with everyone, and overcame the challenge of being the youngest.

"In light of the age differences I always pushed to be more mature. This made me more competitive whether I was playing games with my family or just contributing something to dinner conversations. No matter what, I was determined to gain respect. In some ways this created a churning undercurrent of energy for me in my rush to gain approval, but I think there was a balance from the closeness and security I felt. Sometimes I compare the contrast of how I related to my family with the character of the sea shore. Like the ocean, there's a rush of energy where the waves crash, while like the calm, inviting serenity of a clear blue sky I had a stable, nurturing home.

"My mom ran the house and also worked in a nursing home part time. When I kept her company in the kitchen or helped prepare dinner, she filled the air with remembrances. I felt she was confiding in me like a friend when she reminisced, and I began to see her as a person with feelings instead of a separate icon. I felt I mattered by being important enough to know her thoughts."

"I take it you were closest to your mother?"

"Yes, definitely. I can even hear her voice and see the way she looked at me the first time she told me how she met my dad and some of what was going on in her life before they married.

"She told me, 'Originally I had considered pushing beyond nursing, and had started taking premed classes.'

I remember she smiled at me and paused. Her look seemed like she was wondering who I'd become that she felt comfortable confiding in me about how she had thought and felt, but she continued. 'That was where I met your father. By the end of the first semester we were engaged, and the next semester we were married. I already had my nursing degree, and decided to drop the idea of continuing. At that point I started to work so your father could finish medical school. However, a year later when your oldest brother was born, your father quit medical school also to get a job.'

"My mother claimed, 'I know I made the right choice to be home and take care of everyone.'

"My brothers and sister were usually off with friends or at school activities. So it was often just the two of us in the house between school and dinner. It never occurred to me what she did during the day when I was at school, but she was always there for me. Then, at dinner time the whole family came together.

"Once we finished dinner, the main theme uniting my whole family, before my brothers left for college, was music. Everyone either played an instrument or sang. My mother sang, my father played the piano, my brothers took turns with the guitar and recorders and my sister played the clarinet. We took turns playing, or all joined together in sing alongs.

"I had wanted to play the drums, but was strongly discouraged. I felt there was a talent for music inside me also, but at that point I only stubbornly joined in by tapping my fingers while imagining drums. However, when it came to singing, I joined willingly."

Sam laughed, and I felt like she could easily see me as a little kid whining, "But I want to play the drums." and equally seeing my parents grimacing at the thought of the noise and probably wisely holding their ground. She added like a true authority figure, "I take it you don't play the drums now?"

I shook my head, "No. I found a substitute.

"When I was eight years old I picked up my brother's wooden recorder just after he finished a song. Without thinking I played the song note for note!

"That got me over playing the drums for awhile. At first everyone was amazed and fawned over me. It was exciting and fun. For a week I didn't put the recorder down, or stop playing 'my' song. After the third day though, they were practically screaming at me to stop. With such encouragement I stopped playing the recorder. However, it was the first sign I had a good ear for music."

Sam interjected, "It's unreal sometimes how sensitive we are to our family's approval, but it's amazing how gifts within us are uncovered."

"I hadn't thought about it that way," and paused to consider her input before continuing.

"The next instrument began the same way, but fortunately I was given positive reinforcement, and never stopped.

"It started with my father," I reflected. "He played the piano when he got home from work to melt away his day in the science laboratory of a pharmaceutical company. He played old jazz ballads and boogie woogie until it was time for dinner. He also played at parties with his friends gathered around, and at family affairs.

"One night, after my dad was done playing and had gone into the kitchen for dinner, I sat down at the piano. I had poked at the keys before, but I was suddenly confident I could play what I had heard my father just playing. Before I finished a second round of boogie woogie, the whole family was standing around me laughing so hard they cried. Picture seeing an eight year old playing boogie woogie, and imagine my surprise that I could play so naturally."

"What a scene that must have been."

"Yeah, I remember thinking, 'This is great. This is for me!' I wanted to be just like my dad, and play music with everyone gathered around laughing."

I had a flash of what Sam would have looked like when she was eight years old, and somehow inserted her into the joyful scene of my first memorable accomplishment. I liked the thought. For a moment when I looked at her I actually felt she was half child and half adult.

"Initially, I was as surprised as anyone, and the shock

ingrained the scene in my memory forever. I was amazed that I had somehow tapped into a natural reservoir. If I'd stopped to think about what I was actually doing, it would have seemed impossible. However, I never stopped to question if I could do it or not, but simply dove into playing. The funny part is, once I knew I could do it, and proved it, my ear and my hands were linked forever.

"My parents hired a piano teacher that fall for my birthday present, and I was thrilled. There was never any difficulty getting me to practice and I learned the lessons quickly. Then afterward, by ear, I would sit and figure out the jazz ballads that I heard my dad play. It came to me naturally.

"Part of my motivation was that my mother loved every song. Once I played them fairly smoothly, I could hear her sing along with me from the kitchen while she was preparing dinner. Some of the happiest times of my entire life were playing the piano for her.

"As you can see, my childhood life was simple and idyllic. I played at the beach through long warm days, and played music at night. However, when I was twelve, and my older siblings were either away at college or had already graduated, my life changed. My father suffered a heart attack, and was in a hospital or a rehab-nursing home for the next two years until he died. I loved everyone in my family, but my dad was my idol. From that day I didn't cry once in the next fourteen years, but I poured all my love and grieving into the piano. Even though I still went to the beach, I mostly sat at the piano for hours every day. I became extremely introverted, but I could play anything."

* * *

When my father died, the eulogy my brother gave spoke volumes about his life. Once, when I was seeking to understand who my father was and what he was like, I dove into some old papers and found an original copy. Alone later the same evening Sam and I had dinner, I reread my oldest brother's words. It made me want to introduce Sam to my dad, and the thought resounded in me that he would have been a great guy to have had as a friend.

My brother had said, "The love and respect I have for my father were inspired by his smile and his ability to laugh at something every day. Throughout all of his life, whether healthy or sick, he always enjoyed a beautiful day and always showed his appreciation for life in a way that everyone around him can still feel. He showed his emotions openly, and warm and loving feelings were, and are, awakened in me, him, and I think all of us, when he shared his smile and kind words. My sister told me that this is one of the clearest ways she brings dad into her life, and that he is a model for how she interacts with everyone in her life.

"Someone once said that judging a person by how much love he shared in his life is the true measure of a person's life. By this measure my dad was a rich man. In addition to being respected in his work, he set a standard for life that went well beyond what can be accomplished professionally. This standard for love and kindness came directly from his mother, uncles and aunts, and like a magnet drew friends to him who shared these qualities like his loving wife and nurse, my mom.

"I especially remember the days during his disabilities, when I would sit outside and visit with my mom and dad. In many respects these days were spent the way we all wish we could. There were no longer stresses from work, or being stuck in traffic and long lines, and no more rushing around to be somewhere at a certain time or deadline. Instead, he found enjoyment in some simple aspect of life each day, like listening to books read to him by a tape recorder or my mom, or listening to his favorites on the radio; Sinatra and others singing the old standards from when he was young. He still recognized all the singers and all of the songs, although he could no longer play them on the piano.

"On the other side, it was difficult to be around him when he would express how frustrating his life had become. I know he always wanted and fought to regain his health, and to make decisions that could once again control his life and his destiny. If any one of us could have given him a present, it would have been his self-destiny that the illness stole.

"However, everything in life gives us something we can learn from. I learned to look and find something positive in everything; that kind and loving words instilled love and respect in everyone who knew my dad and that I wish to live my life the same as my dad; and having been with my dad through his illness, I have learned to cherish every day of life no matter how it appears on the surface, and to find the energy to enjoy life and to play a little every day. Learning these lessons - to appreciate life and to always find something good to say, and to smile and laugh at something - all of this was emphasized in my dad's life and has given my life meaning and perhaps his as well. If this is all someone, me, him, or any of us learned from his life, I think it would be enough."

To conclude my brother's thoughts I remember he said quietly to a tearful room, "I see in everyone here a story or a special memory that came from knowing my dad. I know this sweet soul will always be in my heart and I know everyone else's hearts also."

Before going to sleep that night I felt closer to my father, and knew I would tell Sam more about him another time.

* * *

"After my father's death there was no money, so my mom went back to nursing and worked odd shifts every other week. I still liked to play for my mother, but she wasn't home as much. The bills had piled up while my dad was trying to recover, and all their savings had been spent putting my brothers and sister through school. We got by, but I was usually alone, and frequently made dinner and cleaned the house. I felt I had to mature even more quickly, and become responsible for my mother and myself."

I sensed Sam's understanding when she added, "I can tell the challenges pushed you to be who you as much as anything."

Sam's eyes showed an inquisitiveness to know more and I continued.

"Yes, it became evident when I was preparing to go to college. I decided to go to Rutgers, on the New Jersey side of Philadelphia where I had been accepted, but knew I would need to pay my own tuition. I borrowed enough to cover my first semester and set out to make some money. Since playing music was my saleable talent, I interviewed at hotel restaurants and lounges to play the piano."

"It surprised me how receptive they were, and I was soon playing as many nights of the week as I wanted. It was too perfect to plan. Rather than going out and spending money like other students, I was getting paid to play in clubs. I was thrilled. Rather than trying to make friends and meet people, everyone came to talk with me. Through performing I made good money and also came out of my shell. College was a fabulous time of my life.

"Most of the times I performed people truly appreciated my music. However, if I thought no one was listening, I would imagine my mother there and play with a passion that brought tears to my eyes. Here I am, once again tonight, going to play another job.

"That's enough about me for one night. Besides, I need to save time for you to tell me about yourself. I want to hear about what you were like growing up."

Sam's look seemed to see inside me and past my suggestion. Her comment punctuated the look, "I sense the child in you is still hiding behind, and playing hide and seek with, your responsible persona. I appreciate the peek offered by your story."

"You sound like a wise sage." Sam had surprised me by her

directness and my response seemed to come from someone else, "So you recognize yourself in it?"

Sam replied gracefully and with a smile, "I'll tell you mine and you can decide for yourself."

My story had ended before dessert arrived, and we still had plenty of time to linger before I needed to walk over to the Borgia. As I heard Sam's story, her life came alive to me and I felt, perhaps as she had listening to my life, like a mix of being one of her childhood friends, an approving neighbor and a cherished love.

Sam started willingly, "You don't know any of the islands or towns in or around the Puget Sound do you?" Sam barely stopped, "Well, I grew up outside of the town of Port Orchard on my family's farm." Sam used her napkin to draw a map of the State of Washington showing the Olympic Peninsula, the tear-drop shaped waters of the sound and some quickly sketched islands between a bunch of squiggly lines for mountains. She put a star on what looked like an island, but it was connected to the peninsula. She initialed it and tossed it to me saying, "Here, you can have it framed."

"The star's where I was born and raised. The town is framed by the Olympic Mountains just behind to the west and the Cascade Mountains with Mt. Rainier to the east. Over on the west coast and just in from the P for Pacific Ocean is the temperate rain forest. It's awesome. It's filled with ferns, waterfalls and lush growth everywhere, and gets as much as two hundred inches of rain a year. Then, on the east side of the peninsula in the Puget Sound are islands stretching from Anderson, Vashon and Bainbridge Island all the way north along the peninsula and across to the San Juan Islands, Vancouver Island and British Columbia."

Sam reached across for my napkin and each place appeared as she whipped through another drawing. She added a few dots across the water to show the ferry routes to her town and also to a few of the islands without bridges. "Seattle is here and the dots show the ferry."

Sam glanced around, and snatched a napkin from an empty table. Talking as she drew, "My parents and I lived in a cottage by the apple and pear orchards on my uncle's farm across from his house. Voila!"

Again delivered by air, I looked at the third of my growing collection.

"It looks like you were surrounded by nature everywhere."

"Yes, but that's only the cartography lesson. It sets the scenery though for what it was like growing up. My family was practically the center of a close-knit community. I'm an only child, but there were tons of people around the farm, so it was really as if I had a large extended family."

"What's you family like?"

"Well, my immediate family is my mother, father and uncle. They were, and still are, the core of my life. Each of them instilled characteristics I recognize in myself every day. Although maybe a couple that push my buttons from my mother."

"What do you mean by that?"

"I'm kidding, kind of. My mother has amazing strength of character combined with as much flexibility and resiliency as I've ever seen. There are just some aspects of my mother I've resisted, and I get a little crazy when I see myself being like my mother. Mostly though I'm pleased. I'll tell you the short version of her story and you'll understand where her, and probably my, values and beliefs started."

Sam rolled her eyes and kept going with a flourish.

"The rebellious spirit in my mother began the adventure that ripped away her ties to conformity, parents, and traditions in Japan. All, as she would say, for the allure of love."

"Adventurous, and rebellious," I repeated. "Tell me more. It sounds romantic."

Sam explained more matter-of-factly, "She left her family in

Japan as a young girl in disgrace due to an affair with a foreign emissary, and followed her lover to America. But, when he lost interest, she went to live on her uncle's farm outside of Seattle. Eight months later I was born. By then my mother never wanted to see the father again."

"Lower on romance and more toward non-conformity."

"Yes, but at that point neither really mattered. She'd changed her life and was freer than she ever could have been in Japan. Once here, she not only survived, but flourished, as people who are catapulted into life are pushed to do. The farm became her life, but I think it also offered a safety she could structure her life around.

"You said there are sides you resist?"

"Yeah, well, I know, and really I appreciate everything about her, but the structure and organization inherited from my mother's family was too much sometimes. While raising me, she worked hard in the orchards, and not only began running my uncle's business, but expanded the distribution into markets in Seattle. Being around her while she worked so hard, I acquired a work ethic where I occasionally feel I'm hand-cuffed to myself. So, as the spirit of control and proper respect was ingrained in my mind, I also became self-disciplined. I've learned to appreciate her ways as I see the value in my own experiences."

"Sam, you seem pretty balanced. If she was business and hard work, who does your artistic and fun-loving side come?"

"My father. He was the opposite. That is, the man I acknowledge as my only true father since he married my mother when I was one and a half years old. The love for my father was inspired through all we did together. He developed his interests in art and nature side by side with me, and taught me in the process.

"His parents were half Indian from a local tribe and half French Canadian, and his world was the Olympic Peninsula and the surrounding area. He had worked at a number of different jobs from fishing to mill work before meeting my mother, but once they were married, he worked on the farm."

"So he was drawn into the family business too?"

"Yes, but no matter where he worked, his true talent was as an artist. When freed from helping around the farm, he would take me for hikes along the water, or into the mountains. We would bring lunch, and set up for hours of drawing and painting.

"He still proudly claims, 'My daughter was born with a paint brush in her hand, and I'm the proud father who put it there.' His influence and the many days painting with him imbued me with a love for nature, and a way to express my inner feelings. I'll always love him for it.

"While growing up I applied myself to the disciplined art of Japanese flowers and mountains, and also developed an unique approach that combined pen and ink drawings with selective touches of paint. The landscapes and trees surrounding our home provided excellent studies for the hours I spent painting. The scenes I captured of the Olympic Mountains and the Puget Sound contained all the love of my home. My father tells everyone 'his' love for nature is expressed through 'my' art.

"My favorite medium was, and still is, water color."

Sam added with professional authority and irreverence, "I know oils last longer than water colors, but maybe that's what I like, the acceptance that it may all disappear and need to be recreated again, but new and different some day."

Sam thought out loud, "In some ways I will always be a little girl in my parents eyes, but even as a child, Uncle J treated me like a master and teacher.

"He told me ancient parables from his vast knowledge of Japanese lore, and stories of his life too, filled with examples of respect and wisdom for each day's activities. Every day together we exchanged teachings. Uncle J would tell a story about something he saw as poignant for that day's experience, and I would relate what I had seen through my eyes that day. Sometimes it was just fun, but other times we each learned something of life through the other's eyes that carried a meaning deep into our hearts.

"As a memento and reminder of the pearls of wisdom shared, Uncle J bestowed me with the sapphire necklace I always wear near my heart."

"It's beautiful," I acknowledged.

Sam held it out so I could see better. She looked at it as if she was speaking to it.

"Outwardly Uncle J treated the endless stream of kids and adults who came to the farm from the community equally. I was not singled out as a princess publicly, or it might have embarrassed me and subjected me to playful ridicule. The beauty and paradox was I knew Uncle J expressed a special love for me, but he truly loved me equally with all the others too. Everyone felt his or her own special connection to him; just as the one Uncle J and I had. He showed everyone respect by finding wisdom in each person, and thanked each individual for being his teacher.

"Through him," Sam declared, "I learned endless principles about life by how he interacted with his neighbors, but the major influence was the discipline of meditation and movement he taught; what he called the mysteries of his art. This beloved man intermingled the wisdom of his ancestry and a respect for all human and natural life, into a vibrancy that was felt by everyone who knew him."

As Sam continued her story, I could tell that as much as she was exceptionally close to her parents and loved them, she felt doubly so toward her Uncle J. Sam looked to her uncle like a child who believes a friend's parents understand her better than her own.

Explaining that was the case, Sam elaborated, "My uncle was my surrogate mother and father combined. He played a major role in tying together the pieces of my life, and added layers that intertwined the threads from my parents and friends."

Apparently, through her family, Sam became a mixture of discipline and creativity. She had the benefit of living close to nature and the influences surrounding her farm life. The blending of cultures and genetics wove a tapestry of influences that had transported her through life. She was somewhere between a flying carpet and an intricate but earth-bound Oriental rug. Sam was a hybrid with individual distinction like a magician with the spark of a Taoist master and a lumberjack integrated into a clever artist and astute business person.

Sam skipped ahead, "When it came time to look at colleges, I had no idea how my portfolio would compare with other's work. While waiting for acceptance letters, I bit my nails for the only time in my life. Even after I received acceptances, I couldn't paint or draw for a month. I wanted to tell my parents I didn't want to go. Part of it was that they were so certain I'd be a success, which was another way of saying 'We expect you to succeed.' It was as if that was the only way I could be. In a way I felt there was nothing for me to gain. I wanted to go out and prove them right but at the same time I wanted to prove them wrong. It was useless to fight myself though, I was conditioned to always do my best. Well, that was easy in a small town, but at school I'd just be one of kids like me from all over the country."

I nodded understanding, and listened as Sam expressed the fear we all experience when we leave a comfortable home for the unknown.

"Fortunately or not, my self confidence is an impenetrable protector and I dove ahead, but I found watching my fingernails grow back was a reminder of the self doubt. Of course, my family was not surprised when I was accepted everywhere I applied. The initial excitement of going away hid some of the fears underlying my decision to attend art school on the east coast. I had insisted on being near the art museums and galleries there, and I presented that as a compromise to my wilder dream of studying in Europe.

"I really was ready to dive into the world. I wanted to explore life in a city so I could experience the parts of life my small community did not offer. After a great deal of examining all alternatives, I chose to leave my slice of heaven to go to art school in Philadelphia.

"Initially my parents questioned why I had to go so far away. It had been inconceivable to them that their only daughter and almost only family would be three thousand miles away. However, they eventually supported my decision, and would, as they always had, continue to do whatever was necessary to encourage my drawing and painting. Although I knew they'd miss me, I also knew they wanted me to make my own decisions.

"They had shared their wisdom with me, 'We want you to know when you succeed, it is an achievement you initiated. When you encounter setbacks, you will value the experiences and learn from them if you rebound yourself. Always remember that you have our love and blessings in any choice you make.' My family knew, as I realized, that by being unrestrained I could truly delve into new freedoms and fly into life. However, my rootedness would keep me from flying away.

"In a way they blessed me. I remember how their approval had supported my self confidence. My mother's words have always stayed with me."

Sam quoted her. "You've earned our respect by being disciplined and studious. Continue to be responsible for whatever actions you choose and keep in mind how your actions reflect back to your family. We respect you to make your own decisions now."

"By consciously integrating their values into my decisions," Sam acknowledged, "I knew I had a foundation for life. I felt their ability to let go and not control me supported my self-respect and cleared space for me to learn life on my own terms.

The balance was, in fact, that I would always feel grounded near my home and family, but also anywhere else too."

Sam's awareness spoke volumes, "In many respects the distance turned out to reinforce how much I cherished the love and closeness I'd shared with my parents and uncle. The initial loneliness of leaving my family and friends was co-mingled with the adventure of becoming enmeshed in a new world even more outrageous than I'd imagined."

I knew from the way Sam spoke of herself and everyone close to her, that her upbringing had given her the inner strength and focus, quick mind and sensitivity to what's inside a person that I perceived in her. It seemed that throughout her life she learned from people whether they were nurturing or openly hostile, similar or diametrically opposed polar opposites, and in some ways like me, either or both had pushed her into life.

I offered, "It's phenomenal to me that you recognized what these influences in your life were presenting to you."

Sam replied, "Yeah, well that's easy to say now, but back then I also was part fool. Don't get me wrong though, I think being a fool should be a mandatory part of everyone's life; that's how we can break the cookie-cutter, sameness of life. But, it takes a while to wake up, and be a little more conscious. Reacting to life's stimulus as it popped up became a problem at some point, so somewhere along the line I learned to pay attention."

Sam casually stated a whole life's philosophy, "At some point I began to see all the opportunities I was creating, and started to take a responsible role, shaping my life to be what I desired. Rather than just responding to the things in my life, I started on a path where I could begin contributing some of the richness I received, and give some to others.

"I guess like most people, I started by looking to understand myself once I left home. In a way everything and nothing prepared me for all the new people and experiences during college; especially Randi."

Then I was introduced, through Sam's story, to Randi, who was her roommate when she started college. Anyone could see from the love in Sam's eyes they would be life long best friends. The two must have created a bond that was almost inseparable, and it was obvious they were a dynamic force together.

Sam began to explain Randi, but swore she could only scratch the surface until I met her, "Randi's self confidence came from learning to keep control of her wildness and presenting a trust worthy image to everyone, starting with her parents while a kid. She played the game well. She had fooled everyone as a kid so she could go to college parties while still in high school, but she never lost control of situations; in part by staying away from drugs and alcohol."

Sam blushed but spoke like she was only stating a fact, "Her one true vice, however, was sex. Even while young she told me she would teach her lovers just what she wanted. Actually, she only had a handful of lovers in her life, but stayed with each one to explore the possibilities of pleasing in depth. Randi had an explosive balance of impulsiveness and street smarts, but she kept sex in perspective and took precautions. I teased her, saying she was a body scientist, studying bodies for the sake of art."

Sam laughed, "A friend like this introduced me to what seemed like an unbelievable odyssey. I was guided through college life, city life, artists, musicians and more by a wild woman who simultaneously cut me loose and watched over me like a mother hen. Randi was protective and somehow steered me away from trouble before any could even develop, well almost. I was shy and innocent in comparison, and Randi, perhaps like a mother, encouraged me to stay that way.

"We went to a lot of parties. Seeing how crazy others were, made me realize how staid I was, and I started to hate myself for it. I wanted to break free, but somehow it wasn't really in me to let go of my 'proper' ways. I wanted to be like Randi, but I didn't really know how. I was an innocent fool, but I'll tell you, there are days I would trade my whole life for a minute of that innocence again.

"It all happened too fast. One night at the end of my junior year, Randi, I and our boyfriends decided to drive to the Outer Banks in North Carolina for a weekend and sleep on the beach.

"Well, by the time I knew 'it', school was over for the summer, and the guy had decided to transfer to another school, and we'd broken up.

In a surprisingly open and light way of introducing her single motherhood, Sam related a conversation with Randi.

"Randi teased me and asked, 'Sam, after all I'd taught you, tell me again how you let yourself get pregnant?'

"I replied, "Hey it worked out okay. I've got a beautiful daughter and you as a nanny. What could be better?"

"So now you're saying you planned it this way?"

"Yeah, that's my story, and I'm sticking with it."

Sam simply came right out and told me she chose never to call and tell the father she was pregnant or that she had decided to have her child. Effectively the man just disappeared from her life.

This was Sam's way of joking through what someone else might never have told.

Sam said a little too unequivocally, "Alex makes me as happy as anyone I've ever known, and even if I could, I wouldn't change a thing."

She stated her philosophy, "The instruction manual that comes with babies is as limited in any one area, as it is in every area. Raising a child under the best or worst circumstances is a matter of accepting what you've got and making the best decisions as each situation presents itself. A child could have too much, or too little attention, too easy or too hard a life, and any one of millions of influences could become the key to repelling her from the negative or drawing her to the positive."

"Irrespective of what I thought I did or didn't want, my decision to have Alex, and the necessity of being responsible for another's life, changed me forever."

Sam abruptly changed tone and said emotionally, "Look, I don't know why I'm telling you some of this stuff, but the fact is, some days I went through hell and hated everyone, and some days I still do!"

In a sober voice, Sam opened an old fight with herself and confessed.

"I berated myself for sabotaging my life. I've always wondered what I would have done otherwise with relationships. Even something stupid like all the traveling I thought I'd do, or my old dream of living in Europe and studying art there. Finally with my business I'm doing some of it, and that makes it better, but it was a long time coming. Anyway, I know when I meet a person who truly loves me, the right one will stay whether I have a daughter or not. But, once in a while, I have regressed to blaming Alex when something hasn't worked out."

Sam looked like she needed some reassurance, but sounded light-hearted , "Well, this is your chance. Do you want to make it easier on both of us and leave now?"

Sam continued before I could answer.

"Phil, I tend to say whatever is on my mind. Sometimes I end up feeling like an ass, but I'd rather speak honestly and let you know who I am. If you're someone special, it won't scare you away."

I saw a crack between her humor and sensitivity, and to ease any apprehension said, "It sounds like you're human and willing to express yourself; flaws and all. You seem pretty terrific so far. I'll take a chance and stay to find out more."

It looked like Sam had a tear behind her smile which told me I said something right. I did make a mental note though. I knew all too frequently there was more truth in people's kidding than any one ever admits, and I recognized some reluctance in her barb pushing me away. It was easy to see because I'd said the same thing before, and meant it.

Sam's return to her story broke the minor tension, and she began telling me about how the business had started. At the same time we left the restaurant to get some air and head toward my job.

"Well," Sam resumed, "one way or another I made it through art school. After that Randi and I started the business that became the other central theme in my life. Together we faced the task of planning how to make a living in the art world. Randi had seriously joked, 'We could get by pretty well doing modeling for art students mixed with some waitressing."

"I came up with another idea, and laid it out in a single, all night meeting of the minds. There were lots of questions to be answered, but mostly it was serious fun, and alternated from fits of laughter to a few tears. It was a 'no room for fears' business plan party between the partners, owners, workers, and staff all rolled into one; the two of us. That night we started the business.

"In the beginning we represented ourselves and a group of other artists. We sent letters, made calls, met with hundreds of people, and it worked. Surprisingly, the portfolios of our own work and our friends were readily accepted as a fresh approach for adding a new touch to homes being decorated. We actively created a market for our art work instead of waiting for someone to find us. After a while, we built a network with a number of interior designers in and around the city, and finally connected with galleries and even produced some private art shows. We had some rough patches getting started and some slow periods, but we made a living and had fun doing it.

Sam seemed to take great joy in quoting a subsequent executive business meeting between her and Randi.

"Randi had announced, 'It was easy to forecast the whole thing would be a total success; I simply knew you could do it.'

"I knew Randi really did appreciate me, and kidded back, 'I'm just lucky the business people like your cocky, flirting but keep it in your pants, attitude."

"Randi had teased back, 'Yeah, and it'll be worth a million someday, you'll see.'

"I'll take half a million, but I might have to share my portion with my mother."

Sam expounded, "I knew even then how important working with my mother had been, and called on her business sense many times. She had been more understanding and supportive with all I went through raising Alex than I'd ever hoped, and was invaluable while the business was growing.

"Randi was the same, and sometimes more. She was on the front lines and was the glue that held me together. Plus, she cared for Alex when I wanted to escape, and handled the business so professionally I sometimes wondered if she even needed me."

"One basic thought kept us going, 'Keep moving toward it'. Some days I didn't even know what 'it' was, but I pushed myself, or was too busy or wired to stop. Sometimes the scariest times were when it was quiet," Sam confided. "The key was to always wake up every day with a plan, and even if things went haywire, I had some basis to decide what to do next."

It was clear to me that Sam knew how to find the best in any situation, and had created an independent lifestyle that reinforced her ability to take life on her terms. In many respects I got the impression she had taught her daughter from some of the same life experiences as her mother had taught her.

Sam was just finishing her story as we stood across the cobblestone street from the Borgia in the rebuilt, old-fashioned, open air market that was empty of the summer art and craft show, and relatively quiet. We turned toward each other, and with one mind stepped to embrace. At first we held each other tightly, as if we both needed reassurance the other would stay.

Then we held each other more gently, and Sam looked up into my eyes. We knew we were going to kiss, and I felt the kiss answered any doubts Sam had earlier. I felt like an awkward teenager, but the kiss had more meaning than any word I've ever spoken. As our lips touched softly, I actually felt giddy. I remembered a time when kisses were truly special, and held the secrets of love like a childhood oath. Again we meshed together, holding each other tightly, like a sealed promise. There was passion, but it spoke more of trust. Shared experiences and emotions bind two lovers, and in our hearts we knew there was more. With a softly spoken "good night" our hands touched lightly before walking off in different directions.

Interlogue

Imagine yourself in your back yard as a child. Was there an old oak tree whose grace captured the essence of your yard, or an apple tree that grew as you did from sapling to maturity? Did your tree grow up outside your window in the city, and amaze you with its ability to survive? Can you remember the trees that watched you as you matured through life? Did you spend long days climbing into the sky, or swinging from limb to limb pretending to be a monkey? Did playing in the branches inspire your imagination to blossom, as mine did? Maybe you never climbed a tree, but found awe in its colors or how it sparkled when it was covered with ice and snow.

There were a few trees I played in while growing up. I pretended to be an explorer paddling uncharted waterways in the Amazon under canopies of vines interlacing trees like snakes wrapped around branches; or, I was a pirate sailing into a secluded bay surrounded by an ancient forest, where I climbed a giant sequoia to build my lookout to observe from the lofty tree tops and guard against invaders after my treasure; and, of course, I was a knight holding a gnarled, twisted tree to steady my foothold on a steep cliff while the other hand gallantly brandished a sword to protect my village from the dragon who lived in the cave below.

The trees were my friends. When there was no one else to play with, I was always happy to play with them. In addition to being the source of my games, the trees were also my teachers. I remember the time I climbed too high and was afraid to come down and the time I fell. The days after those episodes I went right back to climbing with the certainty that I would not make the same mistake again. Each experience taught me that with determination and courage I could forge ahead once I overcame an obstacle. Even cuts and bruises were worn as badges with pride. Sharing these adventures with the trees made them special, and the bond I created with trees has lived in me forever.

With this initiation I continued to look closely at trees wherever I went in life. Trees came alive to me whether I was in a city park, the country, a forest or against the openness of the beach. When I was older, I started a new game in which I identified personalities in trees, and gave them human characteristics. In this way I examined how elements of human nature were reflected by aspects of tree natures. One of my favorite comparisons was of a bonsai to a tree in the forest. A bonsai, in a way, reassured me about the nurturing contributions of family and society, and a tree in the forest reminded me of freedom and personal resourcefulness.

To me a bonsai is disciplined with integrity and purpose. It is molded and shaped, but unique and distinct. It knows it is always watched over and cared for with loving hands. It is raised with strict rules that would restrict another, but that allow the creative artistry in its soul to develop. All of this nurtures its grand potential into a star to be admired.

Or, perhaps to be an identical seedling, but in the wild; free to live and grow. Now it is shaped by the hands of nature through all the climatic extremes, and watched over by the wind, the sun and the moon. Maybe only one human actually sees or touches the graceful, elegant lines of its trunk and branches, but it finds contentment in the self knowledge of its humble purpose. It may seem to blend with its neighbors to become the forest, but it is truly an individual too. Although perhaps never a star, its common sense connection to nature makes it just as beautiful.

These are but two of the myriad of possible personalities of trees. All of us can identify with at least some aspects of the characteristics that define us as represented by tree personalities. Sometimes these thoughts are like a cold draft that gusts into my mind to sweep out any cobwebs. Then I can clearly see that the branches reaching to the sky in a forest are a single unit containing individual branches and leaves. What appears infinite and represents the epitome of the unlimited, unique personalities, albeit with many traits in common, offers a peek at how separate decisions comprise a singular web.

Each branch a decision, and all influenced by friends, family and society. Decisions such as whether to go to school and which one, or to learn street smarts and old fashion common sense; whether to follow a creative artistic path, or to go into finance. Also, significant people in life can influence the hobbies we select such as playing sports and which ones, playing games or reading books, or mechanical toys versus art projects. It becomes apparent that each choice will impact who becomes a friend, and how relationships begin. A decision, as a child, to draw pictures might lead to becoming an architect and marrying a college classmate raised in Europe who loves traveling the world, or a good natured child who starts in sales in his father's business and stays single while living at his parents and dating his high school girlfriend. Literally, anything is possible.

After considering the outside influences, a wealth of emotional factors creates the dynamics of each person's personality. Am I sensitive and caring, or hard and spiteful; loving and joyful or angry and hateful? Am I giving and open, or miserly and withdrawn?

The clearest way to identify major and minor character traits is to see how someone acts in a crisis situation. The dramas of life offer a way to recognize which aspects we will hold fast and which we are willing to change.

Challenges in life open new opportunities, but ignoring them can be devastating. Crisis in the life of a tree can mirror this human drama. Abrupt changes could be brought on by a bolt of lightening, splitting life into charred pieces, or by being caught in a wild fire. Imagine being swept away in a river of lava, or carried downstream after being torn away from your roots in a flood. And yes, the ignobling indignity of being cut down. But perhaps even then, to accept the most dramatic changes life can bring, and forge ahead in a new direction.

In this parallel to life a tree can continue as handsome furniture in a house or even a museum, or as an instrument in a symphony orchestra vibrating sweetly with the passionate sounds of true genius. There is also the possibility of being sculpted to precision for the straight mast or cutting bow. Or, to be polished each day, after working as the resting place for drinks in a rowdy bar, and trading stories of drunken nights and dancing on your friend, the floor, across the way.

At this point you may be well beyond your quota for considering the meaning of your life's decisions and how life can be mirrored to you by looking at trees. But you've come this far, and the story will resume soon. So indulge in one more tangent.

Imagine jumping like a child with an impish smile into a daydream. Imagine being a tree watching your life story. See yourself playing and growing up under the branches, or climbing the tree to see into a bird's nest. Imagine yourself picking fruit from the tree to help your grandmother make your favorite pie. Remember how you watched leaves fall to the ground to be rolled in or collected for a leaf fort to hide in until it was time for dinner. Remember in youths naivete sitting under the tree with your best friend sharing the dreams of what to be when you grew up. Certainly, never forget your first kiss and dreams of true love when you imagined marriage, kids and living happily ever after. Where are they now? How have all those experiences affected your life and shaped who you are today? And, when was the last time you thought about the results of your life's decisions?

Then, as you get up and go to the window to look at a tree, imagine the process from when the tree was first planted to its present life. Realizing that some series of decisions brought you to where you are presently is sobering. There was some process of hows, whys and what ifs that created this unique person, who has your birth certificate. Once you have come this far, look at what cards you are holding, and appreciate the rules in the game of life you have already learned. People can make more of this life than just unconsciously filling in the blanks of others' expectations. The next step is to consider that although the tree may be rooted to its fated spot in life, humans have the ability to change.

Chapter 3

Sam and I knew when we talked on the phone the next day we wanted to hear more of each other's lives, and decided to get together as soon as possible. I felt so alive when we were together. It was as though a magnetic force was drawing us together. The difficulty was finding time in Sam's schedule. Our lives had revolved around our own situations for so long we had almost forgotten how to make room for a relationship other than with our daughters. My schedule was freer than it had been for many years, but Sam's calender was booked for weeks and in some areas even months. However, she was free for dinner on Tuesday and we decided to take whatever few hours we could.

In one conversation on the phone, Sam had quickly filled in the rest of her pivotal relationships and experiences. It was easier for her to be more cavalier after having gotten over the tough part during dinner. Sam summed it up, "I'd seen little relationship appeal in even the most intriguing men I've known, and simply preferred my friends, work and Alex. I've met potential relationship candidates at social outings with friends or business parties. Maybe I've fooled myself and I've actually driven all the others away, but even when I 'got involved' for almost a year two different times, eventually I choose quiet evenings at home.

"I'd say being with you is better than staying home and I feel in my heart that you're worth taking a risk."

She closed the subject by declaring the rest of her past encounters were almost unworthy of mentioning, and figuratively dismissed them with a wave of her hand. She did assure me she would tell me other stories that were more representative and pertinent to knowing her.

For me, it had been awhile since I had explained why I was a single parent, especially since I had come to terms with that period for my own purposes. But, I was willing to tell it one more time.

I had come to prefer starting fresh with people, and not rehashing old memories. However, this time I wanted Sam to know what I had been through and the subsequent changes in my life. It seemed expressing our lives perspectives would be fundamental to understanding each other, and perhaps it would all seem lighter though Sam's eyes.

One of my theories is that we tell our stories to others over and over again until we finally catch on to the true meaning and value offered to our lives. People often tell, and retell, their same favorite stories. The essence of the philosophy is that each experience in life has a lesson, and the rehashing indicates a person is not sufficiently bored with his or her past to move on with life. The key to the theory is the value of listening to our own words, as well as other's. When a person finally understands the meaning of his or her own stories, he/she is able to appreciate the insight in what was offered and why it was so compelling. Just think, we have millions upon millions of experiences in our lives, but only a dozen or so make it into our top stories in life.

I had replayed my stories many times to my learning partners, as I had come to call my past relations. When I met Sam, I decided I would tell my tale one more time. I felt Sam's acknowledgement would validate that I was truly on a new journey.

* * *

We had agreed to meet at an Indian restaurant on the University of Pennsylvania campus. A classmate of mine from college had opened the place after we graduated, and I enjoyed combining a good meal with a chance to say hello. This time, however, I knew it was his slowest night, and he wouldn't mind if we occupied one of his prime tables, one with the sunken seating and a semi-private setting, for mostly talking. I got there a few minutes before Sam, and we were chatting when Sam walked into the restaurant.

Sam and I embraced. I felt a tingling in my heart, and a warmth within. It was a unique feeling. It was as if my heart was telling me with its intuitive sense to recognize this type of tingling, and to be open to what was coming.

We held each other for a couple of minutes. Neither of us seemed to want to let go, so we didn't. While we were hugging, I glanced over her shoulder to see my friend's broad smile.

I introduced Sam to my friend, "This is Moriah, like the desert wind."

He bowed slightly to Sam and spoke through his smile, "You are more radiant than Phil could have described. Welcome to my restaurant."

"Thank you, Phil says it's the best, and you treat your guests like royalty."

"Ah, well, Phil exaggerates a bit. But keep it up, you're one of my best sources of customers."

"Hey, the food speaks for itself."

Sam met his smile with her own and her eyes danced with a delight that I knew must endear her to most people she met.

Moriah showed us to our table. Almost immediately a waiter brought us a sample of spicy dips, naan, my favorite bread, and promised to bring a sample of entrees to us.

I admitted to Sam, "I've never seen the inside of one of his menus, but I've always been happy with whatever he brings."

I began to tell a story about the science class we took together at Penn, but Sam interrupted and forced me to start right in on my story.

She cajoled, "I want some info on your daughter Anna, and when you stopped last time, you had not even told me anything about her." She then sweetly encouraged me to tell her everything and added, "If you're lucky, and save some time for me, I might tell you more about my life too."

Without further hesitation I picked up where I'd left off at Tang's.

"I performed almost five nights a week during my freshman year. One time a friend, his sister and a few of his friends came to hear me play in a jazz club. I made an immediate connection with his sister, whose name was Marcy, and we began dating. Dating for me usually meant my date would come to see me perform, and then we would go out afterward.

"Marcy came to see me over a couple months, and we fell in love with each other. When she was with me those nights, my heart went into every song, and it was as though I played and sang just for her. All of my feelings were poured into my music. It seemed she heard and understood. We felt charged and excited about ourselves and the world, life, and clearly each other.

"It was funny in the beginning, while the club was being cleaned up, we would go up-stairs above the restaurant where there was a sofa outside the owner's office to talk and then back to the piano so I could play for her. When he was ready to go home after settling his books, we were usually still there talking and playing into the night. I think we were mostly running on youth and adrenaline.

"At the time I thought I offered her my heart and soul, and expressed my love openly. Only in retrospect did I realize that it was mostly through the music, and the music was also a shield. I didn't understand it was creating a barrier between us, and in actuality I was difficult to reach. My playing actually received the love and expressed it, and acted as an intermediary.

"I realized much later that my heart had closed when my father died, but I was completely unaware of the implications with Marcy. Outwardly I exhibited all the symptoms of being head over heels in love. Only after years of questions and introspection was I able to acknowledge a part of me was off in another dimension reachable only through music. So, while I thought I was expressing my love to Marcy, it was being transformed and directed through my music."

As I started my explanations, I stopped for a second. I had a peculiar feeling, and needed to overcome my feeling of uncertainty. And, even though it was all what I perceived as true, I thought I was being too serious about myself. With one look, Sam renewed my confidence that talking about loving someone else was all right, and to continue. The momentary doubt dissipated when she smiled and told me, "Keep going, and don't worry, I'll let you know if you get too serious."

I continued, "By the middle of my freshman year, I realized I was making enough money afford to pay for a private college. I decided to audition at The Curtis Institute of Music in Philadelphia. Perhaps the money gave me the confidence to apply, and even though I made money with jazz, my classical technique was always clean. I was not only accepted but given a full scholarship based on merit alone.

"Marcy and I had been talking about getting a place together. Once I was accepted at Curtis, Marcy decided to transfer to Temple University so we could move into Philadelphia. We looked for a place within walking distance of center city for me, and accessible to public transportation for her. Since I had already saved my tuition for the next semester, my scholarship allowed me to use the money as a down payment on a small house. We chose the art museum area, and searched until we found a place that was perfect.

"That part of town was relatively inexpensive and feasible for people getting started. You know, the area just north of the museums along the Benjamin Franklin Parkway where the factories and warehouses were being renovated into apartment buildings?"

"Yes," Sam acknowledged. "I've visited friends there and

always felt like I was in a small town within the city."

"That's the way I feel too.

"Initially there were many reasons for looking there: It was less than a mile from the middle of the city and Rittenhouse Square; In just a few minutes we could walk to the river drives in Fairmount Park where everyone runs or bikes; And, as you said, the sense of being in a small neighborhood. Almost every section of Philadelphia has gone through rehabilitations from Society Hill to the University City section. But, when we moved to the museum area it was just starting there, and I loved it immediately."

"What was the condition of the house?"

"Pretty good. It didn't require any major repairs, and everything functioned well enough to move in. The previous owner had lived on the first two floors and rented the third floor to a college student. That worked out great too. The student stayed, and the rent money helped pay for general upkeep and most repairs.

"It must have been a good investment."

"It was, but at the time it was home. Whether others thought the area was desirable or not, from then on it was my favorite neighborhood."

"So the two of you settled in?"

"Yes. Starting our home together made us feel united as partners in an exciting new phase of life. We had candle lit dinners on the bare dining room floor, and evenings in front of the fireplace on the pillows which furnished the living room. It was fun starting to learn about life, each other, and ourselves.

Everything was perfect. We were so tickled about life, I think we believed we would find happiness in anything we did together. After a year of living together, we decided to get married in the summer before our junior year. People, especially our families, told us we were too young, crazy, or to wait until after college, but we felt wise beyond our years and were certain we knew it was right.

"We took a four week honeymoon that following August traveling through New England to Maine, over to Nova Scotia, then across Canada through Quebec and Montreal before coming back down through Lake Champlain and Lake George. It was an outrageously fun summer. We bicycled and hiked in each area, and believed we owned the world. During this trip our daughter Anna was conceived, and by November we were already making plans for our family."

"Ah ha. Married and something about Anna all in two minutes."

"Yes, and I'll tell you more about Anna soon, but bear with me for a few more minutes."

"All right. I'll just listen.'

"This is when things started to change. Anna's birth the following May brought on a range of highs and lows in our relationship. I was completely captured by every movement and noise that came from Anna. I was especially in awe of how our love was manifest for the world to see. At the same time, the reality of responsibilities came with a suddenness that was sobering to our previously flexible and basically carefree college life.

"Marcy decided to postpone her senior year to be at home with Anna. Initially I think being a mother was a shock to her, but some natural instinct quickly filled the gaps that everyone else's well-meaning advice missed. Marcy poured all of her energy into Anna, and loved the feeling of nurturing this living extension of herself. I sensed she was content being a mother, and that she also found pleasure in expressing her love through taking care of me.

"Most of my energy was poured into my music, school and making a living. In this respect we were perfectly paired bookends with each of us holding up the opposite ends. We believed we were partners making our marriage fit our lives. The arrangement allowed me to study during the day and perform in the evenings, while Marcy took care of everything else. The situation suited me quite well. Later I realized it was a challenge for Marcy to have me away from the house and focused on areas difficult to share.

"Our relationship continued like that even after I graduated from college since I decided to apply for a fellowship program to continue my education.

"I had put together a proposal for research I wanted to do. My idea had originated from observing black gospel singers who performed at the college in a holiday program one year. I could see an almost hypnotic calm in the singers, while the resonance in their voices came from their bodies like cellos or violins. I felt I recognized the highest place music took me. At times when I was playing music, I reached a level I thought might be the same type of experience. The thought occurred to me to find volunteer subjects for a study and investigate it further.

"The idea was that the body is a musical instrument, and the research was to explore the correlation of brain activity to the vibrations created as the body and vocal cords resonated. I wanted to monitor their physiology and brain activity as they sang. I knew certain creative aspects were associated with the right hemisphere of the brain, and I wondered if there might be a connection to the interaction between singing and the vibrations in the right and left hemispheres of the brain.

"One of my teachers suggested I send my proposal to a friend of his at the University of Pennsylvania. An initial meeting ensued, and I presented the research ideas. Soon after, I was offered the fellowship in which I taught a couple of music classes a week, and took science classes with lab work to lay the foundation for the research work I'd designed. I remember sensing a connection to my father when I started a path into my research. Even though he was gone, I felt closer to him by stepping into his world of science and laboratories.

"Also like my dad, I had a family to support, but I continued performing at night so I could have both. In this way I earned a reasonably generous income while beginning my exploration through the graduate research work. I loved it all and felt I'd created a dream where I could have my cake and eat it too; the research allowed me to explore my fascinations in music and science, I still played music, and my wife and daughter were always home for me. Some nights though, after working, I collapsed into bed, and then first thing in the morning rushed off to school. I thought things were all right, but problems started to surface.

"Of course I see now it also created a gap, and my decisions began to push us farther apart. I still thought Marcy was the center of my universe, and truly her emotional support and love was what held me together.

"I dove into my work with a passion, and knew even then the research would lead to doctoral work, and probably continue forever. I was always thinking about the next phase of research. And, as I had expressed in my experience at Zanzibar Blue, I did finally personally experienced a small taste of what I thought my research would explain.

"Anyway, the years between starting the research and finishing my doctorate degree flew by. After my degrees were completed, I felt fortunate to find a teaching job at Temple in the Philadelphia area so we could stay where we already lived. It struck me as funny that this was actually my first real job. Well, that is if you consider being a college professor a real job. What was most important about it to me though, was that the university supported and encouraged the research I wanted to continue. The teaching position paid less than I made playing music at night, so that continued also.

"Marcy had become increasingly unhappy with our life together, or not together as was usually the case. By then Anna was going on five years old, and was at preschool for a half day during the week. With this break in Marcy's life, she became focused on needing more fulfillment from a relationship. The crisis came to a head when she made accusations that I was having an affair with another woman. She was wrong about the sexual affair, but in effect right about what should have been clear at the time. I was over-involved with music and work.

Ah, the clarity of mistakes with the benefit of hindsight.

"She, however, did have an affair; perhaps as a result of jealousy or simply from a need for more attention and affection. She said the affair had only been for the prior three months, but that it had opened her eyes. The other person did not really matter, and in fact she broke off with him quickly. It was just that she preferred being away from me. She explained she had spent over a year trying to tell me how she felt, but gave up when I just never seemed to listen.

"Either way, she was bitter and resentful toward me, and asked me to move out. She asked for a divorce, and took custody of Anna. Initially, I believed she was the one who was wrong. However, as each fight was lost and most of our communication was through attorneys, it began to dawn on me that there was no right or wrong. The marriage was over.

"My life had been so full, I had been completely unaware and blind to how I treated Marcy. Being so preoccupied with work, I had gone about my days unconscious of how she felt and how we were slowly losing our emotional connection. Years went by like a blur without anything to shake me into acknowledging these flaws or even considering that there was anything to acknowledge."

"I talked with Anna and saw her regularly, but it was difficult integrating a child into my business and social life. Without trying to make excuses, this period of transition was difficult, or distracting, or something I knew I would figure out someday. Anyway, we did not see as much of each other as was intended, expected, allowed, proper, or some adjective that would appropriately fit what I thought everyone expected of me. Anna though, even as a child, always amazed me with her ability to understand people, especially me, and accepted the time we did share together.

"I resolved to strengthen my connection to Anna. I began to let go of my resistance toward Marcy, as I realized fighting was only going to complicate making arrangements for me to pick up Anna every other week. What mattered was being civil so Anna could be nurtured through the transition rather than being the reason for another fight. I was forced to wake up and pay attention to how I was acting and what effects my actions had on the people I cared about.

"As I paid attention, I started uncovering emotions in myself, and noticed others had feelings too. It was too late to change how I had acted with Marcy, but the first glimmer of light was peeking through the clouds. The most surprising part to me was how quickly my insight received reinforcement, and amazingly, I was aware the healing process had begun.

"With my resolution, the next time we made plans for me to pick up Anna, Marcy and I seemed to remember how to communicate civilly again. The regular conversations with Marcy to make my arrangements for picking up Anna became more and more friendly.

"Then suddenly, after being divorced for a couple years, the nature of my life and my relationship with Anna changed, but due to circumstances nobody would have wanted. It turned out that Marcy was diagnosed with an advanced case of cancer and died quickly after the discovery. The last time we talked she was depressed and unwilling to accept that she could die. No matter how little time she had to go through the stages of accepting death, though, she knew plans had to be made for me to take Anna.

"The news was surreal and oddly like hearing about a character in a movie, but it was a movie I was in. However, the full reality was staring me in the face. The news was related to me as Anna held on to me with no apparent intention of ever letting go. The impact of the situation hit Anna and me in different ways. She remained calm and understanding in a way that nurtured me. I cried like a baby.

"The unresolved issues which had never reached closure in my relationship with Marcy had created emotional messes. I understood some reached back to unresolved feelings toward my father.

"My unconscious need for closure was forced on me abruptly. The changes made me question everything, and fear that it was all my fault.

"Fortunately Anna was there in the days that followed. She kept me focused on solutions while my emotions and doubts mounted a final massive attack. Anna was my support.

"Some of the wonder of the resiliency in a human being's nature showed up in me once I reached that low. Almost as abruptly as my confusion came, the clouds of the past started to dissolve. By sheer need to take responsibility for Anna, I found a way to forgive myself and immediately resolved to create new ways to live. Since giving up was not an option, I knew I had to move forward without the old baggage. There wasn't an overnight metamorphosis, but daylight was ahead.

"I realized Anna's experiences during the dissolution of the marriage and then Marcy's death had matured her well beyond her years. Whether Marcy and I had suppressed our emotions or vented them openly, Anna had remained the stabilizing factor in the middle of the volatility. Rather than reacting or screaming for attention she would retain an equanimity. When we were finally done with our nonsense, she would come over and hug us and cuddle until we lightened up. Between that behavior as a four year old and her sensibilities in the crisis as a seven year old, she taught me never to underestimate a young child's ability to understand.

"Sometimes Anna was sad and cried over her mother's

absence, but retained her joy when immersed in play or 'normal' life. Then, as always, Anna seemed as knowing as an adult is expected to be, and carried that ability throughout her life to see things with the simple clarity only a child truly can. Continually she has embraced each new facet in her world like the lead actress in a play. Not only did she know and acted her role perfectly, but she saw all of her supporting actor's roles as clearly as though she had learned the parts as an understudy. Although she stepped into the role of Anna, she could have played any one one of us. This was not done in a contrived way, but flowed from her naturally.

"Perhaps, due to her innocence she did not fall apart like adults who are conditioned by social habits. In fact, even through the challenges in her young life she maintained her innocence. Anna already had incredible insights into life and an intuitive perspective that gave her a clarity beyond reacting. Most amazing of all was what she taught me about the grieving process, all of which was brought into incredible focus through the eyes of a child. It seemed that Anna understood about life better than anyone, and even somehow intuitively about death.

"She began having dreams about meeting her mother in her favorite garden, and believed that her mother still existed and could be visited whenever she wished. When Anna described her dreams, she would give details about the color of the roses and flowers, and even the smells sometimes. Anna's eyes sparkled as she described the love she felt as her mother would hold her, or sing to her, and swing her around, while telling stories of what it was like where she had gone.

"I delved into the mystical aspects of her dreams, and learned there were books and prominent psychologists and psychiatrists who acknowledged seemingly unusual insights as more common than openly discussed. Studies at leading universities and prominent physicians explored these realms through personal interviews with patients who had near death or psychic experiences.

"It was a challenge to integrate the information she related into my prior knowledge or experiences, but the dreams gave her a sense of peace. We went for counseling to a doctor who was recommended as professionally reputable and also considered aware of "other possibilities." After a number of sessions, the doctor felt it was superfluous to worry about this wise child although he thought I might benefit from continuing to explore my understanding of myself and work through the grieving process with guidance.

"Also, so I could understand Anna's experiences, he suggested reading some books on Indian culture or aboriginal tribes where dreams were treated as real events to teach about life. I pursued this area with him and also read a number of the books he recommended which discussed some fairly difficult-to-believe concepts and experiences. Some of what I read also peaked my interest for more research on brain activity.

"However, for the time being, I was primarily reassured of Anna's sense of peace and purpose, no matter what any book or counselor thought. To me, the method was secondary to the essential fact that Anna reached an acceptance that her mother was gone. She was in all visible respects adjusting quite well.

"Of course Anna was to live with me, and I moved back into her, our, home. Her ready acceptance that being with me was a reality also forced me to accept the reality and move on. Caring for the needs of a seven year old gave me perspective. It helped that she was already a child when she came to me instead of a baby who required full time care. The day to day arrangements for getting her to school, making dinner and being home, forced lifestyle changes that were definitely changes for the better, and were actually just what I needed. Once together we became extraordinarily close. The bond of love connecting us grew each day in strength and flexibility.

"Even though I was the parent, I recognized Anna was

teaching me about life. This became especially clear as I came to understand the love Anna had for her mother. It helped me to let go of my anger, and made clear how much I had loved her too.

"I realized that the ego I created while teaching and performing had prevented me from seeing that there was something in me that needed fixing. But, as you can probably tell, I've come back down to earth. I began to take responsibility for my actions, and stopped blaming others for what happened in my life.

"Between Anna and my continued exploration of my psyche with the doctor we had seen, I began to realize that a major part of all my problem had stemmed from the difficulty of expressing my love to those close to me. I vowed to change for the better. Through the changes, I gained the wisdom of at least a couple lifetimes."

Sam was thoughtful for a moment but then nodded, "Yes, from the way you describe it, I'd say you did."

The restaurant was almost empty and quiet enough to hear the other couple there.

"I sense through it all you'll appreciate the richness of having Anna in your life. She sounds as if she's been a healing presence."

Sam had listened attentively, and her expressions while I spoke showed she appreciated my sharing. I felt Sam comprehended the significance of it all.

This was my past that led up to our meeting. If we were to move forward together, this was my chance to give Sam the meaning and then leave the stories behind.

Sam slid around the table, and put her arms around me. I believe in that moment I had a glimpse of Sam's love.

Sam promised, " I'll tell you more about myself the next time we see each other. For tonight though, I just want to let all you told me sink in. There's a lot of meaning to digest in what you related. Phil, just think if it only builds on all the knowledge you've gained from 'owning up' to your past."

* * *

I went home that evening, and briefly felt lighter as though I had released a weight from my heart. But by the time I went to bed, I began to feel troubled and restless. I lay awake for a while, and then drifted in and out of dreams.

I felt transformed, but I also knew there were dark aspects to these stories still hiding in the corners of my heart. I wanted to ask Sam to forgive me for it all, and 'wash away my sins,' but there were still some aspects that I would need to face myself.

First, I reflected on the period coming out of my self-absorption. Before the divorce could have been characterized as my "ignorance is bliss" period. Afterward, when I saw what I'd really been like, there were times of despair and loneliness. Finally I appreciated the push those feelings gave me, without which I might never have changed. I remembered:

* * *

After the divorce but before Marcy's death, I had wanted to blame her, or someone, for what was happening to me. However, after analyzing my problem to death, it became apparent that I had to accept much of the blame and take responsibility for my part.

I realized later the loss of my father in adolescence had pushed me to become independent, but I had learned to suppress my emotions. I had tended to be aloof, distant and cold rather than open to true intimacy with Marcy.

In fact, I must have unconsciously thought that anyone I allowed to be close to me, would abandon me like my father. So, I found ways to push them away first.

I'd had plenty of chances to open up and I began to understand I would continue to be emotionally aloof until I actually did. Without action the learning process could be an endless circle of repeating similar mistakes. Upon recognition, the process started, but it was years before I became close enough to anyone again to truly reciprocate love and accept another's care.

The other issue was expressing my feelings. My habit was to process everything in my mind, and so I lived there. Recognizing emotions within me, let alone expressing the ones I did notice, was like learning a foreign language. Acknowledging these faults brought on an instant karma effect. All of a sudden, everyone was making me aware of my habits. These interactions opened the opportunity for me to start changing consciously.

Prepared with the knowledge of my faults and an intention to change, I then entered the next phase of my life: the search for a new relationship. The process included a few stable relationships that lasted from six months to one year.

As each one realized she was unwilling to wait for me while I was coming to terms with my past, and how I was currently relating to her, she left. Then, the search continued. The good news was that as their paths crossed with mine, it left me, and the ones who related their progress during our continuing friendship, a little closer to being able to participate in a healthy, loving relationship.

Each woman I met was actually quite caring, and some of the ice surrounding my heart began melting away as I accepted I could receive love. I began to learn to express love in return, and even accept feeling the pain of heart ache when none of the relationships lasted. Each lesson took me closer to my new attitude.

Experience and understanding helped me believe it was possible to see the process to completion. Every step encouraged a belief that eventually the fruits of learning would be harvested and shared. In retrospect, I had truly turned a corner, but while caught up in the process, acknowledging the progress was slow. The learning process often seemed much worse than it was.

At one point it was almost beyond my comprehension that the theoretical possibilities desirable in a relationship would ever meet reality.

The process had arrived at the point where I thought any sensible person, meaning me, would prefer solitude unless I could meet someone as perfect as my mother. Well not really my mother, but the list had gotten so long it seemed like only an actual angel would be enough. In fact, an angel who was also great in bed, creative, funny, intellectual, independent, physically active, trusting, loving and the list went on and on like that for pages, with footnotes, a bibliography and references for other areas still uncharted.

During the process some comedian called dating, and of course still working too much, the connections with my past and the encounters with my other relationships had kept me on a roller coaster of occasionally despairing to eventually reaching a knowledge of myself. All the while my connection with Anna was still in the bonding stage, but improving. The recognizable improvements finally came when I neared the point of giving up. I decided to devote my life to my precious daughter. Anna was still with her mother most of the time. If I was going to devote myself to her, I needed to start by at least seeing her more.

Once I was reunited with Anna, I felt guided to understand myself and the people in my life.

* * *

The second set of memories came as a nightmare from the night of Marcy's funeral. I felt like I entered purgatory to relive the prior life episodes again. Finally, though, I was able to see the meaning in the emotional pain that had been blinding at the time.

Earlier that night I knew I felt refreshed and reborn with Sam, but by myself that night I wondered if the jerk I'd been was still in me. I wondered if the sweetness I felt would again turn to bitterness if hurting unconsciously was my nature.

During the dream, I floated over the scene, but as a detached observer:

I could see myself the night of the funeral, crying myself to sleep. I was questioning, "How could God allow this to happen? Why her? What purpose could her death serve?"

I flitted from crying questions to trying to rationalize answers, and for one of the first times in my life, I was asking God for answers to my questions.

When my father had died, I was just silently numb, and eventually escaped into my music. This time I was angry and felt alone.

"Why was everyone close to me dying, and leaving me alone? Why? What was the explanation? Why me? Why were they leaving me?

"Why Marcy? It was too much to have another person so dominant in my life die. "I cried that night pleading to understand. "Why did I push her away from me? Is it my fault? She was the most caring and loving person I had ever known, and now she's gone too."

I felt abandoned, alone and naked with no place to hide, especially from myself. I thought, "God, she was so beautiful, so intelligent, so alive and happy. Why did I alienate her? How did I become separated from someone who loved me so much?"

I cried, "What a monster I am. Oh God, I'll do anything, but don't let this happen to me again."

I flipped back to my father. "How could he leave just when I needed him? Maybe if he had been there when I was growing up this wouldn't have happened. Why did he leave my mother and me? What was the point of it all? Was there something I was missing? Maybe, somehow, that was my fault too."

I swore, "I'll appreciate everyone in my life from now on. I won't push people away, or allow them to push me away. I'll allow people to get close to me, and welcome their care and closeness."

Then I switched again, "Oh God, what about Anna? How can I care for her? I should have been the one to die. At least Anna would have had Marcy to really care for her and really love her."

Before the dream faded, I watched myself as I held my throbbing head, trying to stop the ache, squeezing out the dull pain, and feeling the hurt. My head was where I had kept everything; my emotions, my experiences, my self control, my fears. It was as though it was all seeping out. Like each one was a drop leaking from my brain and running down my face; first came my hurt, then my fears, then the loss, the loneliness, the separation, the doubts, the pain. I was living all the pent up emotions in me, and feeling them all at once! I laid there, holding my head, while the waves washed over me again; again the doubts, the heart wrenching I'd controlled and endured silently, and the pain.

I had yelled, "Stop! What do I need to do? Is there a way out, through, and beyond? Tell me, oh God, please tell me!"

* * *

Gladly the last one I remember before falling asleep for the rest of the night put me back on an optimistic note:

The years between the divorce and Anna coming to live with me led to introspections, and prepared me for the necessary decisions to turn over a new leaf. Then when Anna came to live with me she helped me to look at the loving side of myself and other people. It was as though I had donned rose colored glasses.

It became clear that I had to stop looking for my happiness through seeking approval. This was opposite to my behavior while playing music where I had sought approval and attempted to keep everyone else happy. I realized that even though I found enjoyment in my activities, I was still judging myself by the standards of others, ranging from the expectations I believed my father would have had, to my desire to please even the most difficult person when I performed. Only by being accepting of myself and knowing self-happiness, would I stop the swinging from being good or bad, and between judgment and approval, that made dissatisfaction habitual.

Anna loved me unconditionally and I realized that is what children teach us about life. Through the process she became my role model. Her example showed me I could do it. I knew that unless I took responsibility for my own happiness my life would be doomed to always looking and searching. No matter how independent my life had been, there was a knowledge within me that it would be vital to share aspects of life in an intimate relationship some day. Once my expectation that someone else could solve my problems started to dissolve, I knew I could attract some one equally self respectful and self loving to share a relationship. The new way was to know it was always within, no matter how challenging it might appear.

The solution was to stop and listen to myself. The process with Anna and the self realizations finally did give me a sense of completion in my relationship with Marcy and myself. I knew I had a clearer foundation to being by myself or to being in a healthy relationship.

Every step in my life was in some way preparing me for the next. My experiences growing up led to college life. My music opened doors to my relationships. My relationships taught me about aspects of my life that needed changing to communicate and feel love. Even the failures moved me forward with integral knowledge for what was next.

I gained a respect for each person and acknowledged that even in unpleasant situations, if I could grasp the keys, I would leap into a new realm. Previously going with the flow and accepting fate made for intriguing, but unconscious, decisions. I learned to recognize when to take control of my life's decisions, and go beyond reacting. I was aware that it was not only a possibility, but what I desired to accomplish. Life had my attention. I realized I had not dissolved all of my old habits, but I was committed to raising my standards which meant starting to create some new habits and being increasingly aware of the process.

* * *

When I woke the next morning I sent Sam a dozen, long-stemmed, red roses.

Chapter 4

During those first few weeks, Sam and I went out together a few times, talked on the phone our other free nights to share our thoughts and experiences for the day, and plan when we could see each other again. In a way it was like an old fashioned courtship. A chaperone was unnecessary since we were either in public, or we were leaving early to get home to our daughters. Since sex was not even a possibility in those few weeks, we had put our energy into understanding each other and starting a friendship. No matter how often we could get together or how long we talked, each time seemed to fly by.

Through the intricate details of telling each other our life stories, we felt as though we had lived the experiences. We also explored our similarities: our passion for creativity, close knit families, wanting balanced relationships, being independent and being nurturing to our daughters. We blended compatible levels of intelligence and common sense, and we laughed easily and frequently. There was also a common appreciation for long walks in wooded parks, by a river, lake or ocean, or anywhere in nature. The sports we both enjoyed included swimming, preferably in a open body of water, some skiing, although sitting by a fire looking out at the snow or the view from the top of the mountain was equally preferred to the actual skiing, even a friendly game of tennis if followed by a picnic or barbecue.

I knew there were also differences to challenge us, but any

evolving couple would encounter some. I had considered one significant question was whether the reason for getting away with Alex was to make up for how much energy Sam put into her work. Sam was still finding ways to expand her business, while my priority, after over-working, was to find a happy balance with Anna between being together and our individual activities. I wondered if Sam and Alex were at greater extremes or if like Sam's relationship with her mother, the disciplined work ethic set the basis for their understanding.

So, if the pieces came together at what seemed to alternate between information packed bubbles and a snail's pace, each question was another treasure to explore. In a way we were like wanderers from the relationship desert, approaching from opposite perspectives, who were either looking at an alluring mirage, or an oasis that was not only physically drawing us in but also intellectually, emotionally and intuitively taking us home.

* * *

The following weekend Anna and Alex had each made plans to visit with friends overnight. This gave Sam and me all of Saturday free with no other responsibility until Sunday. A couple, Larry and Jan, who were close friends of Sam's, had invited us to lunch at their house outside the city and we accepted.

It was a perfect day in early October, the kind that makes you happy to be alive. The temperature was seventy degrees and sunny, and all the pieces had fallen into place for a whole weekend free. It was wonderful to get some fresh air outside the city, but all I really wanted was to be with Sam, hear her laugh, and find a way to show her I loved her.

Being together felt so right. I caught my words recognizing that I used to think like that when I started with someone new, but this was different. But it was, and no old cynicism or fears were going to get in the way. And they didn't, and I was - in love, of course. I still pinch myself to make sure I'm not dreaming when remembering that day. I will always be able to picture everything that happened that day as though I am living it right now.

We laughed and drank with her friends over a beautiful lunch on their deck overlooking a wooded backyard with a stream running from a small pond with ducks flapping about.

Lunch was a sensuous delight of various grilled foods, fresh herbs from the garden mixed into all the dishes, fresh breads with olive oil and dips, a Caesar salad and desserts from a nearby French pastry shop. Needless to say we were well satiated, and felt like bears having eaten enough to last through hibernation. Besides eating, we laughed so much we each took guesses at how long it would take for our smiles to wear off. We all vowed to plan many encore performances to equal that one, or live trying.

On the way home Sam and I decided to stop at a park before going back to the city. We thought we would walk around and work off some of the lunch, and also hopefully create some appetite for the meal I had promised to make that evening. We were still feeling playful as we strolled through a grove of trees, and found a quiet spot to lay in the grass on the edge of a rolling field. The sun on our bodies combined with the warmth that flowed from our touches and kisses. We had kissed before, but in that moment kissing was all that existed. Like electricity flowing through us with no past or future, the heat rose in our hands, our faces, our loins and our hearts. Like fusion energy, atoms collided with each touch. The energy in our bodies was more than enough to fuel an ordinary fire. Any spark, and we risked bursting into flames of spontaneous combustion.

We were oblivious to the world around us, but it was probably the highlight of the day for our audience of trees. Trees are very sensitive to love, and although it cannot be confirmed, I think the trees had visions of spring and actually grew a few new leaves that day to replace some of the ones floating to the ground around us.

Eventually we drifted back to the car still feeling the electricity and heat infusing each little touch and kiss. It was questionable when we would be hungry enough to eat again, but we stopped at a store on the way back to the city to pick up a few ingredients for the evening's fare.

In the store we were still playing around. We felt like kids who were free to buy anything and everything their hearts desired. We picked out a variety of appetizers, fresh fruit for my special fruit salad, and some cream for whipping. We filled a basket with cherries, blueberries, raspberries, melons, fresh mandarin oranges, bananas, pears, and lemons to squeeze on the other fruit for freshness. As we shopped, we tasted each flavor in our minds and some with our mouths. We were having fun just thinking about the flavors food sensuously allows us to experience through the glorious habit we indulge each day.

Once back home I excused myself to get washed up and clean off the elements from our play. Sam offered to put the food away, I excused myself to slip into the shower. Only a moment later I heard a knock followed by the opening of the bathroom door. From behind the shower curtain I heard Sam ask in a sheepish voice if I would like some company. She slipped out of her clothes, into the shower and into my arms.

The immediate sensation sent waves of tingling excitement throughout my body. There was a marvelous mixture of being absolutely turned on and a sense of peaceful calm. As I wrapped myself around her, she drew me into a world of passion that enveloped my being. The hot water poured over us as we held each other's naked bodies for the first time, and I could feel her heart beat. Our hands explored while our mouths sought tasty bites. I was taking in her scent, her soft skin as our lips brushed and nuzzled each other's ears and neck.

There was confidence in Sam's body, but also a shyness if

that is possible in a shower. Looking into her soft brown eyes I could see a blend of innocence and a warm sensuous knowingness.

In this one action she had decided to take the risk, letting go of doubts and whatever fears one might hide behind. Instead she chose intimacy and the awakening of love. Standing there naked, she was allowing a feeling from within her soul to say "I sense you are my soulmate, you may embrace my body, and if you are awake you will see beyond, and know my heart and soul are open to you."

While her touch aroused an immediacy within me, I knew there was no need to rush. I sensed we had all the time in the world. This was all amazingly clear to me in one, intuitive instant.

We took turns washing each others' hair, and then bathed each other from head to toe. This was not to be an "energy conscious" shower! We washed each other we took time to hold and nibble. As we embraced, the steam grew around us and within us. The pressure continued to build. On wobbly legs we discovered sensations that brought us to the edge of exploding from the solar core at the center of our orbiting celestial bodies. But, that was only the beginning.

We dove into a couple of huge terry towels, and I practically carried Sam into the bedroom.

Sam saw some massage oil on the bedside table. When I bought it on a vacation, I had thought the aromatherapy masseuse had the most amazing hands I would ever find, but I was wrong. With my body still moist and flushed, I surrendered to a full body massage from a true artist. My body and spirit were being calmed and tamed, but at the same time I was also ready to explode. While still glistening and lubricated, Sam slid on top of me. Her breasts melded with my chest. Then I poured massage oil on her back, and pressed her body deep into mine. Intimately entwined we reached the heights of heaven on earth.

It was loving and outrageous.

When we laid back, we still couldn't get enough of each other so we just lay there talking and touching and glowing.

To our surprise we both had thoughts of food, and eventually found our way into the kitchen to nibble and graze. Still in robes, we threw together the fruit salad, and by candlelight noshed on it and the other goodies right from the containers. It was so simple, but truly romantic. Of course doing anything together would have felt romantic at that point. We lingered in the kitchen for a while until we found we were practically making love on the floor and decided to retire to the bedroom for the evening.

* * *

I was in awe of the beauty we found in each other. While in past relationships we had probably attached feelings of love to our sex drives, it felt like we had opened the door to feeling love in our hearts while making love. It felt like Sam and I had transcended the absurd mating games prevalent in a world where one in the couple is expecting this and the other that, leading to ever widening gaps between expectations and reality.

Before meeting Sam I had reached the first step, like giving up an addiction, of swearing off sex and relationships. I had become aware that old patterns for relationships were not bringing me happiness. Since the initial illusion of happiness in each new relationship had always dissipated and inevitably led to more pain than pleasure in the past, I had begun to be wary of problems almost immediately upon meeting someone new. These interactions had been repeated with each gradually adding to my understanding until I knew there had to be a better alternative. Eventually faced with no other alternative, I committed to seeing beyond the immediacy of short term self gratification.

I had known people who had fallen into some of society's deeper relationship issues, where habits of power and control actually disguise insecurities. One pushes the other into the role of a victim. For others, the fears of changing for an unknown alternative are worse than staying in a dead end relationship. All of this may sound melodramatic, but I had known men and women who would have given anything just to have someone to hold them and listen to them.

Role models for loving and respectful partnerships seemed scarce, but I knew they were possible. It was easy to look around and find relationships that were not working, or working but marginally happy. Throughout history, for thousands of years civilizations had reinforced roles predicated on basic survival. But, in a traditional system centered around survival and procreation, where was love, respect and a passion for living? They said, "You will learn to love one another," but this was no longer enough for me.

I had reached my nadir, when I had been ready to quit relationships and focus on raising Anna. However, Anna was the spark, and now Sam was the flame. I had committed to raise my standards, be open to finding a loving relationship, and not settle for less. Part of me had always known this, but was waiting for me to ask.

The past weeks of budding friendship, and the day's intimacy had melted any remaining ice, and opened new feelings in us. It was like waking up and finding a wonderful dream was real.

Chapter 5

We woke up early the next morning cupped like spoons although I was certain we had not fallen asleep like that the night before. We awoke together, and with few words slowly reminded each other of all the sensations we could remember from the night before. We had until late afternoon together, so we took all the time in the world.

I suggested, "Perhaps time is an illusion when lovers first meet."

Sam added, "And sleep too. I feel deliciously rested, but I think I only slept for a few hours; you slept longer. I watched you for awhile. You seemed so peaceful."

"So time and sleep. Anything else?"

Sam thought for a moment, however long a moment is, "Yes. Food. I completely forgot about it, but now it's all I can think of."

"Is that a hint?"

"Maybe. It's your place. Did we eat all the food or is there something we can make for breakfast?"

I considered what might be left and asked, "What do you like to eat? That is, unless you're adventurous, and want to try my regular morning eating habit."

"Uh oh, is this something I should have known before I decided I liked you?"

"Well no, I don't think so, it's really great. But, well, it takes someone willing to break with convention."

"Okay, what is it?"

"It's this green stuff called the Ultimate Meal, and I mix it with fruit, water and juice in a blender to make a smoothie. I really love it, and so does Anna I might add. The only trick initially is getting over drinking something green, but considering a lot of people start the day drinking something black - I think green is preferable."

"What are my other choices?"

"Sam, I would fly around the world to get you anything you want."

"Good answer. Ok, I'll tell you what. I'll try the green stuff if I can have a bagel and something black to drink too. If I'm going to have something that sounds like it's healthy, I want my stomach to have a familiar chaser."

We decided I would run out for the bagels and Sam would shower and start the coffee.

After the great adventure of the green smoothie, which Sam agreed tasted just like the fruit and juice it was mixed with, we decided to walk to the Art Museum and along the river.

As we were walking, I reminded Sam, "It's your turn to tell me more about your life. You mentioned to me there was one particular day a few years ago that accelerated events. It must have been one hell of a day considering where you are today. What happened?"

"My God! Phil, I haven't told anyone about that day in a while and there is one part I haven't told anyone yet, but this second as it comes into my mind I can feel it like it was yesterday. The amazing part is that much of my life now started in that one day."

Sam began, "With perspective, I had felt like I was taking from the world, and missing the satisfaction of giving something back. People, who reach a level of contentment, rarely choose to fly forward into life without a push. Well, I must have been really ready because I got pushed, shoved, and definitely had a fire lit under me. As events turned out, I was prepared to launch into a new adventure rather than just sitting back and enjoying the ride; I just didn't expect what or how it happened.

"Not surprisingly, the moment a person has an unusual thought, synchronicity will soon be knocking at the door, quite insistent about bounding into the person's life. Actually it would be fine if destiny only knocked, but with it's flair for the dramatic, it believes a pre-recorded wake up call is for those less girded for an imaginative approach.

"Wherever I signed up for my mold, my maker added a slip of instructions requiring a periodic recharging, a good shaking to avoid settling, a systems test to make sure all the parts were working, a transfusion to add some high test blood to the system, or a reflex check to keep the mind from dozing, and make sure the world is still turning, the clock coo-cooing and not just whistling in the dark, or if none of the above, a mid-life crisis with more mids than lives.

"If you haven't guessed already, I was about to receive a couple of wake up calls that would set the stage for the first of many changes. And, as if that wasn't enough, the process would also take me up and through some new dreams.

"You know the saying, 'Be careful what you ask for, you may get it?' well, I'm not sure exactly what I asked for, but I got more than I ever expected. A word of advice, if you find yourself asking, take the precaution to be as specific as possible. If not, fate, if there really is fate, or just a lack of a better word for an often unexplainable part of life, has a bizarre sense of humor. If left to its own devices, it can conjure up a ridiculously circuitous route to get you from point A to point B when it was only right around the corner.

"So, if you actually dare to dream and grab the steering wheel of life to drive, sail, walk or fly, be specific as to the way you most desire. You still might end up on a wild horse, riding at break neck speed across the countryside, but at least you'll have put in your two cents. People rarely test fate, so who knows, maybe fate is willing to consider input. Fate probably isn't going to ask for it, but might accept some if it's offered."

I thought, "This is fun. I wonder if Sam wakes up with light hearted philosophy spilling off her tongue every morning, or am I being treated to another side of her reached only through the proximity of a lover."

I asked, "Do you think or talk like this often?"

"Well," Sam considered, "No, not really, but I've given it a lot of thought. Before that day I'd been flowing along with only minor complaints, and didn't realize anyone might be listening if I did contribute to the suggestion box. After that day though, the game changed for me, and I started giving it more and more thought. Listen, that day really grabbed my attention, as you'll find out.

Sam began, "I had been covering the business for a week while Randi was ill, and running back and forth between my place and Randi's to nurse her back to health. I stayed healthy while mothering Randi back from what seemed like death to her, but as recovery was nearing, was a kind of stomach virus or flu.

"Each evening I was fighting the city traffic and city parking, which is an oxymoron, to get to Randi's and also brought whatever work stuff was absolutely necessary.

"For years we had met near Randi's place, on South Third Street, at a local restaurant that we still consider one of our offices, but eventually we found more convenient places because the parking is truly horrid. The only relief is a parking lot that's not cheap, but as Randi acknowledged, 'It's less than the ransom notes the other lots issue if you ever wanted to see your car safe again.'

"The quickest way around to the lot is by cutting through a small side street behind Randi's place; otherwise the one way streets take you everywhere but where you want to go.

"To quote Randi again, 'Finding a parking space has the same chances as winning the lottery, and even finding one barely slows the transfer of wealth from car owners to parking lot owners.'

"For the most part I had pretty much given up on finding spaces, and even abandoned my positive thinking approach. Hope was replaced with acceptance that parking is impossible in a trendy neighborhood.

"Don't get me wrong, it's a great area, but Randi moved there when it had just started with a number of art galleries. Since then it has been flooded by a plethora of good restaurants and bars serving everything from rock, blues, jazz and country, to food designed to please the United Nations. I'm sure you've been to the movie theaters showing foreign and art films, or the eclectic performance centers. Anyway, she bought a unit in a renovated house. Next door is an old warehouse that was carved into apartments. All the refurbished places are sandwiched between the previous urban renewal and the not yet renewed; you know one side with expensive, architecturally redesigned homes, and the other the dangerous neighborhoods that are joked about as being war zones."

"Yeah," I interjected. "I like a few of the places around there, but I hate to drive anywhere near it. Something draws me back, though, in spite of the congestion."

"Randi says, 'People flow into that part of town like gamblers to the tables. Everyone wants a little action, and feels like there is a little risk.

"It had been perfect for Randi, who bought in when it was still fairly rough. Even now it still has enough of an edge for her, in spite of it becoming touristy. Randi's a local, and I've become acclimated, or at least built an anesthetized tolerance. I'll even admit I like it on a good day.

"Well, while driving through the heart of this circus, I saw something that would have surprised even Randi. It was almost beyond my comprehension, and actually shocking to the point of outright disbelief - a parking space.

"After squeezing into the space, and reading the sign a few times to be certain it was actually a legal space too, I walked around the corner to the entrance of the building. I have a key, but I make it a habit to always buzz just in case Randi has company.

"As I was waiting for the elevator, I was wondering why I had felt an unexplainable sadness on the ride over. At the time I had shrugged it off, attributing it to some weariness from the long day.

"Even though Randi was sick, I was ready, although uncharacteristic of me, to complain. It had been the longest and most trying work day of my life. At the time we had been getting increasingly busier, but that day had pushed my limits.

"After getting Alex ready and off to school in the morning, I had been to three ends of the city for four supposedly short meetings on top of a breakfast meeting and two separate lunch meetings. I knew it was my fault for not insisting that Randi cancel her half of the days stuff, but I had acquiesced when Randi pleaded, 'Sam listen, I'll make it up to you, but please, it took me four months to arrange the breakfast and lunch meetings, and it's bad enough I can't even go.' She insisted there were tons of potential profits from these connections, and that all her ground work would go up in smoke for at least another four months if she canceled.

"Randi was right. In two of the meetings I had firm handshakes on more business than we usually did in a year, but I hadn't enjoyed it one bit. Maybe if I'd rearranged my own meetings, the day would have felt better. I felt obligated, though, and thought her meetings would be shorter.

"When I walked into Randi's, she all but jumped into my arms. She still looked awful, but glowed with a smile that made me laugh. It felt good to laugh. It was either that or cry, and I didn't cry very often back then. Before I could say a thing, Randi launched into telling me that Albere, her lover and significant other for the last six years, had just left.

"We had a running joke that they had only made it together that long because Bere was always traveling all over the world, and they only saw each other a couple of days each week. So really they had only been together for two years.

"I was certain they hadn't just slept together since Randi truly was sick. The exuberance was because Randi and Bere were discussing marriage. I told her I didn't want to hear about it, and could we skip that topic this time?

"They had been discussing marriage for three of the prior four years together, but Randi always questioned, 'Why change something that's going so well,' and 'if its not broke, don't fix it.' To me there was also an element of plain old 'cold feet.'

"Randi could tell what I was thinking, and it wasn't pretty, until she started waving something in my face that looked like blurs of airline tickets. Apparently this time it was different."

"Randi explained, 'We're flying to St. Martin to spend a weekend at his mother and her husband's home. For the first time, I'm actually going to meet his mother!'

"With that I started getting excited too, and curious. The other running joke or question we had was the mystery of Bere's family. The basic story is that Bere's mother, who is French, was the mistress of a Saudi prince, who she met as a young woman while working in the resort town of St Tropez. The affair continued for years, but when she became pregnant, he bought her a small estate on St. Martin in the Bahamas. Bere's father had visited her there as often as possible until his mother eventually married a man from the island. Even after that Bere always maintained a connection with his father. We assumed his father helped him start the international flower business Bere runs importing or exporting roses, orchids and other extraordinary flowers.

"His upbringing and the blood that flowed in his veins created the perfect man for Randi. As a lover Bere was a cross between an Arabian Stallion and a flower bearing French romantic. The caring, gentle man in him came from the slow, island family life with most of his days filled with walks and playing on the beach. He also has a general respect for people that Randi believes infused his life with happiness.

"I said to Randi, 'It's a little shocking to think of you two married, but it's easy to imagine you together forever.'

"Randi was exuberant, and almost forgot about her anticipation of finding out if the meetings were successful. With her mind racing, somehow, the business news was anticlimactic for her also."

Knowing that meeting Randi would give royal confirmation of our relationship, I interjected, "They sound like a great pair. I take it I'll meet them some day?"

Sam quipped, "We'll see." and winked.

Sam skipped ahead, "After going over the highlights of the meetings, Randi was beginning to fade. Even with her excitement, she was still weak from the stomach virus she described as 'inquisition torture level seven point five'.

"With Randi promising to get some rest, I had perked up and was ready to get home. I still had a premonition type feeling that I needed to get home for something, even though there were no messages when I checked. All I wanted in the world, as I was leaving, was to slip into a relaxing bath before anyone else wanted me.

"That night Alex was working on a school project and was planning to spend the night with a friend. I had thought, perhaps a bath would help melt away the never ending day, or as Randi describes, 'Days from hell are like an unexpected visitor that stays too long.' I thought that defined my day so far.

"As I was leaving the building I thought about my Uncle J's farm where I had spent my childhood. The streams of visitors there were always welcome and usually stayed long. I smiled to myself, and my thoughts went to the sapphire over my heart. I felt a tingling at the thought of my uncle, and made a mental note to give him an overdue call.

"Then as I was walking toward my car, the scene around me began to change, and I quickly began orienting myself to what was unfolding.

"As I stepped up to my car, two men who were walking toward another car turned and came directly at me. It suddenly became clear that this was more of a back alley than a side street, and that nobody else was around.

Sam hesitated and looked at me as if deciding in that instant who I was before she continued.

Her voice became serious, "One man was tall and thin and had his hands in his jacket pocket. The other man was bigger and heavier, and was carrying something I realized was a short metal bar. I turned toward them and they stopped about six feet away and confronted me."

"The thin man told me, 'Don't yell and we won't hurt you. All we want is your money.'

"Various thoughts went through my head, but I talked slowly saying I would do as he asked. I slowly got out my purse, and took out all the cash. I had been taught that if something like this could be settled with just money, to give it to them and not take the risk that they had a gun. The thin man looked like he was holding something in his pocket, and he was definitely a bit shaky."

"He told me, 'Put the money back in the purse, and throw it to me.' He checked to see that it was a decent amount of money, seemed satisfied, and said, 'Thanks babe,' and nodded to the other guy to head off."

"The heavy guy told him, 'You take off, there's something else I want.' Turning to me he grunted, 'Maybe the other guy won't hurt you, but if you don't yell I won't kill you.'

"I wasn't going to scream. My pulse began to pump, but I took a breath to stay calm and focused the way I had been taught. I had been there before. My vision became what is termed soft, which allowed me a broader peripheral look. I could see the attacker, and the other guy off to the side and still watching."

I had gone from enjoying Sam's story to being mesmerized and nervous even though the attack had taken place three years ago.

"I knew this guy would try to hurt me, and prepared to fight. I remembered vividly a similar situation when I was sixteen, and faced two attackers coming at me with a club and sword. It was while my Uncle J was training me for my black belt in Aikido."

I cried out, "You're a black belt in Aikido!" Astonished, relieved, definitely impressed, and with compounded respect, I stammered, "That's what you meant when you said your uncle taught you his 'art'? No wonder. You're amazing. When were you going to tell me?"

Sam shrugged calmly, "Now I guess. I would have told you, but it just never came up in our conversation."

"Forget it. What happened next, and what does someone in Aikido do?"

"I had taken the first step which was to become centered and focus. It is common in Aikido to have multiple attackers of equal skill rushing toward you with weapons. Part of the Aikido theory is to let attackers use their own force against themselves, and simply help redirect them."

"Multiple attackers are simple?"

Sam ignored my comment. "I could hear Uncle J's voice: 'The consciousness is actually more significant than the physical, and the key is the intention, which is to have compassion and recognize the consciousness in the attacker.'

"My thoughts flowed and I observed succinctly like a student, there is anger, pain and fear within him.

"My uncle's voice blended with mine, 'If you react to the fear, anger and violence it only acknowledges that the attribute exists within you, and has the effect of drawing the experience to you. Become compassionate to the perpetrator and understand him. Allow yourself to see or feel what's in him, but allow him to keep it. Stay focused, and the attacker retains the fear, anger and especially the violence.'

"I felt like Uncle J was with me, but also like I was facing him. This time the voice was like an echo in my brain, but I was unable to identify who or where it came from, 'Let the violent actions he attempts be his own experience. Know this education will lead to a permanent resolution of how he and you view this side of life. Whatever the causes or outlets for these ugly aspects of our society; attempted rape, senseless violence, bigotry or misogyny, face it all now, for yourself and anyone else connected to you or him.'

"Probably he hesitated when there was no reaction from me. For me time had stopped, but in reality only seconds had elapsed. All the thoughts and voices came and went in the flash of an instant like a potent bubble of information hitting me; the last was clear, 'The essence is not to be passive; help him unearth what is in his heart without judgment; stay focused on remaining separate; act, don't react to him; stay centered.'

Sam added simply, "This common brute was certainly no match for me, but in my heart I did not really want to hurt him. However, I was willing and about to help him learn a lesson that would have him questioning his feelings toward violence after the encounter."

I began to sense what Sam meant. She was exuding such confidence, I simply knew she was, and would somehow always be, ok. In fact I realized I felt some compassion for the attacker, who obviously had no idea what he had gotten himself into.

"So what did he do?"

For a moment Sam spoke as if she was a ghost who re-entered the scene, "I found my balance and compassion as he flung himself toward me striking with the metal bar. In one swift move I deftly ducked and spun allowing his momentum to carry him just past me. I then kicked up hard directly into his ribs. This added to his momentum, and took him head first into the next car. He collapsed without a sign of movement."

Sam winced unconsciously and I could see a slightly glazed look in her eyes.

"Foolishly the other man came rushing at me from behind, but I saw him, or more to the essence, I felt his energy coming. This time I squatted, grabbed his arm and flipped him over me and onto the ground."

As the impact of Sam's words hit me, I could hear the hard thud of the man's body landing on the asphalt.

Sam's voice became mechanical; with clear precision she recited the rest of the episode.

"My purse flew to the side, and spilled the contents on the street. Like an injured animal the man looked wildly at the purse, and then at the other guy lying by the car, and then at me. Whatever went through his mind, he got up and ran away leaving the first man, who was unconscious and bleeding from a gash over his eye.

"I stood there in ready position, but it was over, and all of it in less than a few minutes. Still I stood there as if expecting another round of attackers, but there was no one else in sight except me and the man lying in the street. I checked myself, and surveyed the situation. I knew what to do next, and began without hesitation.

I found the keys to my car and went around to open the trunk. After sorting through my workout bag I grabbed a few of the long cloth ties used during my Aikido workouts and walked over to the man. He was still not moving so I used the first one to wrap his head to stop the bleeding, and the second one to tie his feet just to make sure he waited for help. I didn't bother to tie his hands when I realized his ribs were probably broken, and he would be in too much pain to move.

"I stood up and looked around again. It felt like someone should care, but the same city and the buildings just stood there like they had before. I felt air being drawn into my lungs like it was a unique feeling, an awareness of the cool air entering through my nose and filling my lungs, only to be sighed out into a silent city street.

"There were only a few more things to do. I got on the car phone and called the police to bring an ambulance, giving the location but a false name. I got out to collect the money, and get my things together. Then I got in the car, and drove away."

Sam looked into my eyes. It was as if in her look she was asking me for forgiveness for hurting someone or leaving him or something. I pulled her to me and she came willingly. She felt so fragile and innocent in my arms, as if looking for moral support and strength from me. And I, I had never felt so weak in all my life, as I held the most sensitive, self-reliant person I'd ever met.

When we resumed walking, Sam took my hand for comfort and reassurance and whispered solemnly, "I've never told anyone about what happened."

Chapter 6

We walked in our own thoughts for a while and watched at the swiftly flowing Schuylkill River. There was a crew team gliding on the water stroking with all their strength as their coach barked at them from a motor boat. We sat on the grass and colorful leaves from half naked and half multi-colored trees. We watched a V of Canadian Geese splash land and regally paddle to a calm eddy by the shore. We were entertained as a black retriever, followed closely by "Hey! No! Sit! Don't go in," dove into the river for a swim and to chase the geese. Mostly though, we were silently sharing our thoughts and emotions.

My curiosity broke the spell and I asked, "So what happened next? Why do I sense there's something else?"

"The next part gets pretty involved," Sam warned, "Do you want me to share the rest?"

I checked, "Are you ok telling more?"

We laughed together realizing we were more than okay, and Sam began again.

"This episode started a series of encounters with catalysts for change. I guess one jolt wasn't going to be enough. The next message arrived when I got home. I was going to have the benefit of some 'real' perspective. Fate was not going to take the chance, that even though I handled the attack, that the initial shock might wear off once I slipped back into my busy, everyday life. So, I got a combination punch strong enough to evoke actual changes, and to crack any possible outer shell of indifference; rather than add another coat of shellac to harden even more. The questions created a domino effect to make sure I was awake.

"When I arrived home, I went directly to the bathroom, threw off my clothes and dove into the shower deciding the force of the water would help wash away the violence and feel of the day. The centered, balanced master in me kept asking: why did I create this experience? and what am I 'supposed' to learn? I could feel the yin, female, right brain wanted to explore every emotional energy waiting to spring out. At the same time the yang, male, left brain wanted to move forward, act, or maybe just create a diversion to escape the reality that my ability to protect myself had been challenged; even though I had survived.

"Before I had a chance to digest it all, I got another dose of both, emotional exploration and action. I later thought my brain was competing with itself to see which side could outdo the other. I wondered if I could call a truce so I could think it through, or maybe erase all thoughts.

"The minute I stepped out of the shower I got the call from my mother. Only moments before, my one true desire had been to forget anything my mind did, or did not want, and throw on flannel pajamas, make some tea, snuggle into my favorite corner of the sofa and hope my eyes would close after reading a little. That was not to be, in a flash I was a whirlwind in action; although, I guess, technically an inactive whirlwind is not a whirlwind."

"Anyway, I knew something was wrong and listened to my mother, who was still putting the pieces together herself. The essence of what she knew at that point was Uncle J had fallen from a ladder while doing some pruning in the orchard. There were definitely some broken bones, but the main concern was he had been found unconscious."

There was a shift in Sam's tone from the lightness at the beginning to a sense of revisited concern as she continued.

"My mother explained, 'Apparently the neighborhood kids showed up for their Aikido lessons after school, and searched around for him until they found him in the orchard. When the ambulance arrived, his condition was not clearly discernible. He appeared to be in shock, he was alive, but not responding, and looked to have been that way for a good part of the day. The doctors are considering the possibility of brain or spinal damage, and have a specialist standing by for when he regains full consciousness. They first want to know definitively is if there was any damage to his head or ability to function. They did the basics, and put a cast on his broken arm and identified bruised ribs. He is under close supervision, and now we are just waiting. The doctors are taking every precaution, but they are subtly saying his condition could be serious.'

"My mother's bluntness was a shock to my senses, but her last line started me packing. I told my mother I'd call her with my arrival time, and hung up. I started throwing clothes in my travel bag with my free hand, and called the airline to find the next flight to Seattle; it left in forty-five minutes.

"Fortunately, I kept a prepacked bag with a travel set of personal items, and so, I was out the door in minutes.

"As I screamed across the city, my focus was clear. The possibility, even if it was a remote possibility that he might come to and wake up just long enough to know I was there, gave me an urgency to see him. Maybe he would respond to my being there. Uncle J was always a vital inspiration in my life, and if there was anything I could do, it was at least to be there. I called Randi to say I'd explain more in the morning and to tell Alex I'd call her early at her friend's.

"Whatever the circumstances, I was in action. I knew I could assess the situation once I was there, but in Philadelphia I would only be able to second guess myself. In a way I couldn't believe anything bad could happen to Uncle J, but I needed to be there, and ready to respond to any contingencies.

"An hour later I was sitting on the plane taxiing for takeoff. I was at the pinnacle of feeling all of the nervous energy from the day and the news, not to mention the car ride and running through the airport. I had gotten in the car at 6:30 pm, and was on a 7:08 pm flight that would land in Seattle at 10:01 pm.

"To top it all off, being out of control on an airplane during take off and landings makes me nervous.

"As I had no choice but to sit and wait, I closed my eyes, and took a dozen or so long deep breaths. I adjusted my posture, relaxed my neck and shoulders and began a centering type of meditation Uncle J had taught me.

"There are many meditation techniques; some are integrated directly into the Aikido training, while others are for any time. But, what I love about all the meditations is the deep level of stillness and peace. It's like being transported to another world.

"The one I did was simple, and I drank it in like a natural tonic. It could really be sold as a cure for common stress, except it's free to anyone who asks to learn."

I didn't want to interrupt, but on cue I asked, "Oh, I'd really love it if you'd show me one."

Sam nodded, but was still emotionally back on the plane.

"On a normal day that would have done the trick, but my limits were already trashed. As the plane was leveling off, I made the trek to the restroom to pee, but when I sat down, it was the flood gates from my eyes that opened. The flood came from deep within and flowed like a waterfall from somewhere in my soul.

"I cried for at least forty minutes. That was my low. If it wasn't for noise from others outside waiting to get in and some air turbulence making the tiny room even smaller, I could've cried for hours. I found a catharsis in crying that no meditation could offer.

"I remember I felt like there was ground under my feet as I made my way back to my seat. Everything was happening so suddenly, but I had an intuitive feeling that Uncle J still had more to live for. I blew my nose one last time, and already sensed a spark from within giving me a renewed optimism.

"I sat back, and decided to put my whole life in perspective. Well maybe not my whole life, but the events of the day had my attention and I swore I'd find meaning in it all. My uncle had been prominent in my life that day. I wanted to know why the same day he had an accident it was like he had been with me on the street.

"I never thought I took him for granted, but in my busy life it had been difficult to find time to visit my family. Then a phone call later, and immediately I'm flying to be with him. I didn't even care about the next day's work."

I laid back in the grass, and thought about how infrequently I saw my brothers and sister; everyone was so spread out and caught up in life. Sam laid her head on my shoulder and stretched her legs. I wondered how often Sam visited now, but decided not to ask. Big, fluffy, white clouds floated over us leaving an open blue sky before the next group piled in to cover the blue again.

Sam marveled, "I always thought it was amazing a man like him existed in today's crazy world of never ending schedules and, well, everything. The people in his world still interact with each other in simpler, more personal ways, while working or playing together. People who come into his life always seem happier in their own lives; his underlying joy for life is infectious."

Sam thought out loud, "Until those experiences, I had been floating along quite happily, but then I wondered, what's going on that everything is being shaken up? Where's my joy for life and people? I realized the curtain was rising and a spot light was swaying around in my mind attempting to focus on some new issues moving toward center stage. I just hadn't realized there was such an immediacy.

"I asked myself, are the dramas popping up to alert me to

make life changes, and rewrite or add some zip to an overly familiar script of my life?

You know what you mean?

"It was like each piece was coming together to present a pivotal question to me, and I was beginning to take it personally.

"Like, did I stop noticing or become desensitized to what mattered?

"Apparently, a meeting was being called with a new director, who was requiring answers, and not accepting any old rehearsed lines. Maybe it was a quality versus quantity of life theme for the new production, and it looked like it was taking the nature of a courtroom trial. The first witness to be questioned would be the city. With the incident I had just confronted being submitted as evidence, the jury looked ready to judge summarily against the city, but the city was only a witness. I wanted to plead innocent, but the issues ran like a trail through the woods until a broader ruling on life could be found."

I shook my head, but got the general idea. "So what happened?"

"Ok, well, as I sat on the plane, I questioned, 'What makes me happy? And, where are the sources of that happiness?'

"I realized, for me, sharing experiences and ideas with my friends and family was number one. All the occasions shared with my father, my mother and uncle, Randi and others too, were the keys and central to my being. And, of course, Alex had also influenced every aspect of my later life; although I hadn't ever recognized it outwardly, or maybe even inwardly, until that moment. When it was all said and done, that was the foundation of what mattered to me in life.

"Acknowledging my most basic support patched a few of the loose bricks of my self confidence.

"The rebuilding continued as I thought of how my father introduced me to art. Also, with more than a little help, I had learned how to run a business sensibly from my mother; not to mention her as a role model for raising Alex. There alone, being a mother, what an amazing achievement in itself; seeing the miracle I had created every day, and how my influence contributed to molding her life.

"I had found in other tough times that listing all I had to be grateful for gave me a boost, and still needing one, I continued.

"Close friends like Randi filled roles ranging from best friend and partner to roommate and being a second mother to Alex. My other friends were mostly artists, from art school or business; especially Jean Pierre. Even though he was dean of my art school when we met, our friendship bonded as though we had known each other forever.

"He's like a second father to me," she added before going on.

Then Sam confessed, "As I've mentioned, the relationship area has always seemed to take a back seat in my life, actually a distant, way back seat."

Passing that topic quickly, she professed, "Financially things had been stable or improving for awhile, and the meetings that day figured well for the future.

"And, due largely to regular Aikido workouts, my health got an excellent rating. It's especially gratifying to watch Alex progress in Aikido; that is when she'll still let me work out with her."

I started to ask, "What about Alex?" and ask for an explanation, but decided to save that conversation. Instead I affirmed, "You sound like your life was in good shape."

"Yes, so overall I decided a fair grade to give myself was a B or B+; I hadn't won a Nobel prize, or done anything particularly socially redeeming, and for that matter my art wasn't in a museum, yet.

"But, the other hand, and positively more satisfying, was the knowledge that like my parents and uncle, through all the aspects of my life, I treated people with respect and kindness. I knew 'that' brought a simple joy into everything, and made even small accomplishments rewarding. Based on that criteria, whatever I had to show for my life, I would always deem everything a success.

"I was rebounding pretty well once I finished my game of 'feel good' which my mother taught me. The rules were to either find what you are grateful for in your own life, or appreciate how fortunate you are compared to someone with 'real' problems. If thinking was not enough, the next step was to go to a soup kitchen, shelter or hospice, and find some way to share a smile and kind word. To quote my mother's wisdom, 'If you have problems and need cheering up, go find someone less fortunate than you, and your perspective on your own life will brighten immeasurably.'

"It occurred to me that through speaking, feeling, being, and acting dynamically with grateful appreciation, I could accomplish anything I put my mind to. Then I thought, what if I was 'up' in every moment of my life?

"I thought, 'Who knows, maybe it could even become habitual.' I'm generally a positive person, but that sounded passe' compared with finding joy in each moment and sharing it with others. Maybe others would start to get excited and approach life the same way.

"It sounded invigorating in a life sustaining way, but terribly exhausting. Maybe, I would make 'How am I happy now?' my new theme question, and leave buoyantly springing into life for another day."

"Yes, that was enough. I had carried the game far enough and stopped. I was not ready to be that happy yet. I was willing to acknowledge I could smile more, possibly be 'up' more, and if pushed, show a little more love to loved ones, but, hey, I kidded myself, keep it in perspective - no one wants to be too happy. Maybe a few positive affirmations would be acceptable."

I laughed at the way Sam's mind worked. I could picture her

sitting on the plane talking to herself. I could also feel the emotional roller coaster starting up from the steep drop it had taken.

Sam sat up and continued, "I decided to start with a few resolutions. The first one was to move my family to the top of my 'to do' list. I realized there was a gap between the value I placed on my family, and the disproportionately small amount of present attention being paid to them.

"The second related to getting into nature more and out of the city. I actually considered walking out of the city and never looking back.

"Maybe the attacker was really a friend in disguise, willing to sacrifice a few bruises to dramatize the point. Maybe it was time to make a change, and the city was too harsh an environment. Nature had, after all, been my greatest friend and teacher while growing up, other than family.

"Nature had really been my first love. In the city I'm tuned to a different frequency. Maybe nature and the idyllic orchards of my youth had been calling to me, but I had tuned them out. Maybe the city helped me create the illusion that life was 'ok', fun, fulfilling, but perhaps only a sliver of happiness in disguise. Maybe the bigger factor was missing, which was to re-enter nature, and it was always just within reach.

"I wondered what effect the city had on Alex's values; growing up surrounded by a city consciousness. I wondered if Alex's experience growing up as a city girl created an imbalance that would tear at her until integrated with a dose of nature.

"Of course I was conscious of the increasing violence and crime in the city. It was as plain as day. All anyone needed to do was listen to the news, or just look around. How easy it had become to ignore some parts of the world that were right in front of everyone's faces. All the while caught up in life, and just one more thing demanding attention. Sometimes change is just too much trouble until it becomes the only alternative left.

"And what about people's personal sensibilities. At what point did everyone build such a tolerance that it was possible to be surrounded by so many problems, and appear to stop caring. Certainly if any one person stopped and tried to solve all the problems, he would quickly become overwhelmed. The makeshift solution became some token gesture, like sending money to an anonymous, non-personable charitable organization rather than getting involved with your own hands.

"As I sat there trashing the city, I realized I really loved the city also. I was not going to be chased or run out of town, at least not because of the attack. First I needed to settle the score with myself; not just with a couple of thugs, but by seeing if I had finished what I came to the city to accomplish in the bigger picture. What was the reason every step in my life had led to Philadelphia? Perhaps the city had been presenting issues for me to open the discussion on change sooner, but I had ignored the gentler reminders. Now that the lessons on my doorstep were getting more dramatic, it clearly made sense to pay attention before the next wake up call was even more serious or even life threatening.

"I quickly dismissed a fleeting thought of moving back to the farm as impossible at least for the moment. I was willing to concede that the city had been dominant in my adult life in the same way nature had been in my childhood; both offered many positive advantages. I was unwilling to just switch back suddenly. I resolved to find a way to balance the two and make a transition smoothly, but life would still need to be centered in the city, at least for a while.

"Perhaps nature's patience was simply at a low tolerance point, and was jumping on the circumstances to get equal time in a debate that had been shelved for a long time. A first step was to plan more trips out of the city with Alex. I considered we should visit the farm together for longer than our usual long weekend, or special event trips. I was getting the message: for

Alex and my own sake, remember the balancing influence of nature. Of course, since Alex grew up in the city and seemed happy spending most of her time with her friends, a change to being together in nature would be a tremendous opportunity/challenge.

Sam gave a thoughtful pause and smiled, "Alex is becoming such a beautiful, young woman, and even though she's occasionally exasperating, I love how independent and mature she is.

"Whether it was Alex, me or any of the pieces, events and people, clearly too much had come together to be a coincidence. I realized it is easy to question the decision afterward, but the real question at the heart of a retrospective is: 'Would I do it differently given the opportunity again? And even better, what can I start doing now?'

"Once I asked those questions, I felt my attitude, which had already turned, improving by leaps. After pondering the first question, I decided whatever was done, was done, and I accepted everything that I had done in my life; the good with the bad. However, if things were starting to change in my life from the comfortable plateau I'd reached, and it appeared to be the case, I thought, 'So things always change,' I'll just need to pay closer attention. If I'm starting into some new adventures, I want to be consulted and contribute some ideas of my own.

"My mind switched to my business. It seemed to be the primary factor tying my life together, and influencing my decisions. I knew I loved what I did, and that morning's meetings looked like a real financial breakthrough."

"Then I asked myself, 'What can I do next in my life using my current knowledge and experiences as a launching pad rather than a lily pad?"

"I admitted to myself that I couldn't remember the last time I'd really asked that kind of question. I told Randi later, I literally had a feeling like a purring in my brain. It was different than I had ever sensed before. It felt like an engine designed to propel a race car to speeds of 180 mph, but had only driven around the block for groceries, was finally being tuned and prepared for a race.

"When I related this story to Randi, she added her theory on how the brain works.

"Randi claimed, 'There is actual scientific research proving that asking questions starts the brain working like a computer. Thoughts and ideas will flow in continuous loops until acceptable solutions and answers are presented. Even afterward, it does a few victory laps just for fun and hopes you enjoyed the purring ride enough to do it again. The brain then waits in neutral doing the mundane tasks it is assigned, patiently waiting for the next question.'

"Her proof was that a friend once told her, 'When a Nobel scientist was asked to what he attributed his success, he responded that everyday when he returned from school his mother would ask him, 'What questions did you ask today?' and that led him into his life's work of exploration.'

Once I challenged my brain, it started doing loops to offer some answers.

"I was sitting on the plane looking out over Iowa, still only half way to Seattle, when the storm struck. The other passengers were calm though because it was a brainstorm taking place in my head. Rather than the sky erupting with buckets of rain and lightening bolts, the gray matter in my head had flashes of electrical activity jumping through the forest of dendrites, leaping from neurons to receptors across synaptic clefts while enzymes stood in awe.

"Well, there was the first idea, then a second, and a third, and, and, and, - hold that thought - I was scrambling through my bag for my journal to outline a new life changing business project. For the first time my focus was on how to give, and make a contribution where everybody involved wins. Although still not quite Nobel prize material, it was a major first leap forward.

"The notes I made were the initial working outline to start a new project. Basically, I knew art students did some incredible work for school projects, rarely got any recognition and were always broke. Next, charities were always doing art auctions as fund raising projects, but most of the money generated went to the auction company and to just a few better known artists, instead of a wide variety of talented struggling unknowns.

"My idea was to turn this around so most of the sales would be split between the art students and the charity fund raisers. In a nut shell, students at art schools in the area would be asked to contribute some of the thousands of incredible school projects to be sold at art actions for charitable organizations. The students would get the proportionately largest percentage of the sale, the charity next and finally there would be enough left for Randi and me to make money too.

"In addition to the money, the students would get some recognition and encouragement to do more than the minimum number of projects. The money the students would earn could defray the ever increasing cost of art supplies, and possibly tuition also. The work would still be put on slides for the students' portfolios. At the same time, the purchasers of the art would have access to, and support, the next generation of creative genius.

"People buying or collecting art would simultaneously be supporting their favorite charities, and we'd be bringing original art to a wide brush of people. The charitable organization could invite its existing list of patrons and supporters to enjoy an evening of original art. The art schools would gain in reputation and visibility, and attract students who would see an additional funding source. The auctions could be an outlet for awakening more kids to see creative endeavors as a way to reach their hearts' dreams. Also the business could make and encourage alumni or others, through the auction process, to set up ongoing scholarship pools, or even begin funding summer art camps similar to the ones for classical music.

"I ran some quick numbers and realized, if I took a flat $25 for each piece of art sold and let the students and charity split the rest sixty/forty, and, if I could do twenty auctions a year, and, if I could sell an average 300 pieces an evening for an average cost of $200 each.... Roughly it would generate $1.2 million per year to be split; $150,000 to the business, $420,000 to charities and $630,000 among all of the students.

"Then I realized, if the idea expanded into twenty metropolitan areas, then just multiply by twenty, and the money split would be $24 million with $3 million going to the business, $8.4 million to charities and $12.6 million to the students. In the big picture everyone would win.

"Sitting back for a minute, I thought, pretty good work for a depressing plane ride. I felt like I was truly rising, like the phoenix from the ashes, from the challenges of the day.

"The pilot announced the plane would be arriving in thirty minutes, on schedule, and thanked everyone for joining him and the crew. I made a few more notes to go over with Randi, and then wrote my thoughts on how to approach Jean Pierre. He was still dean of the art school, and his support would be the cornerstone to all but guarantee the success of the project. Jean Pierre could not only win support of the school's board to sanction the project, but he was connected to half the city through the boards he sat on. He also had contacts with the other art schools and most of the movers and shakers in the city.

"I wrapped up my notes as the plane descended over the lights surrounding the Puget Sound. I realized the idea had been a tonic for a flight which would have been interminable had I dwelt on any possible bad news. Once the plane pulled up to the gate, I felt some trepidation, and prepared to hear the news on Uncle J.

"As I walked up the ramp from the plane, I saw my mother's face, and instantaneously knew Uncle J was still alive. We hugged for awhile with neither wanting to let go. I think each of us wanted, and also needed, to be rocked and held like only a mother could. For the moment all that mattered was the love we felt toward each other. The episode with Uncle J made us both realize how fragile life can be. The geographic distance could never lessen the connection of mother and daughter, and we did talk often, but in holding each other, we knew being together filled a deeper call from within.

"We then headed for the car, to go straight to the hospital where my father was waiting, and find out the prognosis and how it all happened."

Chapter 7

As Sam and I strolled by the river, I felt an intimacy from sharing thoughts and the emotional episodes. I knew it would bond us beyond our budding physical connection.

"From your other stories I already know Uncle J is alive and well. Please though, I still want to know what happened and how. I'm also enjoying hearing the process of how your business and personal decisions developed."

We crossed the river at the Falls Bridge and started back toward the museum and home on the other side.

Sam continued her story, "My mom told me Uncle J had regained consciousness, and the doctors had taken him for additional tests right away. She had asked, and received special permission to return with me to visit, since it was about 10:30 pm when we arrived.

"In the car I had begun feeling tense about the situation again. My thoughts seem scattered compared to the plane ride, but talking with my mom, especially her assurance that he was at least conscious and alert enough for the recommended tests, assuaged my concern.

"We chatted briefly about Alex, Randi and the business. At one point I began to mention I had a new business idea, but decided I would tell her about it later. As excited as I was during the plane ride, once back to earth, I was aware of a swing to be quiet and just listen to my mother's voice.

"I asked my mother to tell me the story of how Uncle J got

his farm and the connections to his community. This was an easy out because I knew my mother loved to tell the story as much as I loved to hear it. The drive to the hospital would only be another fifteen minutes, so it needed to be the short version.

"My mom knew it was probably a ploy to keep the conversation light, but she truly loved the chance to tell the story of how he was the center of his community and how it had all started. It was like a favorite bedtime story that a child never gets tired of hearing, or the parent telling. I hadn't heard it in years, and it brought back a warm, fuzzy feeling. My mind was flashing to the possibility of an extended trip in the summer, and staying at the farm like when I was a kid. She began:

* * *

When Uncle J arrived in America from Japan, he was a young man tired of fighting. His family was a line of Aikido masters, but his country had wanted them to teach the art, as he referred to Aikido, to soldiers for fighting. He believed the purpose was for disciplining the mind and purifying the body as a means to spiritual growth. His refusal to teach would disgrace his family, but so would leaving. He chose to leave.

How he journeyed to America is another story, but once he arrived he found work as cook, cleaner or anything else needed with the railroad on a repair-maintenance crew. After one episode where he defended himself easily against one of the workers who had been a boxer in the army, no one ever challenged him physically again. What surprised Uncle J was that everyone now wanted him as their friend, and had really disliked the other man.

He was encouraged to run their nightly poker game, since they knew he did not want to play, and no one would mess with him. He acquiesced. They agreed to give him a few pennies each night, and sometimes the winners gave him more. He saved all his money, and almost all of his pay, since he preferred meditating in his free time to the costly pastimes of drinking, gambling and women, where the other men spent their money.

The funny part is, to hide his money which was beginning to accumulate, he would buy gold or silver, and have it melted by the smith, who made the eating utensils for the crews meals. He put a little into each mold, so the precious metal actually became part of the utensil. The smith received one when Uncle J left in return for keeping the secret.

A couple of times dishonest or disgruntled workers or poker players went through his belongings looking for money, but they never thought it was actually in their hands at each meal. As you can imagine, Uncle J was meticulous about cleaning up after meals so that all the utensils were always returned.

He finally quit the railroad, after a maintenance job was finished, which happened to be in the Seattle area. He decided to look for land to buy, and went to a number of sheriff's sales. One day he took the ferry across from the city to look at a farm being auctioned. The farmer had died with no known family or heirs, and it was being auctioned by the state. The day was stormy and colder than usual, and Uncle J was the only one to show up. He bought the 200 acre farm and orchard for a song.

When Sam's mother arrived to stay with him, he was the happiest man in the universe. She became a daughter to him, and he decided to pass along the family heritage by teaching her Aikido.

Neighborhood kids who helped at the farm started to join in the lessons, and before long other kids from the area joined them. It became a place where responsible kids would come after school to learn, and then stay to do school work, or talk and play games.

When the parents came to pick up their children, they would stay and chat. At some point the neighbors started bringing pot luck dinners, and whole families would stay for the evening to play games and talk, or practice and teach each other Aikido. The last hour every night, which was always by 8:30, everything stopped and everyone there would come together and sing.

They met in the long, rectangular farm building that was a cross between a barn and a work area. Parts of the building were used for sorting and packing fruit, and another section was used for canning. Those areas led to a green house and a storage building. The packing area had a large semi-finished section with a large fireplace along the length of one wall, some wood work tables and chairs around the room, and an open area in the middle for Aikido. This was where everyone met, and it officially became the community center for the whole county. Many friendships, and even a few marriages started there.

It turned out there was an additional benefit to Uncle J as well. He would charge each child or parent a little bit for the Aikido lessons, in part because he believed they would value what they learned more, and partly to help him through the winter and spring months when cash flow was low. But, he also had another plan.

When it came time for the farm work, he needed reliable help. Here he had a ready made, disciplined army who would have worked for free just to show their love and respect for everyone's Uncle J. People laughed about how they knowingly participated, since they knew it was his plan to return all the lesson fees and always more for any work that was done. Besides money, everyone also received some pay in the actual fruits of their labor. By the end of the summer almost everyone in the the community had come to help at least once.

Everyone looked forward to the fall for the highlight of the year. After most of the work was done, everyone came together for a whole weekend of hayrides, bonfires, eating, singing, music and dancing, story telling, games and seemingly endless fun and laughter. Often one of the highlights during the weekend was a production of Shakespeare's, A Midsummer Nights Dream, or The Tempest which are still two of the favorite plays they do.

Amazingly, it is still going on even in today's society. Three generations participate. Grandparents, who were some of his original neighbors, still help with the harvest and farm work, while their children's children come to play, and learn Aikido from the master, Uncle J.

* * *

"After my mother and I pulled into a parking space at the hospital, we practically tripped over each other to see who could politely, but quickly, get to see Uncle J first. I smiled at my mother, who although always a little stoic, had a heart that opened with great love when it came to her family and friends. If watched closely, she could even be playful around Uncle J.

We hurried to find out about his condition.

"When we entered the room, Uncle J was sitting up in bed smiling. My father picked me up, and smothered me with hugs. Delicately, I then did the same with Uncle J, avoiding his injuries as much as possible.

"I sat on the bed, and held his free hand. I laughed and shook my head, and asked scoldingly, 'How did you get yourself into this mess anyway?'

"He looked back with the sparkling eyes of a child, who had gotten caught playing in a mud hole, and replied teasingly, 'I just don't get to see you often enough.'

"We all laughed, but Uncle J pleaded for us to stop, he whimpered half seriously and half jokingly, 'It really does only hurt when I laugh.'

"This had the unfortunate effect of making him laugh even harder, as we all said in unison, 'Good,' and laughed again.

"I said affectionately, 'It's just such a sweet feeling to be with you, and know you're all right.'

"My father pulled up chairs, and insisted Uncle J tell us the story of what happened in the orchard before the nurse came and made us all go home.

"Everyone loved his stories which always left people laughing, crying, or thoughtful; separately and sometimes all together. Yet this one turned out to show a new depth of possibilities. The family all sat down for the first telling of Uncle J's 'near death' experience.

"He was quite alert, and began to explain what happened: 'While pruning trees in the orchard, a bee flew into my pant leg. I knew that a bee would not sting a tree, so I remained calm and focused on being a tree. It worked, of course. I was amazed at the sensation of feeling the bee walking on my skin and buzzing around and against my leg.

'I knew I was okay, but the problem remained: How do I get the bee out? The next thing I did was talk to the bee and ask it to fly on its way. The bee still seemed confused, or at least had not yet found the way out. Next, I decided to visualize the bee flying out the bottom of my pant leg. At first, the bee became very quiet and didn't buzz as frantically. Either I was beginning to communicate with the bee or the bee was just getting tired. Whatever the case, I took it as a good indication. I could feel the bee begin walking slowly from my knee down to my ankle. Finally, after I had been calmly balanced on the ladder for over an hour, the bee crawled out and flew away.

'In a way it was fun. Whether the bee understood me or not, but I'm certain it did, I felt like we accomplished the task together. But, as I turned to watch the bee fly away, the ladder shifted and I fell to the ground.'

"Uncle J continued, 'The funny part is the bee came back and landed on my chest as I lay on the ground. The bee watched as I took inventory of the situation. I realized in the fall I had apparently broken my arm, and there was a fair amount of pain in my ribs, neck and head.'

"My parents and I winced empathetically. We had been taught, though, by Uncle J many times that pain was the body's message to the brain, and to respect where and what the meaning indicated."

"Uncle J mused that the bee seemed to say, 'You created this part yourself.' The bee, however, was mute when Uncle J asked, 'Ok, here I am. What's the next step?'

"Uncle J related stoically, 'The first thing I decided was not to move. Since it was unlikely anyone would find me until later in the day, I decided to go into a deep meditation. The trance-like state would give me a chance to focus my energy and make it easier to remain still.'

"The doctors might have explained that part as shock causing him to black out, but Uncle J said he reached another level deeper than any meditation he had experienced.

"He said, 'At some point I was no longer aware of my body, and imagined I was in a room with my parents. Together we reviewed my life. It was actually exhilarating. I remembered scenes from the farm, and all the way back to childhood. Then my parents said it was time for them to go, and left, but I didn't return to this reality yet.

"The next part was crystal clear and misty at the same time. I was given insights into life through a lucid meeting with my first master in Japan. In the scene we walked to a pool where a waterfall crashed and mist sprayed everything. We walked straight through the waterfall and into a cave behind the cascade.'

"He exclaimed, 'I was dry but for a few drops of water, and I actually had the sensation of feeling the water on my skin. The cave had fine rugs on the floor, and was illuminated without apparent lights. Then, I turned to a wall which came to life like a movie screen, where I again saw more scenes from my own life. The scenes shifted fairly quickly, but elucidated different highlights of my life. In particular I relived the honor of being given the sapphire stone now residing over Sam's heart on her necklace.'

"Uncle J switched tone and became very deliberate, 'Next I

saw scenes from the future.'

"He spoke thoughtfully, 'I'll tell you more once I meditate on it all, but first I saw Sam at the farm. Then there were a jumble of scenes for me to untangle, but it quickly became clear again. I saw myself traveling to Japan to visit my original village, where I met two families who were preparing to travel to the farm in Washington.'

'After that the screen went blank. As the images all faded, I turned to my master, who blessed me. I saw in his eyes the wordless directions for me to return to Japan.'

'In the instant before the scene disappeared, I knew a quest to complete a circle in my life could only be filled by returning to face the life I had run away from.'

"Uncle J had a reverence while describing his visions, but also a casual comfort as if he accepted this mode of communication. The part he did not tell yet was that he imagined more of my future than just seeing me at the farm.

"He finished, 'The next thing I knew, I was fully aware and in the hospital about an hour ago.'

"We asked him a bunch of questions until a nurse politely told us we had to go. As we were leaving, Uncle J insisted, 'Come and get me out of this hospital the second there is someone to release me.'

"He was only kept at the hospital for the night. The next morning after completing some tests the doctors gave him a clean bill of health. Other than the broken arm and bruised ribs, which would heal, he was fine.

"The next few days I stayed at the farm to help take care of Uncle J, and generally had a lovely family visit. My father reiterated Uncle J's kidding, 'The only reason Uncle J did the whole thing anyway was to get you here.'

"Many friends came to visit, and all were happy to help my parents take care of him once I returned home. Since I had run out so quickly, I decided to make it a short stay, but promised another visit when things returned to normal.

"Before I left Uncle J insisted on taking a short stroll with me. We walked to the edge of the yard to the tree swing. He told me the parts of his dream that spoke to my life. It was just enough to get me thinking, but nothing that would allow me to anticipate or change the path that was developing. My interest peaked, but I knew clearly that each day and each endeavor would still be in my hands and would always be my own journey of self realization.

"I listened intently, but had to hurry back to the car where my father was waiting to take me to the airport. The whole flight home I was filled with the questions and curiosity the peek into my future raised. Of the details that Uncle J foresaw, only a sample had been mentioned to me. In a way I felt my past, present and future had come together, and that the gold ring of my merry-go-round of dreams was within reach

"After my return from the false emergency with uncle J, my business expanded dramatically as the two contacts Randi had pleaded I keep her appointments with, began referring new artists and new clients. First doors opened to business in the New York area, and soon after the business expanded into Europe to find new artists, and to bring the American artists to buyers abroad.

"Also, the auction business I designed on the plane had a gala kickoff season the first year, and grew geometrically the second year. Fortunately, Jean Pierre and his team of art students covered most of the details for the auction.

"The added bonus was that once Lou and Jack, Randi's two contacts, began meeting at parties and gallery openings, they became friends and realized it might be fun to come out of retirement and get involved in the businesses. Initially, their interest had been purely to connect people they knew who created art, and others who were regular buyers without getting involved. Each of them had separately sold their businesses and retired without the need to make money from the referrals they gave to Randi and me. Their connections had created tremendous business for us. Their occasional help was also a welcome addition filling in spots to keep everything run surprisingly smoothly. Most of all, though, their friendship made having them around fun.

"Everything seemed to bring my thoughts around to business, but one phrase Uncle J had said to me echoed in my mind suggesting my priorities would start to change.

"I am certain Uncle J smiled knowing his little spill awakened my attention. He always reminded me how all the events in my life were the only possible way to prepare me for the next experience, and every one was absolutely necessary."

* * *

We were only a few blocks from the house when Sam finished her stories. The day was slipping away, and we both had to return to things like time, food and sleep.

Chapter 8

After meeting in September, we talked on the phone frequently and met for dinner when Sam had an evening free. I felt closer to Sam every day. But, due to her busy fall schedule with the auction business, it was the end of October before we were able to spend the night together again.

Sam called and announced, "I convinced Randi to cover for me this weekend in return for reciprocal coverage the next weekend."

Sam hesitated but I could tell there was more.

"What do you think about going to the beach for the weekend?"

I began to picture a romantic get-away, but before I could answer, she surprised me with the rest of her suggestion.

"My idea is that we take Alex and Anna and visit where you grew up."

"That sounds pretty adventurous," I blurted.

"I guess I just have an adventurous streak. Alex hasn't met Anna yet and I think the beach would be a great place for them to meet. Well, what do you think?"

"Um, sure. You just surprised me, but I just decided I like surprises." I paused for a slight dramatic effect as it sunk in that Sam was speaking casually, but there was an element of asking for reassurance. "I'll call my mother and tell her we're coming."

"Let me confirm with you tonight. I need to tell Alex my idea and make sure she'll agree."

"You're too much! You weren't certain I'd agree?"

"No. I knew you would if you were free. The challenge is to get Alex away from the normal preoccupations of a sixteen-year-old to spend the weekend with us. Alex would probably prefer being with her friends or having me all to herself, but I know she is curious to see what you and Anna are like.

"By picking a place that is neutral territory, where Alex is away from her friends, it will be easier. At the beach she won't feel any peer pressure to be cool, or feel the need to fight being with a thirteen-year-old and her father."

Sam warned, "Adolescence and the associated hormones have created an undercurrent throughout Alex's life which periodically create a disassociating impact on our ability to relate. Probably all of the power plays can be attributed to puberty. On the surface, Alex seems almost perfect, but I know it has been at least a couple years since she had lost part of her child's smile and joyfulness. Through any difficulties though, I'm sure it's just a phase mothers and daughters go through.

"Although I'm preparing you that she might revert to being a moody and difficult teenager, being in nature at the beach should take her out of her element. I think, like our trip I told you about, a mature, young woman will shine through. In fact, once Alex forgets it should be 'incredibly boring' she'll be fine."

As Sam talked, the idea of us all going to the beach seemed natural rather than surprising.

"My mother has the ability to make visitors feel welcome and that it's okay to be yourself. Even people calloused from the city, which I don't think applies to either of you, have felt an exceptional air of safety to open up. She is always a gracious hostess, and enjoys company. People have been known to let go of their defenses. Maybe Alex's image of what a teenager should do will melt some."

I did not mention to Sam that occasionally guests had

become so captivated they had asked to extend their visit forgetting the energy required to play the role of hostess. This had been the case a number of times when friends or a seemingly promising person for a relationship had come to visit. Some actually wanted to adopt my mother; thrilled to find the mother they felt they never identified with through birth. After a while, I found I was reluctant to bring any woman I knew near her. I was afraid they would agree to a mutual adoption and I would never be able to break off the relationship if we chose to go in different directions. Actually, two women I never talk with anymore still stay in touch with my mother.

With Sam, a part of me wanted to have an ally in my mother in creating that type of connection, and maybe even her confirmation and approval. I knew Sam would feel comfortable with my mother, and would fit in easily. Anyway, it was Sam's idea to jump in and meet her so soon.

Perhaps Sam wanted to check my foundation, especially after hearing the stories about my childhood, and confirm if her first impressions were supported. She could also see for herself how much she could learn from comparing the apple to the tree it fell from.

By making the arrangements close to the last minute, we alleviated the possibility of getting caught up in too many mental gyrations. Three days later we just hopped in the car and went.

We decided to start in the late afternoon on Friday, but before the rush hour traffic would be leaving the city. The two hour drive flew by as Sam and I caught up with each other's news of the week. Our talk was interspersed with talking to Anna and Alex or listening to them get acquainted.

As we crossed the broad, blue bay on the causeway to the island, the familiar smell of salt water from the ocean brought back a flood of memories. The sight of the seagulls gliding over the boats and heading for the docks all along Barnaget Bay, made me remember many long days out on the water. I remembered shaking off the weariness from a day in the sun with the prospect of having fresh-caught fish for dinner.

In a matter of minutes we pulled in front of my mom's house, and Sam remarked, "What a wonderful old-style beach cottage. It looks like the main part must be a hundred years old, but in absolutely great shape. The whole street is just like a picture of Cape Cod with all the weathered gray and brown wood shingles."

I was proud of my old home. "The house has maintained the original look even after a fair amount of work has been done over the years. It was remodeled and insulated for winters just before my parents bought it in early 1950 so it was livable all year. When my parents moved in, they added a porch in the front, a den in the back and, soon after, a deck between the den and the kitchen and dining area. Still, even with changes, it and the surrounding houses have kept their charm."

Anna was already running up to the door to see her grandmother, and yelled back to us, "She left a note to go right to the beach and meet her there."

The tour of the house would need to wait. I knew the note was planned to get everyone to the beach right away rather than stand around the house getting acquainted. My mom also knew I would want to see the ocean immediately upon arrival, like someone who is compelled to see an old friend.

Anna yelled, "Alex, come on let's race," and started running to the beach.

They were off. They covered the short block in a minute, and were up and disappearing over the grassy sand dunes, while Sam and I just watched and laughed. There was a lightness in the air near the ocean that always seemed to melt away the thoughts of the city and work.

Sam let out a sigh, "You were lucky to grow up here. That's the first time in a long while I've seen Alex run with such abandon, and we've only been here five minutes."

Then switching to herself, "Just imagine what I'll be like after two days."

My reply was a thoughtful, "Umm" as Sam, turned and nuzzled against me. The tough decision was whether to savor the moment, or rush off to the beach myself.

After another moment or so, I suggested we head to the beach. Knowing the temperature would drop with the sun, I reached into my overnight bag and grabbed a couple sweatshirts to throw over our sweaters. I handed Sam one and said, "Come on, I'll race you to the beach."

As we made our way over the dunes, the soft light of dusk was laying a coat of pink and rose over the dark blue ocean as though to warm the ocean as the temperature dropped. I exclaimed, "Every time in my life I see the ocean I'm amazed at the awesome wonder, and how each day its mood and personality are distinct."

Sam was absorbed in the scene, and I followed her eyes as she looked up at the pink clouds streaming from the ocean to the bay. Turning around and looking back down the street, we watched as the sun hovered over the bay.

Sam looked in each direction, as if trying to choose between two favorite flavors of ice cream, but she was able to savor both by taking alternating tastes. During one of the looks toward the beach, Sam said, "I take it that's your mother headed toward us. Any last words of advice?"

That was the closest Sam came to nervousness over meeting my mother. I waved to her and waited with Sam for my mom to reach us. The girls, who had been talking with her, headed toward the water, and were looking for shells and sea glass.

I took a few steps to meet my mother, and gave her a long hug, "Hi mom, it's wonderful to see you. You look lovely!"

Then turning to introduce Sam "Mom, this, of course, is Sam."

Sam was right behind me, and following suit in what

seemed like a natural sequence, mimicked me by saying, "Hi Mom. It is wonderful to see you, and you do look lovely. " She also gave her a hug.

We all laughed, and even though my mom knew Sam was joking around, she had a sparkle in her eye. My guess was she enjoyed the sound of having Sam call her mom.

Still smiling broadly I shook my head, "Sam, you do have a way with introductions."

I said to my mom, "You should ask Sam to describe how we met at the Expo, and how we sorted out the presentation we gave. Turning to Sam, "I think you were trying to confuse me and test me at the same time."

I noticed a slight rose in Sam's cheeks and teased, "I think it was almost the only time I've ever been at a loss for words."

Sam grinned and nodded in mock defense, "I hope Phil did me justice. Actually I was just happy to find the room and escape from the crowds." Sam winked at me, "You must have said something right."

We all laughed again, and the warm greeting set the tone from the beginning for a light-hearted visit.

Even though I only saw my mother ever few months, we talked on the phone at least every couple of weeks. From the episodes we shared during my father's illness, we interacted more like friends than anything else. I had told her a little about Sam, but had decided to let them meet and form their own impressions. Also, in part I did not want to jinx what I thought the relationship could become, or conversely I did not want to overplay it if things did not work out. Truly though, I knew our growing affections were showing through like the morning sun, and each time together was weaving an ever-tighter bond.

My thoughts were brought back when my mother pointed to Anna and Alex, who were still looking for treasures where the waves washed up a variety of sea life, "I received a warm greeting from Anna, and also briefly made friends with Alex.

They are both adorable, but it's a grandmother's prerogative to sing their praises." Turning to me, "It seems like Anna is in heaven showing Alex around 'her private beach.' Then she said to Sam, "It's just the way Phil always was, and still is when he comes home to visit. So, when was the last time you visited the sea shore?"

"I visit the beach as much as possible when I travel, but I haven't been to the New Jersey beaches in a long time. There have always been so many things to do when I'm at home, as funny as it might sound, it is easier for me to visit the beach on my trips to California or France."

Sam added graciously, "The beach and ocean here look cleaner and more beautiful than any of the others." With an honest, and understated flattery, she added, "Perhaps it's just the people though."

I interjected, "Was your vacation to the Baja in Mexico with Alex your most recent visit to an ocean?"

Sam thought for a moment and acknowledged, "Yes, it's been a little while and I'm sorry to say but that was the last time."

I turned to my mom, "You'll enjoy hearing about their trip. Maybe we can get Alex to tell us about it this evening. It would be fun to hear it from her perspective."

Sam agreed, "That sounds like a great idea. I've never heard Alex explain it from her viewpoint."

"It's interesting, when you're on a trip with someone, you think they have the same experiences, but she may have seen or related to the same things differently. It reminds me of something I was once told, 'meaning takes place in each person's mind, and can be very different for each; varying from being influenced by a previous experience to having the fresh perspective innocence offers.' For instance one person might have expectations while another might appreciate the simple differences each day offers, like a sunset."

My mom smiled at me and kidded, "No wonder you two get along, both of you have interesting theories and philosophies to share. I'll make a point to remember that one."

As if to confirm Sam's statement, the sunset was doing its best to offer us a brilliant exhibition of its daily show.

"I make it a point to see every sunset, and sunrises too when it's clear. I've always found each one a marvel far exceeding most other forms of entertainment," my mother remarked. "The pinks look exceptionally vivid this evening." And exclaiming, as she often did even without a new person around, "See how the sunset sky is like a rainbow, running the full spectrum of colors from the reds on the bottom by the bay, the yellow and green in the middle and the crystal clear blue up above. My theory is that there are rainbows in many places if you take the time to look. Humm, that kinda fits in or augments Sam's thought, doesn't it?"

We nodded in agreement, and studied the sunset. The question crossed my mind as to how much painting Sam fit into her schedule.

I asked, "Did you bring your paints?"

Sam acknowledged, "I always carry a sketch pad with me." And, as if she read my thought added, "Even with all the running around I do, I have made it a habit to do something with my own art everyday. It's like a best friend who can always share a special moment with me and blesses whatever each day presents."

She added with a sigh, "With all I do, drawing or painting is a special meditative world I enter welcomingly."

We were all quiet for a moment. I contemplated how throughout my life I retreated to the solitude of the beach to rejuvenate myself. I added, "I guess we each create our own special places or ways of finding peace within ourselves."

The quiet moment was broken as Alex, with Anna close on her heals, yelled to Sam, "Look I found a sea horse, and Anna found a star fish, and they are both still alive!"

We all looked at their prizes like they had found precious gemstones, and Anna said, "Dad look, Alex found some blue sea glass her very first time."

If I was looking for signs that things would go well, the sea glass, which was deep blue and perfectly smooth from the sand and ocean, was a good luck omen. It was common to find white, green or brown glass, but fairly rare to find blue. We were all sufficiently impressed with their finds, and each of us took a closer look as if we were seeing a sea horse and star fish for the first time.

Then Anna said, "Come on Alex, we need to go put them back between the rocks in the jetty. We only get to keep them if they are already dried up," and off they ran again back toward the ocean.

I yelled after them, "Come back up soon. We're going back to put dinner on the table."

Anna waved an acknowledgement as she kept running to keep up with Alex.

We all grinned, and my mom understated, "It looks like they get along okay."

"Well," my mother sighed, "I guess we should start toward the house. Almost everything is prepared for dinner. I hope everyone is hungry. I always find there's something about the sea air that gives people a hearty appetite, either that or the long car ride." Turning to me she added, "I'm sure I don't have to convince you to play a song or two on the piano before dinner, and maybe a couple of other times this weekend with me and Anna too. I'm sure we can find some music Sam and Alex know so they can join in."

With that we walked toward the house, moving slowly as we studied the colorful glow over the bay left by the setting sun. The warmth of the day was beginning to give way to the coolness of an autumn night at the beach. Before entering the house, I went around the side to pick up some firewood to give an extra warmth to the evening. Once inside, we all headed to the kitchen to finish the preparations.

From the smell of my mother's cooking I felt a childlike security of being home. I could see from Sam's face the universal influence had captured and relaxed her too. Adding to the sense of comfort was, after the door slamming, the sound of the girls voices. They had their hands full of the sea shells, sea glass and other assorted treasures, and went straight to sorting them on the living room floor.

I went into the den, sat down at the piano, and found the feel for the ivory keys with a rendition of Autumn Leaves by Johnny Mercer. As I finished the intro to the song, I could hear my mother joining in from the kitchen on the first note of the song. As we finished, Sam, who had come in to listen, applauded appreciatively.

I felt the sense of timelessness that playing the piano with my mother brought out in me. I could have just sat and played for the next few hours, but I knew there was time to play one more before dinner.

I switched from the melancholy, which had introduced a sweet emotional tone to the way I felt, to a more upbeat song. I played a rendition of Bewitched by Rodgers and Hart. My mother came into the room to sing the song and I joined her in the chorus. The sassy foolishness of what probably bordered on bawdy when it was written, was like sprinkling flowers in the room. After the song, my mom, who knew music made me forget about eating, bent over to give me a hug, and then took my hand to lead me back to the kitchen. Sam went to tell Anna and Alex to wash up and come in for dinner.

In a few minutes we were all seated around the table. My mother lit the candles to add to the festive feeling, and we all sat quietly for a moment before saying the blessing over the food. Something in my heart stirred as I listened to my mother's thankfulness, and a sensation of being truly blessed by all the love in my life swept over me. The essence of just being in everyone's presence filled me with joy, and a desire to make it a common practice in my life. I wanted to know this kind of simple happiness of life in some aspect of every day. Before starting to eat, I made a resolution to make it a reality in my life starting right away.

After dinner and cleaning up, everyone agreed to another walk on the beach. In late October the moon, which was three quarters full, looked like a big orange and sent beams of light over the ocean creating a shimmering light which made a flashlight unnecessary. The few clouds, in an otherwise clear sky, floated on the soft breeze out over the ocean leaving a clear view of Virgo, and Orion coming up over the horizon. Anna wanted to start a bonfire on the beach, but compromised on a fire at the house that first night and a bonfire on Saturday night.

Since it was low tide, we were able to walk easily on the flatter, hard packed sand near the ripples of waves that lapped at the beach. The larger waves were breaking out eighty feet or so on the sand bar. The pool in between was like a big pond and quite calm, and the sound of the powerful surf breaking called to us across the pools.

One of my favorite sounds in the world is the sound of waves breaking. If I want to change my mood or relax when I am in the city I play a recording of the ocean, close my eyes and picture what I was seeing first hand that night. To include my mom, Anna, Sam and Alex in my imagery would make my picture all the more pleasant to recall.

We walked a short way and then turned around, but rather than head back to the house we stood and chatted against the back drop of the stars and the ocean. We sang a few songs, and talked about beach stuff like the times whales or dolphins migrated by, or how the wind from the west would fan spray off the tops of the waves creating rainbows in the surf when the sunlight was at just the right angle. We talked about sleeping on the beach in September when the crowds were gone and it was still fairly warm.

Whatever we talked about, we stayed at the beach for almost two hours. Finally we headed back for some hot chocolate, and sat in front of a roaring fire singing songs and telling stories. The evening flew by, and we all decided to get ready for bed so we could get an early start the next day.

My mother offered to wake everyone early to go see the sunrise with her, and we agreed as long as we could go back to bed for awhile afterward. Anna and Alex each had rooms upstairs across the hall from my mother's room, Sam got to sleep on the sofa-bed in the den with the fire to keep her warm. I slept on the futon bed on the front porch where I could hear the ocean sing me to sleep. After a flurry of activity and taking turns in the bathrooms, the house settled into a peaceful silence.

For the weekend Sam and I had made a clear decision to sleep in separate rooms rather than introduce that aspect into everyone's first meeting. I was content having sex be a minor role, although I must admit I felt a rising in my loins at the thought; maybe we could find some privacy sometime during the weekend.

I lay in bed and read for a while, and wrote in my journal some of the highlights from the day. As I was about to turn off the light, I heard someone walking toward my room. In a moment Sam was peering into the room, and coming over to me. She leaned over to kiss me. Her silk robe fell open as she slipped into bed with me. The feel of the silk and the press of her body against mine felt like perfection to my touch. At first we just held each other quietly, drinking in each other with light touches and caresses. I gently rolled over on top of Sam, and sitting astride her, I slipped the robe away from her. I leaned over and kissed her shoulder. I continued with soft kisses down her arm, back up her side to her shoulder again, and then her neck. I held her breasts softly while kissing and caressing her. Sam moaned softly, and rose up pushing herself against me. Sam sat up toward me and her lips sought mine. We found ourselves lost in sweet kisses. We caressed each other's face and neck with light touches; each slowly increasing our desire and heightened our senses. Being on the front porch made it unlikely anyone would hear us, but wordlessly and quietly we communicated our sensuous messages.

After enjoying the luxurious attention, Sam playfully pushed me over on my back, and crawled on top of me. Sitting over me she slowly ran her fingers through the hair on my chest and down my sides and back up my arms to my chest again. I had my hands around her lower back, and slowly pulled her onto me. Sam melded with me. We interlaced our hands as Sam arched up over me. Sam moved tantalizingly slowly at first, then faster, and then very slowly again. I sat up to hold her tightly and she wrapped her legs around behind me so that our embrace was like a oneness of bodies fused into one energy and one being.

The most minute movement by either of us was felt by the other, and we became living extensions of each other. When we breathed, it was as if we were in one breath. With our hearts pressed together, it was as if we had one heart. With our heads next to each other, it was if we could read each other's thoughts, and know exactly the other's thoughts and feelings. Pressed together as we were, it was if we were inside each other moving as one body. I felt Sam shudder again and again as she held me tighter than even before. As she squeezed me, I exploded into her sending quickened shock waves through both our bodies. We were molded together, and held the moment, suspended in time and ecstasy. Then we were motionless. Sam asked me to lay back, so she could lay on top of me to savor the feelings that were still tingling through her.

As I relaxed, she curled up with her head on my shoulder and we returned to gently running our fingers over each other. The feeling of contentment lingered as we lay listening to the sound of the ocean and each other's hearts pulsing a joyful sound in an otherwise silent night. As I started to doze off, I remember feeling a gentle kiss as Sam slid out of bed to return to the den and maintain a semblance of decorum.

The next thing I remember was being awakened in the morning for the sunrise as we had agreed. Everyone was still half asleep, but we all hurried to bundle up so as not to miss the big event. When we got to the beach, the sky was already full of colors from the first light of dawn. After a few minutes, we saw the tip of a huge red ball beginning to pierce the sky from the water. The sun, sky and ocean were presenting the most beautiful bouquet of colors all along the horizon, but at best they only matched the way Sam looked to me that morning.

Either from the awesome beauty or because we were not awake, we all watched in silence. As the sun rose, the sunlight reflecting on the water looked like diamonds, and when the waves curled and crested, the light poured right through illuminating tiny droplets as they danced off the top of the waves.

We knew someone else was up early because we could smell coffee and breakfast beginning to mix with the sea air. Everyone seemed to look at me at the same time for a signal to go back to the house with the expectation that I would make breakfast. I had promised the night before that Anna and Alex could go to the bakery with me to pick up croissant, bagels, pastry and whatever treat they each wanted. I remembered going to the bakery with my dad as being a special privilege, so perhaps I was passing on a tradition. Anyway, food had already taken precedence over going back to sleep, but I made a mental reservation for an afternoon nap with a good book.

We returned with the goodies, and sat down to feast on the bakery treats and eggs with grilled potatoes and onions on the side. I explained I made occasional exceptions to my morning smoothie.

While eating I encouraged my mother, "Tell Sam and Alex the story about Dad's mother and how her parents came to America."

It was a favorite in the family, like the story Sam had told me about Uncle J and her mother.

My mother began: "The decision they made to leave Europe was a dramatic move. Without it you and Anna might never have been born."

"The process started when your great grandfather left alone on the long ocean voyage for an unknown life. He had decided to leave the apparent social and financial security of his home, to embark on an unknown expedition to a new world. Actually he left the Ukrainian city of Odessa on the Baltic Sea because staying was no longer an option. If he stayed, your great grandparents would have been separated permanently because the army was encouraging lifetime conscripts to the army, but not asking anyone's opinion in the matter, so he left.

"He sailed off to New York City to work for a distant uncle. The plan was to save all of his money, and send for his wife and four children. He missed them with all his heart and worked hard so they could be reunited as soon as possible. The following year he sent the money required. His wife responded by letter, which was the only available communication, and gave the day he would be reunited with her. He then waited the month and a half until the boat was due to arrive.

"He was jubilant the day he went to meet her at the dock, until, to his shock and disappointment, his mother-in-law walked down the gangway toward him instead of his wife."

We laughed, but I could imagined the tears he must have held back.

My mother continued, "His mother-in-law told him to keep working, and to send for his wife again. Then, she moved in with him."

I added, "I can picture him enduring knowing he would be rejoined with his wife and kids, but to live with a testy mother-in-law while waiting must have truly pushed his patience."

My mom agreed, "You can imagine how devoted he was to his wife when you realize that the story was repeated. The next time he expected to meet his wife and children, his sister-in-law walked toward him instructing him to send for his wife again. That might have been my, or anyone else's limit, and when I think about it, I question if he considered giving up, or if she really wanted to join him. However, the next time he waited for the boat, his wife and children ran to greet him and they were finally reunited."

"She told her husband that even though he had promised to send for her mother and sister after she arrived, they were not easy to get along with and it was her way of assuring their passage.

My mom added, "They went on to have another three children, and eventually moved the entire family, mother-in-law and sister-in-law as well, to Philadelphia for another opportunity for work.

"Of course, one of the children was your grandmother. I think she faced almost as many difficulties as her parents.

"She eloped with the one true love of her life at eighteen years old. Eight years later, after having three children, her husband died of TB leaving her to raise them and work. Of course, one was your father. She knew how to survive.

"Some years later, she remarried, but he died, as did her third husband; both due to illnesses.

"Whatever the case, we really had the benefit of a very resilient teacher, who could not only survive many hardships, but shine through it all inspiring us with a love that was always felt by everyone she knew."

Later I told Sam the part my mom left out. My grandmother stopped visiting for a year after her second son died of a sudden illness. Then, when my father, her first son, was attempting to rehabilitate from his condition. During my father's illness when we all felt so helpless, she came for extended periods, but again stopped for over a year after he died. Of all of the challenges in her life losing her sons was the hardest.

My mother was still explaining, "Later in life, she moved to Florida with her fourth husband where they bought a small apartment a block from the beach. For at least one holiday a year she flew back to Philadelphia to visit her brothers and be with her family. In Miami she worked as a legal secretary part time, and every free day whenever the water and air temperature were at least seventy-five degrees she went to the beach for a swim in the ocean."

I added, "After she retired from the law office at eighty-nine, she practically ran the Coop, which is the corporation that owns the condominium building, where her apartment is. What amazes me is how, rather than giving up on life at any point, she found a way to get through it all."

My mom said, "Family is still what is most important in her life. During all these years, she has always stayed in contact with her friends and all sides of the family. I think that's what got her through everything."

I said, "Whenever I need inspiration, or think I have a problem, I think of her and her parents too. I truly appreciate how much we have to be thankful for."

I picked up with a thought, "It amazes me what they did to survive. Maybe relationships at the turn of the century were based more on physical survival than now, but people who lived through both periods, needed to adjust to all kinds of changes.

"In a way though, I think the emotional baggage is more elusive than the physical hardships. Physical survival can at least be addressed through working harder or moving to a place with more opportunity. On the other hand, when people have an emotional problem, it is usually so well integrated in with other personality traits that it is obvious to everyone but the 'owner' of the trait. Anyway, I think, people are now aware of the emotional challenges, and taking steps in a way that parallels the physical changes embarked on by my great grandparents.

"One of my other philosophies is that people change under two primary circumstances: When forced to, or due to boredom. In other words, people wait until the physical or emotional problems leave them no alternative but to change, or someone has repeated the same ordeal so many times, they would rather die than do it again."

In the silence that followed my theoretical ramblings, I thought to myself, people like Sam and I are making progress on understanding ourselves and each other. I felt a momentous exodus had begun to take place from my/our known, but now unacceptable, past of relationships to a new world of freedom to choose. Rather than being conscripts to emotional habits, we were venturing into previously uncharted waters.

As we began to clean up, we excused Anna and Alex, who went back to the beach, and our conversation quickly regained a light air, as we talked about what to do next.

The day stayed clear and was warm enough that we were able to wear shorts and tee shirts during the middle of the day. It was a perfect fall beach day. We spent the day either on the beach, in the kitchen or on the back deck, and it was filled with talking, reading, walking and of course, as at any mother's house, eating. Later in the afternoon, Sam went off by herself to the bay with her sketch pad and paints for some quiet time.

During the weekend, Sam and I created a little haven around us. Anna and Alex got to know each other, and set the basis for a friendship between them. There was a mutual admiration between my mother and Sam and Alex, and everyone got along great.

We all appeared to find a respectable portion of socializing and privacy, and by the end of the weekend we felt closer, having shared such a special time together. By the time we left on Sunday, everyone was planning the next time we could take a trip to the sea shore again.

Before going to sleep that night I called Sam to thank her.

"For all the times I've been to the beach, it seemed new to me through sharing it with you; and Alex too."

"I knew everything went great, but it's really lovely you called to tell me. I also appreciate what you mean about having a new perspective to familiar experiences." Sam offered, "It's refreshing to see how I've been living through your eyes. I've especially been rethinking the meaning of the stories I told you last month. I felt I relived the episodes while relating each one to you. Retelling the part about being attacked near Randi's place in the city, even though I handled it, makes me question running around the city again. While my career has been incredibly dynamic since then, it's also so time consuming I've still only made it home for short visits. I've decided to talk with Alex about going there the end of December for a couple weeks or so. I feel I need to talk with Uncle J. Maybe I still need to better understand what happened back then, and get his perspective on my life since then. I have an uncanny feeling the changes Uncle J talked about are still ahead of me."

"So what does that mean now?"

"I felt very contented this weekend, but in a way it was unsettling as I sensed the different parts of my life need to be more balanced. I guess I have some work to do. I know I'm always progressing, but meeting you has been reopened the questions in a new light. I'll keep you posted, but for the moment, I'm going to sleep."

Chapter 9

The next time Sam and I saw each other was a few weeks later. Sam came back to my place after listening to me play at the Borgia one night, but she needed to leave very early the following morning. After that, although we still talked on the phone almost every day, we only saw each other one other weekend in December. Alex had agreed to Sam's idea to visit their family for the last week of the month and the first week of January.

While Sam was away we still talked on the phone, but only once or twice a week. We also exchanged these letters:

Dear Phil,

I woke up before the sun today, and dressed quickly so I could walk through the orchard with the first rays of dawn's soft light. Layers of mist rose and flowed past me and the trees, making me, or us, feel like dancers with veils. Every tree, bush and blade of grass glistened when the mist parted. The light illumined fallen leaves and bare branches that held spectrum-filled drops from a shower that had sprinkled the little rainbow catchers everywhere during the night. The clear morning sky still showed the last stars, and there was a rose border where the fields, trees and mountains met the sky. As the mist melted away, the sun silhouetted the Cascade's ridges away to the east, back-lighting the snow-covered peaks.

I walked for over a mile from the farm house to a hill overlooking the Sound where I often used to go to paint. As I walked, I took long, slow breaths, drawing cool, moist air to savor the taste of fir and earth riding on every drop.

I began my meditation with sweeping movements to move my awakening flow of Chi, my life energy. It was as if I was a tree rooted to the earth while lifting my arms into the heavens. The awesome balance of life in nature seemed to merge into me, blurring the boundary between my body and all else. Each sweep of my hand reached as though touching the lines of light topping the ridges. With my eyes closed, I engraved an image of the shapes, colors and emotions enveloping my senses as if painting on a canvas inside my mind.

As the sun jumped out from behind the mountains, the flood of light washed away the delicateness of dawn's details, and my thoughts and focus shifted to the farm. I observed the curls of smoke I knew meant the fireplace was being lit to take the chill from the room for the pre-breakfast Aikido workout.

I wandered back, guided by the patterns in the smoke weaving into the sky and dissipating into nothing. When I opened the door, I found Uncle J, my parents and Alex waiting there for me. I joined them and sat quietly on the floor.

Uncle J began by reading a poem from the Tao Te Ching. The essence of the thoughts stayed with me for the day; to be like water, strong and resilient through acceptance, flexibility and not resisting; to realize, that by always flowing to the lowest places, all is equal and only as vital as the lowest; to be as humble as the ocean, the king and queen of water, for only by accepting the gifts that flow from every river, stream and spring is life willingly given to support the greatest sea.

Then we began the graceful, meditative motions, quietly and slowly bringing the inner dance to the surface. Though each of us moved within our own space, we felt a communion of our energy, thoughts and love for each other and all.

It is later in the afternoon, and I came back to my room to

explore my thoughts after having lunch with my mom and dad. I feel completely at ease here, but there is also a level of discomfort. I feel as though I have reverted to my childhood, but still as an adult. Something doesn't quite fit. In a way, it is like being a child who knows too much. It is tricky to be content now that I know what responsibilities await me. Having experienced the adult games in life makes it harder to enjoy some of the simple ones, the way it used to be. At first I felt like I had returned to heaven, but there is a tug as if there is some place I'm supposed to be. Balancing the two sides, the familiarity and contentment with the conflict and tugs, may calm the current feeling of being slightly out of place either way.

In some respects I realize I've felt that way with you also. Perhaps I've been responsible for myself, and entrenched in my own habits for a little too long. I recognize and feel how wonderful you are, but, at the same time, I feel a pull to retreat. There is part of me that believes this is too good, and I wonder if I know how to keep it going. I know to trust myself, but there is a part of me that's resisting. For example, I'm thrilled when I'm with you, but then I get caught up in everything else I do. Mostly, when I'm away, you disappear from my thoughts, and then I worry that maybe you'll really disappear from my life, but then I go back to what I'm presently doing.

I ask myself what it means that I don't really miss you or think about you when we're apart. I love our intimacy or even knowing we'll talk on the phone about our day, but I am also happy when you're gone. These conflicts within me are disconcerting. How do I blend you into my life when I am equally content being alone, and just thinking of myself (and, of course, Alex).

I just returned to my room for the evening, and read the first parts of this letter. I considered leaving out my thoughts after lunch. It sounded too harsh to me; I wondered if questioning being with you might be hard for you to accept. I feel the need to express that side of me though, and tell you what I truly feel. In a way it is easier to tell you my thoughts in a letter; so I'll keep going.

It is actually kind of strange. I still haven't really told my family about you. I wonder if that means there's something in our relationship, or us, that I am having trouble facing. Maybe it is just the distance and being away for the past couple of weeks, and now being here for another week. Maybe I think you will have changed when I return, or something will be lost by being apart this much relative to how long we have known each other.

You are truly a wonderful person, and seem so patient with me. Part of me wants you to fly out here right now (but don't), and another part of me feels like I can handle anything life throws me except how to adjust to having a relationship in my life. I wonder if I'm too set in my ways. I feel inexperienced with all this stuff, and what to expect.

Well now I really feel like I've opened myself up, and thrown my thoughts and questions on the table. It truly is wonderful out here, and I wish you were here right now.

Love,

Sam

When I received Sam's letter, I read it three times right away. I had never heard Sam, or anyone, describe a morning in such beautiful poetry. I was drawn to her descriptions and insights. But, I was also upset by her uncertainty and the conflict within her regarding beginning a relationship after being unattached most of her life. I realized that, although we were getting along well, it must have been a hurdle for her to accept a "significant other" entering her life. I sat down and replied as my thoughts began to flow.

Dear Sam.

Anna and I returned to the city today after visiting my mother at the beach for the weekend. Your letter shook me up, but in a way it was also comforting to hear a deeper truth that I had wondered about, but was still unspoken. My first thought was that you were pulling away from me, perhaps as you said, due to the distance and seeing each other infrequently. But, then it became clear that there were other questions within the letter, inviting intimacy and trust in a way only your truth and openness could offer.

It's funny, as my thoughts begin to flow, I feel more closely connected to you than I have ever felt in a relationship. I realize we are coming from two opposite sides of the stage. I've run away from commitment, or pushed others away, while you've committed to everything you do, and in the process you seem to throw your passion into life, finding fulfillment in each of your choices.

When I have looked at my life in perspective, I simplified it into two types of existence: being accepting, generally happy and satisfied, or being frustrated, generally unhappy and dissatisfied. The second results from inconsistencies between the present and my desired expectations. The contentment of the first way to live allows me to focus on a desired goal but I am non-invested or non-judgmental in the way it results. Then by accepting whatever presents itself as a means to the next 'whatever', creates the ability to be ok, or maybe even happy, with what is happening in each now.

I sense I'm intellectualizing what you expressed in feelings, but this is how I'm realizing I work. I start with an idea or theory, and then see how it comes out in the real world. What I'm saying is, you're the one I want to explore all this with whether we're together or apart, confident or afraid, open or resisting. A part of me knows we can be playmates and teachers to each other, and I'm willing to explore the adventures with you to find out.

I just read over what I wrote, and appreciate what you

meant about wanting to tear it up, but also finding it easier to express myself in writing. There is a feeling of being anonymous and a sense of freedom allowing my thoughts to flow naturally. I have been writing in my journal more and more lately, and find a flow of consciousness springs from within me giving me perspective. I keep finding life is an education as I observe what each person and situation shows me, especially what I see in myself through another person's expressions and thoughts.

The journal entry I wrote last night was so much fun I wanted to share it with you right away, and I think it will lighten up the first part of the letter. I became engaged in a most unusual conversation yesterday at the beach with a man I'd never seen before, who was surf-fishing for striped bass. I asked how the fishing was going. Somehow we ended up talking about how nature, in this case fish, can show aspects of human personalities. He was explaining how most bass stay lean from chasing down the coast with the cold water on their tails, and die young while always on the move reacting with the school or to the herd instinct. He continued saying that there are old, fat fish called locals that stay in their deep holes through the winter and slow their body temperature and remain inactive through a hibernation-type period. His wife joined us, and we dreamed up a little vignette between two striped bass. We named the fish Mark and Marion, and it goes something like this. By the way, it is open for input if you wish to make a contribution.

Mark: "Where did every one go?"

Marion: "They all headed south with the warmer water the day after the storm."

Mark: "I must have been caught in the storm's strong current. I was swimming lost and alone for days. Is that what happened to you?"

Marion: "No,"

Mark: "Then why are you still here by yourself ?"

Marion: "I live off Cape Cod all year including the winter."

Mark: "How do you survive when the water gets colder? What do you eat? Don't we need to stay with the school?"

Marion: "I hibernate like a bear, nothing and no."

Mark: "Oh? What's a bear? Never mind. I mean, from your size I know you've lived many seasons, and obviously from your weight you eat well, so okay, I can tell you've been successful, but how do you do it and stay so vibrant and vivacious too?"

Marion: "I've never explained it to any of the others because they usually just pass by for a day or so on their annual migration, blindly following the fish they eat and the water temperature they prefer. But to answer your question, I stay in this hole all year. I was taught by another "local" that I asked when I was a young, and an especially curious, fish like you. She is a cognitive psychologist, who is excellent at helping others find perspective and understand the lessons of what we create in our lives. I highly recommend talking with her in the spring, but for now I'll teach you the trick of gradually lowering your body temperature as the water changes thus slowing your metabolism.

Mark: "Wow. I'm not sure I understood all that, but it's getting cold here. Can you show me, and explain the philosophy and science side of it later?"

Marion: "Sure, but you'll have a lot of time for contemplation throughout the winter. Staying alive is the easy part. Being silent, still and alone with only your thoughts is the tough part. Look, all you've ever known was following the crowd, eating, reproducing and facing whatever each day presented; without a thought to being an individual. Your friends and family will continue to live facing the daily conflicts and turbulence of life as a fish. You though, must look within yourself for answers and resolve any fears if you intend to grow and be happy with your new life; although you'll still be a fish, you'll be more of an individual. I know this sounds like a lot now, but first you need to break the old habits, accept change, and find a contentment in this new way of being. Then, like I am now, perhaps you'll pass on what you know to another some day."

Mark: "You're right, that's pretty overwhelming stuff, but I get the basic idea that I can survive and be happy by myself once you show me this hibernation thing, and then we can talk more in the spring."

Marion: "You seem like you'll be a quick learner. We better get started now. I hear a cold front is moving in a few days from now."

You're probably wondering how I managed to meet someone fishing and have a conversation like this, but I'm sure you realize I couldn't have made all of that up myself. Well, maybe I could. Anyway, we decided to continue our philosophies on life over lunch - fresh caught stripers I might add.

The essence of what we discussed is that life is a balance between conflicts and resolutions, and between being alone and being with others. The thought is that most people find happiness in resolving the conflicts, but that implies a need for a series of conflicts to resolve in order to be "happy." The key is to find happiness and peace within yourself, and then break the pattern of creating conflict with others.

Finding a solution involves more than changes in physical location, and emotional signposts can be found by being aware of physiology, words and expressions. The nature of the bass seemed like a pretty close analogy so we played with it for a while. The dialogue was a summary of a much longer play we considered writing, but decided to save for another day.

What I really want to say in this letter is, I know once we're together again it will be like we were never apart. Let's get together in person as soon as you return. We can find out if the perspective from being apart and the letters will have brought us closer.

Love,

Phil

PS. I told Anna about the fish dialogue in the letter, and she told me to say "Hi" to you - and from Mark and Marion too.

Chapter 10

Sam asked me if I could visit for an hour the night she returned to Philadelphia. She and Alex had arrived on the "red eye," and Sam put in a ten hour day to catch up on work that had piled up. Even though she was exhausted, she appeared energized once she saw me. It was as though a cloud blocking the sun evaporated the moment we held each other.

I said, "It's as if an emotional memory is stored and then released in each other's presence."

Sam agreed, "It's true. I'm thrilled to see you. Sit next to me and let's just talk for a while, but let's keep it light. I want to go to sleep soon."

"Okay I won't get into philosophy tonight, but really, something is missing when we're apart that creates a tension, and now I feel immediately revitalized being together."

"Phil, you're so sweet to me. Of course, you're also a goof-ball. Tell me again how you met someone on the beach, and came up with theorizing fish."

I left after about an hour, but we decided to make it a priority to see each other at least twice a week from that night on. When we were together, there was an awesome compatibility, and we committed to consciously nurture the loving basis we'd begun.

* * *

One night the following weekend when the kids were staying with friends we decided to spend a quiet evening at

Sam's place. We made a simple candle lit dinner that promised romance and the dissolving of a work week that had pushed us each to our limits. For dessert we decided it would be fun to make a complicated double chocolate mousse pie that had captured my taste buds at a friend's dinner party. Having acquired the recipe and all the required ingredients, we set about gleefully with expectant delight to make the dessert while the rest of dinner was cooking.

It turned out that my, our, independent nature, which we thought was a key strength for building a working balance between interdependency and mutual support, was trickier than we could have guessed. As I started melting the chocolate and preparing the ingredients, what appeared to be fairly straightforward directions were not working quite right. Sam offered a few suggestions that altered the recipe, but I was determined to adhere to it.

Unfortunately, when Sam kept suggesting what to do or how to fix the recipe, I listened to her input, but became increasingly annoyed and agitated. With some difficulty I, we, did work out the dessert, and it was almost as tasty as anticipated, although somewhat lacking texturally.

However, by that time there was a low level tension that had mounted between us, and Sam had retreated to other tasks in the kitchen. Perhaps the tension was perceived as rejection due to my taking control of the kitchen, and in effect attempting to control Sam.

Had I been aware of my need to be right and seeing the challenge as mine, not ours, I might have realized the tricky recipe and our intimacy would have benefited from teamwork. Maybe I was being too linear when an analogical approach would have been more appropriate. Maybe I was being stubborn and trying to force the "ingredients," both interpersonal and pie, when the recipe required a little patience. Certainly accepting her as a co-creater in the process rather than as an assistant would have created greater harmony.

The smaller emotion of annoyance that was glossed over, began to fester. Little comments, during what should have been a relaxing evening, had an edge that was unsettling. By the time we got to dessert, we could not explain why we were uncomfortable and self-withdrawn. It had gotten to the point where there was little eye contact, and we were not enjoying the meal. Our limited responses tended to 'step on' the other's opinion or input, and conversation was unpalatable.

In perspective it reminded me of the way many people interact with children. I have observed that children are often 'talked at' or interrupted. In a similar way questions are left hanging as the adult speaks with self-import on a tangential subject. The act of talking over the child is subtly degrading to the child's self esteem. It can even be done in a manner that the adult thinks is complimentary, but actually implies amazement that the young person could be smart enough to have such an inquisitive or insightful perspective, rather than answering the question.

I have observed similar patterns in society where 'without intention' such attitudes gradually create defacing and low self images in children and women. The effect is a squelching of imaginative or intuitive thinking, and willingness to offer thoughts. Often the perpetuator has a latent or blatant insecurity, and need to control people and situations. As this is commonly played out in the everyday power plays of society, the resulting judgment tends to alienate and tear apart the parties. The disassociation can be remedied as the isolation and pain eventually push the individual to listen, understand and hopefully interact with kindness and appreciation for others as a way of life.

These examples are clearly extreme compared to our misunderstanding, but the subtleness of even seemingly insignificant behavior can grow to be debilitating. What some might accept as normal was the first turn of a snowball that could have melted away or started an avalanche. Since we could not even identify what was going on, we certainly could not resolve it, and the drama continued.

Sam left me to clean up the huge mess from making the dessert and settled in to read the book that was currently engrossing her. This was also fine on the surface, but I was aware of feeling disconcerted and a little resentful.

Once I finished with the kitchen work, I went to join Sam, but found her so interested in her book that she really just wanted to be left alone, or so I thought. Since we both appreciated each other's need for quiet, privacy and a love for reading, even this was reasonable to me, in spite of thinking we would keep each other company that evening.

The next part, like the prior ones, held no obvious pitfall as I proceeded to find a book to read before dozing off to sleep on the sofa.

I was awakened around three in the morning by Sam, who was in tears. In reality she had been sensitive to my frustration while I was making the pie, and had felt excluded and rebuffed by my comments. Then, rather than say anything to ruin the dinner, which neither of us really enjoyed anyway, she stayed quiet and the building emotional discomfort went untended.

Sam explained her preference had been to share a quiet, romantic evening, but after dinner she was frustrated and thought that I should have at least made some effort to reconnect and smooth things out. Of course that was impossible since I still had not clearly identified an obvious problem. It would have been easier if there was something apparent.

We began rehashing the evening's mishap. We were both sleepy, becoming irritable and started defending ourselves. In conjunction it seemed we could easily find where the other was at fault which had the direct effect of compounding the problem. As we were getting nowhere fast, we suddenly stopped talking at the same time, and just looked at each other. The look bordered on a glare, and we said "What?" at the same time.

Somehow we found that funny, and realized how absurd we were being. Sensing we could be on the cusp of a issue fundamental to our relationship, we looked for a way to turn the situation around.

The first step in reconnecting was to make physical contact with each other. Sam wanted to be held to show I cared. I, on the other side, felt I needed to communicate first in order to feel like holding Sam. We needed a bridge. It may sound funny, but we decided to rub each other's feet. For me, this was a fairly non-invasive approach that also showed a willingness to compromise from a humble position. Sam and I were also aware of how much feet appreciate attention considering how much they are ignored; despite supporting us in every step of life. While we were rubbing, we started talking. The whole scenario unfolded before us, and begged us to find solutions.

The second step was for us to reaffirm our intentions toward each other, and know we wanted to find solutions. We were learning this was an integral part of anything we were determined to venture into consciously. One of the most difficult things to do in life is to change a behavior, but it is impossible unless everyone involved is truly willing to change. Even then, change is still extraordinarily difficult.

So, we started talking. We began by identifying the clues and traced how the increasing, emotional difficulties had progressed to that point. We realized the miscommunication had gradually become overwhelming within acceptable ways; at least when viewed one at a time. What we thought was being respectful of each other's privacy, and thus remained quiet so as not to ruin what we thought was the other's enjoyment, was actually a whole category being overlooked. Boy, had we missed the boat on all counts.

We each contributed ideas, and initiated a rough draft of

rules. Our resolve to go to the heart of miscommunication, and not just this one mishap, was one of the biggest challenges we faced. Our minds raced through the ways to do it. We even got out a tape recorder so we could hear inflections in our voices for clarity of our thoughts.

We set some guidelines that created a base for communicating in our relationship. Over the next week or so we synthesized it all into a workable approach that built on what we started that night.

The first was to take the risk of speaking openly from our hearts and minds. The spoken word is precious. If the truth is expressed with love then even the most difficult problem can be faced. Communication could flow freely if we did not suppress thoughts or build our's or the other's case in our minds. It was agreed we would rather face turbulence in its early stages than wait until it exploded. We decided openness would encourage us to focus on common solutions to problems. In each respect it was clearly preferable to letting questions fester inside us, becoming frozen, with walls growing between us, or being so overwhelmed we might not even talk.

We agreed the bottlenecks commonly happened when partial explanations were designed to spare the other's feelings. We decided "holding back" in any interaction implied a disbelief that the other was smart enough, emotionally ready, or had the maturity to grasp the level of understanding. An underlying premise was that we intuitively know anyway, and since any gap would inevitably need to be filled, the idea was to nip it in the bud sooner than later. Consistency of intentions, words, and actions would tie the pieces together, create the crucial basis for trust and build the basis in trust for intuitive understandings.

We decided an initial signpost for knowing we were on track was, looking into each other's eyes: "seeing eye to eye."

The second part considered the possibility, and to us the reality, that we subconsciously knew what the other thought or felt through the subtler communications of inflections and body language. This instinct and intuition of human nature would give us a broader knowledge of communication than mere words. Recognizing changes in physiology, eye contact, body posture and more could give clear signs of how communication was progressing, or stalling. In a way, our awareness could identify what was missing in the words. The verbal method of communicating is extraordinary, but woefully lacking if this plethora of other aspects is ignored. As long as we stayed focused on a common solution, our sensitivity to each other would be a contributing factor. We acknowledged that an awareness beyond the spoken word could bridge the gaps and elucidate what was intended.

The third aspect was to pay attention to emotions, especially the "smaller" early ones, during our communications. Emotions flashed warning lights to tell us if we were getting off track. This awareness would allow us to confront and deal with small annoyances as soon as they were recognized. In this way we could prevent bigger emotions like anger, frustration or anxiety. We could turn a potential road block into a new pathway to find our common goals. If one of us felt a disturbance opening in the discussion, then we would need to stop, and ask the other what he or she was feeling. By sharing the emotion, we stood a better chance of identifying and resolving issues, and in the process strengthen our connection.

Fourth was to show self-respect by speaking clearly regarding what each of us truly wanted. We had realized that often when we compromised ourselves because we believed it was what the other wanted, we assumed wrongly. If necessary we could look for compromises after we spoke our preferences clearly. This avoided acting on assumptions, erroneously hoping, figuring out, or somehow thinking we knew what the other wanted. This step was added to prevent doing something that neither of us preferred, but did to make the other happy.

We each had previous experiences that had gone to the extent of being resentful of another, but thinking the other was happy. In actuality neither party was happy. By realizing those situations could have been prevented or resolved initially, we recognized the key was to respect ourselves by speaking up for what we really wanted and then act decisively or find a conscious compromise. We maintained that the result of self-respect would be mutual respect.

Fifth was to listen to the words and sounds that came out of our own mouths. We realized people often listen to the other person just enough to prepare what is in their mind. Instead of a conversation, what ensues are two monologues. A dialogue involves asking questions and listening to the answers. This included using imagination to get a sense of what it would be like in the other persons shoes, and then looking back in a mirroring effect. There was more to the idea than just listening to ourselves and to each other, although that might be enough. We believed any suggestions we had for the other should be heeded by oneself first.

The last step was to recognize that sometimes the first five steps not only did not work, but actually were infuriating or downright painful. We would then need to accept that old habits of manipulation and control could creep in wearing disguises that could fool anyone. Clues included recognizing the times when the two of us were talking at the same time, or if one kept repeating the same point in different ways. There were a few ways to head off a fight once it approached this stage. We decided one of us had to stop and just listen to what the other was saying until he or she was done. Then, one of us had to ask a question that could turn everything around . If all else failed just start smiling and tell how much we loved the other; even when we felt like spitting nails and fire.

After working through the thoughts we shared that evening, we felt closer than ever before. We felt as though we could overcome any hurdle. That night we finally found our way back to bed around five in the morning. Rather than feeling exhausted, we felt alive and quite amorous. We continued our foot rubbing and expanded until we had rediscovered almost every inch of the other's body. Making love sparked a melding of our hearts and minds in addition to our bodies. After we rose to the pinnacle of physical pleasure, we held each other and expressed the intention to take the next step together in our relationship.

* * *

Our misunderstanding that eventful night challenged each of us to understand a boundary that before had held us back in relationships. Due to the process we opened a way to overcame a previously insurmountable hurdle, that was so deeply embedded in us, it was not even recognizable. Until then, the virgin underbelly of our self-doubt and well hidden lingering need for control either went unrecognized or denied. Unknowingly we had been sabotaging our real desire, which was to love and be loved. There was a bursting volcano of suppressed and ignored emotions that offer signs throughout our lives. Like putting a hand over a shaken soda bottle starting to spray, the emotions will always shoot out somewhere and can never really be covered indefinitely.

Some people go to their graves with regrets over misunderstandings they never truly understood, or walk away from relationships because the risk to resolve even minor issues requires being humble enough to admit to an imperfection. Would we have said, "Okay, bring them on. We might as well face them all!"? Yes. Had we know that was going to happen that evening? No.

That evening, though, we became aware of how emotions can actually assist in recognizing stumbling blocks. We found an appreciation for the valuable clues in communication which, once identified, could help uncover and resolve hidden issues.

The impasse in communication had started so simply, we were lulled into being fooled about where to look for the source, and so ignoring the challenge was not a choice. We became immersed gradually and were in over our heads before we knew it, but in the process we learned ever more about ourselves and each other.

The following week Sam was away and we exchanged letters.

Dear Phil,

Since the evening with the chocolate mousse pie, I've been questioning if we can really be together. You're a wonderful person, but that's not enough. That evening brought up more questions than can be resolved with a bunch of even the best thought-out guidelines. In the last few days I have done a lot of soul searching and putting our relationship in perspective. While I did this, I wrote it all down so I could have it in front of me. This is it. Please know as you read this that I really do love you.

What I realized is, I don't need you. I'm really quite happy with my life the way it is, and I like the comfort of knowing I'm self-sufficient. I don't need you to protect me, provide for me financially or be my brains to make decisions for me. I've never needed to listen to someone just to placate them or fill another's need for self-import just for the purpose of having a companion. If you weren't around I could find stimulating conversations with my friends and acquaintances who find my conversation engaging, and readily listen to my thoughts and opinions, and respect me for my insights.

Also, men and women, often compliment me on my fitness, looks and tell me I'm fun to be with. So, I'm sure I could find another lover or companion. But, even if no one wanted to be with me, I'm content to be by myself, or with Alex. I find great pleasure in painting, reading or writing and being in my thoughts about life. I am content to go out to a movie or concert by myself or stay in and watch a movie or listen to music.

In fact, I often prefer walking in nature by myself. I love to sit by a river, ocean or stream especially to watch a sunrise or sunset. I love listening to the birds sing, the wind rustling the leaves, rushing water over rocks, and I especially love the silence of a star-filled night.

Besides all that, I've raised my daughter at least mostly by myself, and I don't need your help or any advise from you in that area, or really in any aspect of my life. I don't need to impress you, or anyone for that matter. In the extreme, you are purposeless, insignificant and almost completely unnecessary. I've survived just fine without you so far in my life, and could continue the rest of my life without you.

The essence of what I feel with you though is the enjoyment of your friendship, and the realization that I prefer sharing all of the aspects of my life with you. I am drawn to the thoughts you share with me which push me to question myself. I am inspired when we conceive of new ideas that break through the prior boundaries I have known. My body lights up and I come alive when we make love in a way beyond any experience I've known. There is a tenderness in your touch, and an intimacy that washes over me and floods through me.

Combining the sensual connection and the coming together in thoughts and mind is one of the finest joys, and has awakened all the emotions in my heart and soul. I realize I want to make changes to include a passionate relationship that has been a missing part of my happiness.

I also sense the creative artistry flowing through your blood, and feel inspired to renew myself through my art. I feel a desire to make changes in my life to paint more, and nurture the expression that is the heart of me.

I watch the way you relate to your mother and Anna, and

appreciate the kindness in your voice and understanding in your interactions with them.

I realize we share a desire to bring an awareness to creating a quality of life that pushes beyond our present limits. We share and love the artistic perspective our work opens for us to view the world through. We share values and beliefs expressed through showing respect and appreciation for the loving connection we have with our families and our daughters.

The feelings I've expressed reaffirm my commitment to join our lives. The other night raised questions, but I realize what we began is a process. In a way, I prefer that to thinking we know all the answers. I considered we could wait until everything is perfect, but I'd rather acknowledge our willingness to work through the imperfections indefinitely, together.

I find a freedom of expression in writing to you. To reflect and put my thoughts in perspective helps me to relate exactly what I want from a source within me. These words on this paper scare me when I look at them, but each one speaks volumes I know you'll understand. To me the words say, "This is Sam, accept these words and you can accept her." Maybe if I keep reading them I'll accept me too.

I need to be up early tomorrow for a meeting, and I want to mail this letter right away before I decide not to send it. I'll be back early next week, but write back to me when you get this. Even if we talk on the phone, I like seeing you in front of me - so write.

I love you!

Sam

I responded:

Dear Loving Friend,

Sam, I am knocked for loops by the depth of your thoughts. The sober acknowledgement of your truth set me crying through sweet smiles. Each word stripped away a veil revealing my fear of whether I can ever be equal to you, and secure enough in who I am to promise to commit to all you present to me. In other words, can I ask and expect you to take the risk, and bear with me through my imperfections, while I find a way to hold up my end of this high-wire act called love?

I truly love you. I even think I know what it means to say that to you. So if you are willing to accept me, and that I am aware each step will require patience and ever more love, then I will put my heart and soul, mind, body and spleen into always finding a way to come together with you in each step of anything life presents.

When we have little setbacks, just show me this letter and remind me I knew there were risks to overcome in making this commitment to my word, "our" reality.

I feel I've been searching for some intangible solution while at the same time running away from an indefinable problem for most of my life. I'm not saying you're "A" or "The" solution, but beyond these words I see a glimpse of true happiness with you that can tame the beast of uncertainty within me. Being with you has been easy, but also has brought forward dormant questions and pacified fears.

I feel you push yourself, and me too, beyond limits of being in old habits. The comforting, side is I see new possibilities with you to overshadow all the fears combined. Being with you opens me to expect a miraculous change even if it comes one slow step at a time.

Even if we spend a quiet day together, or even apart, I always know the potential exists for any experience to vault us forward. But, even if we don't vault dynamically into the unknown, I am willing to enjoy a boring or quiet life together just the same. The key is we could find unlimited experiences together or apart, but the thought of sharing it all with you, and seeing life through your eyes, drives me to be willing to embrace each day together.

With you all the other conflicts seem external to what really matters. It seems my life has been a struggle of overcoming or dealing with those conflicts through people and situations. Now I feel that we can meet the challenges as a team and come together to find resolutions. But, even if there were no conflicts, I am willing to share that too. To quote Elvis Costello, "What's so funny about peace, love and understanding?" I know, you're wondering when I listen to Elvis, but I can even play music by Elvis and Elvis too, and threw it in to show you there are many sides to me, and I'm sure you also, for us to discover. Anyway, perhaps the greatest hurdle is for us each to accept ourselves, as we are now and however we evolve. I am willing to start now with you and I know we will find a way by loving ourselves and finding a way to be at peace with each other.

Love always,

Phil

Sam and I actually spent as many as five days and/or nights a week together over the following two months, and became so close we had to remind each other why we had two homes. The amazing part is Anna and Alex got along better than if they were sisters. Although they were mostly busy with their own friends, Anna enjoyed visiting the nights we stayed at Sam's place. On one trip to the beach Alex even invited a girlfriend who became friends with Anna too. Seeing Anna happy and comfortable with Sam, Alex and whoever was around, showed how easily she accepted, and was accepting of others in almost any social situation. Most importantly though, she was a great indicator for showing the general spirit felt by us all.

Anna was just one indication we were becoming adept at recognizing old habits or emotional responses characteristic of collapsing communication. With our keener awareness, we noticed if we were taking a step toward separating or retreat into egocentric isolation, and challenged ourselves and each other to create new pathways to resolutions. Even when tests of our convictions lead us to scream in frustration at an occasional insignificant miscommunication, we found those episodes eventually brought us closer together. We realized that behind even a volatile personality outburst we could look to the other to be an unshakable support.

With each success we gained confidence we could overcome the fears of uncertainty that welled up in each of us, and choose mutual and self respect. As lifetime battles were averted or repositioned, we created a resilient tensile strength for the foundation we were building. We felt we were awakening an understanding of the process of communicating with love in an evolving relationship.

With all going so well, we committed to merging our lives into a new home together.

Chapter 11

Sam, as instinctual as a lioness commands, but with a wistfulness in her voice concluded, “So, we’ll find a place together?”

“Yes, I’m ready. And you are, too?”

The decision was already an hour old, and initiated by Sam within the first five minutes we were together. We were just verbally confirming, as if each time we heard it, it became more real. We were like children, knowing we would get the special present we asked for for our birthday, but still wanting constant confirmation, say, every ten minutes, until it materialized before us.

Sam declared, “Let’s get out of the city - somewhere between Philadelphia and New York City. We’ll get a fresh start in a new place.”

“What about Anna and Alex?” The realist in me asked.

That raised a momentary eyebrow.

“Oh, they’ll love the idea, eventually, especially if we do and present it well, or maybe with a little bribery, at least for Alex. Leave it to me. I’ll figure everything out.” Sam finished with almost enough certainty to convince me.

I laughed, “We are doing this together, right?

Before Sam felt compelled to defend herself I added, “You do have an amazing talent for bringing ideas to fruition. Just remember, I get to make an occasional decision too.

I teased some more, “Your track record in business speaks

well for what you can do. What's the plan for us now? What's the common factor?"

Sam warily pronounced, "I'll just do what I always do with people: know what they want before they do."

"So you're a mind reader now?"

"Maybe," Sam affirmed with a smirk.

"Ok then, what am I thinking?"

"How lucky we are, and how Alex and Anna will love the idea."

"Absolutely correct." I agreed wholeheartedly. "What else?"

"Well, let me see. You're thinking how wonderful the two of us are going to make our new home."

"Amazing, Sam, you should start a new business reading minds on the side. Anything else?"

"Yeah, about a million things like: how will we handle money, our work, finding a place, schools, telling our families, - stop me if I'm missing anything."

"No. I think you're covering all the bases now."

"So Phil, are you nervous?"

"No. Maybe. No, I'm sure we'll do it. Right?"

"Look, I've been ready to leave the city for a while now, and you seem like a good excuse."

"Excuse me?" Intoning my best wounded voice.

"No, really, with the original business, Present Works of Art, I'm out of town so much, I could live anywhere. And, by the way, you can keep your idea of me starting a new business to yourself. I'd rather sell Present Works or the auction business than start another."

Sam was on a roll, "But, if I need to be in Philadelphia, I can always crash at Randi's. And, whatever it takes to make this come together, I'll, or should I say, we'll, do it together. We'll find ways to get the kids to visit their friends, and we'll find a way to view it as opening more doors rather than closing even one."

"How will Alex react to the move?"

Sam responded lightly, as if positive thinking would assuage a sensitive subject, "She'll resist initially, but her sense of adventure will win out giving her as much drama as she wants to create. What about Anna?"

"I think she really will be the way you described Alex, she'll resist some, but be happier once the process begins. She's so mature in some ways, and still like my little girl in others. I'm just enjoying each day she still wants my company before her hormones kick in more than they already have - which is probably any day now. But, to begin with, we'll talk it out, and find ways to balance her old friends and new activities."

Sam's first choice was to find a country house on a couple of acres between Philadelphia and New York City. She felt the charming farms spotting the rolling hills on either the Pennsylvania or New Jersey side of the Delaware River would combine beauty and accessibility to the cities for both of us.

The location sounded like fun to me, but Alex did not handle it well at all. She was incredulous that Sam could be so unaware of her need to finish her senior year with her friends. Sam surprised me, as with a flash she disarmed the shortest dual in history, and dealt with it by simply declaring to Alex, "We'll make arrangements for you to commute into the city to school, with me, by train, alternated with staying with your friends, Randi or even arranging for you to study at home one or two days a week; whatever it takes to make it work for you."

Alex was as pacified as she had been angry. She seemed either overwhelmed at how great extra freedom might be for her, or baffled as to how easily her battle had been won. She retreated and seemed to enjoy looking for the new house. I wanted to know if Sam came up with that solution instantaneously or if she had anticipated Alex's problem, but Sam was on to some other question already.

Anna was more accepting, and had complained occasionally about the school and the kids in the city before anyway. She was either okay with the idea, or was waiting for more solid ground before making any demands. With promises she too would see her friends, there was a general peace agreement.

One part of the transition, schools for the kids, was solved. Anna and Alex would not admit it readily, but they were burned out on the city also. After a few weekend trips to search the countryside for a new home, they showed signs of being eager too. On one trip, when Randi came along for the ride, her enthusiasm was so contagious that both girls' esteem for the move leapt another notch up the charts. Even though I had only met Randi a few times, from the first she had approved and admitted me as one of the family. Alex and Anna flocked to her like she was a "hip," favorite aunt and they wanted to impress her with their maturity. I thought she was pretty "cool" too.

It was Randi's diplomacy that acknowledged my compromise to commute back into the city. I had explained, "I'm fairly certain I can arrange a teaching schedule of three days a week."

Randi chimed in, "That will make it easier for you to take care of the house when Sam is out of town."

Sam made a feeble attempt to protest, but everyone knew I'd be home more than anyone else except maybe Anna. We all agreed our new house would need office space for me, and probably for Sam so at least some of her work could be done at home.

That day, around one of the unceasing curves in the roads, we found a house under construction on three acres adjacent to a forty acre horse farm. The owners of the farm needed to raise money, and were selling just one lot. The design was to blend the new house and landscaping into the setting of the two hundred year old farm.

The main part of "our" house looked like an old two-story barn from the road, with a few windows that shuttered like ones on a barn. The southern exposure view looked out over the horse farm toward the fields and woods. Two story of windows opened a feeling of being outside with only the deer, fox and a world of birds able to see into the house. Connected to the main house and creating an L was a one story section with the family room, and den which could be an office. All the rooms in the back opened to a brick patio through sliding glass doors. With the neighboring farmer's fields on the other side of the trees separating the properties, the three acre lot seemed like fifty.

Anna and Alex went to investigate and check the place out. Before we knew it, they were back with reports on the neighbor's daughters who were about the same ages. Anna was already planning to learn to ride the horses at the farm.

Over the following weeks we got to know the family who owned the farm, and we worked through the negotiations quite smoothly. The owners of the farm were asking a fair price, but more importantly they wanted a say in who their neighbors would be. The connection was mutual, and it all seemed like a dream unfolding.

Everyone fell in love with the charm of the surroundings. Even Alex thought it would be "an excellent hideaway."

We made plans to move in at the end of May when school was wrapping up, and immediately put our places in the city up for sale. Really I should say Anna's house, since legally she owned it and I was only her trustee.

We found buyers fairly quickly after a series of ridiculous open houses, and a flood of prospective buyers. Both of our homes were in excellent condition, and we made it easier by asking prices that created interest quickly. However, our asking prices were at the expense of annoying the neighbors who thought market values should still be near the highs a few years prior, but they were being unrealistic. Sam and "I" had owned our places long enough that there was a substantial profit even at prices designed to move them. We had made the decision, and did not want to get caught up in fighting for every last dollar.

It felt like a big step in committing to each other, and in our hearts we knew we were ready. Sam and I had a few escapades of "sharing finances" angst as we encountered unasked, but probing relationship-type questions. Although old habits from an already distant past, each question required us to dissolve the old reactions, and re-form new ones. Sharing finances tied right in with those old patterns, but looking at it reasonably, it was just another hurdle we were jumping over.

Besides, Sam claimed, "I'm working hard enough for both of us. I'll make up for any shortfalls in money."

I'm certain that was meant to be reassuring, but we both knew if I worked as relentlessly as she did, and returned to my workaholic days, I'd earn in the same ballpark as Sam.

Many friendly machinations stayed in our minds, and were accepted unspoken. Sam's mind was set on moving, and focused on our new home. Any and all related issues were welcomed, addressed and recognized as part of a larger process. There was no question, moving was tough, but everything fell into place and we did it.

* * *

As if we, or anyone moving to a new place, didn't have enough to do, Sam and I threw an open house for our friends. Anna was Sam's assistant in planning the soiree. As Anna's assistant, I was given the jobs such as calls to invite our guests.

We invited Randi and Bere, Larry and Jan, the couple we had lunch with when we first met, Jean Pierre and his wife Cynthia, Jack and Lou, Tanya and Rose, our neighbors Alan and Linda joined us, and a bunch of musician friends, Ben "Mr. Upright," Aaron my long-time drummer and two regular guest vocalists Eddie and Lois, and a couple friends, Josh and Fran from school. Everyone came and we all spent a delightful afternoon and evening together christening our new home with laughter, music and lots of love.

The day was filled with tours, explanations of the farm going back to an original grant from William Penn, and rides arranged by Anna with Bucks County Carriages, who provided antique horse drawn carriages and drivers to take us through the surrounding country lanes. The night was filled with food and music. We bought or made enough food to feed twice our number, and were still eating, singing and playing or just kibitzing into the next morning.

Late around the kitchen table with fellow stragglers, I began sharing my theory on how science paralleled some developmental psychology theories about how infants develop into adults. Randi was motivated to develop another parallel about how relationships begin and mature.

The ramble began. "The history of science, as related to relationships, is an example of a cycle within a cycle. Sometimes a day, sometimes a lifetime, sometimes a generation and sometimes thousands of years are comprised of similar attributes and patterns. I will start with the development of scientific thinking known as Ptolmaic astronomy, move through Copernican astronomy, into Newtonian physics, then Einstein's Theory of Relativity and E=mc2 and finally the subatomic realm of Quantum Physics, and show the comparability with the development of an infant through adulthood."

Either the wide eyes were wondering if they had tuned in to a late night science fiction channel, or my theories were about to be listened to readily. I chose the second and started in.

"The parallels start with Ptolmaic astronomy as compared to an infant. Each believes that the world revolves around him. The leading astronomers of that period thought the earth was the center of the universe, and that the sun and stars revolved around the earth. For an infant the world does in fact revolve around him. In fact the entire universe appears to come to a complete halt when an infant first cries for attention or help.

Another striking similarity is that this limited view of life does not last very long before being disproved or at least significantly revised.

"As a young child quickly realizes, life no longer stops for a cry unless it is an actual emergency. This realization coincides with finding out he is just part of a complex network of lives comprised of schools, other orbiting children, food stores and many other enlightening discoveries showing there is more to life than the family that cares for him. This acknowledgement was quite a shock to the scientific and world community when it realized the earth did in fact actually revolve around the sun, and that the earth was just a part of a huge galaxy and universe, as Copernicus reasoned.

"The next major step in science was observing how physical objects worked, including everything from apples falling off trees to how laws of gravity applied to the motion of planets. Newtonian physics laid out consistent rules for every 'thing' and is still the basis for scientific explanations of the physical universe. Consider this phase of a child's life. Schools and experiences teach children the rules of society, and simultaneously the child learns how things work physically in every aspect from their bodies falling out of apple trees to the speed and movement of small earth-type objects like baseballs or tennis balls. Multitudinous aspects of the physical universe are explored in every experience. A funny aspect with this stage is that there are so many exceptions to the rules that life and scientific results tend to require a large margin for error."

Nods of interest were scoring much higher than nods toward sleep as I headed into the home stretch.

"The relativity theories introduce questions regarding how we perceive the physical world based on our perspective and the gravity we place on all that seems to matter. From here we take a quantum leap into life and/or science.

"A strange dichotomy takes place next in adolescence and in

science. There are actually two sets of rules operating at the same time. At this point the maturing child is uncomfortably aware that there are different rules for adults and children, and explanations of being able to do something "when you have your own children" or "when you're an adult" are completely unsatisfying. A relatively similar discomfort appeared when Einstein and his friends made an equally simple statement that the components of the physical universe played by a different set of rules than the objects whose form they comprised. By defining two equally provable, but diametrically opposite sets of rules for an object like one's hand and the atoms comprising one's hand, people were wringing their hands for quite some time. Initially, like the child, there was a rebellious attitude.

"As you know, once a child has had a taste of adult behavior, or once a scientist's curiosity is awakened, there is no turning back. Once maturity is reached, the adult is now aware of being connected to a larger universe of families, society and, in many respects, the entire earth. The adult is also aware of how rules apply for different ages.

"The key to the quantum leap, especially as maturity develops, is the ability to observe the process. As an aware participant, a person can, at least potentially, even go to the next step and determine the outcome of the lives of others, as for example parents and teachers. This is precisely how quantum physics is defined. The observer to an experiment can and does have an influence on the outcome. The scientist has a full working knowledge of the physical and sub-atomic rules and possibilities, and as the mature adult, is lord of at least the kingdom of the experiment being observed."

There was a smattering of applause followed by others' insights or questions. After hearing my philosophy, Randi laid out a spontaneous view of how she saw the history of science, as compared to relationships and sex. Her expose' even went more than a couple of steps beyond my ideas. She subsequently agreed to allow me to quote her freely.

Randi compared the Ptolamiac view of the earth being the center of the universe to the attitude when two lovers first meet. Initially, with someone new, the whole universe revolves around the other person and often sex. Whole evenings might be spent sitting on the sofa talking into the night, or in bed, without much of a thought of leaving the love nest. Even having food delivered allows complete and uninterrupted attention to what is in reality an infantile perspective of the world.

The first steps in the childhood of the budding relationship are nurtured by days at the park, or evenings in town. Here there is a re-entry into the outside world to intermix with the universe, but still from a different outlook than the pre-lover/lover dating period. This stage recognizes the relationship, and making love, actually revolve around a schedule of other centers such as work, social obligations and planning activities which must merge with the surrounding world. Still, dinners out, rather than dinner parties with friends, tend to be private and nestled in the corner of a quiet restaurant. Nights out might be spent dancing closely on a crowded dance floor. Days out might be on secluded picnics where feeding each other treats and rolling together on or under a blanket, shielded from voyeurs by well-situated foliage, maintains a self-contained world.

"Hey," Randi had exclaimed, "who hasn't done some landscaping one time or another."

As the Newtonian phase begins, the explorations into sensuous delights begin to know some rules and boundaries of the physical universe. The lovers become less interested in endurance tests, and teasingly begin to enter the waters that lap at the shore of enthusiastic ways of learning to please. The physical connections planned around busy schedules take on a quality over quantity. Here the child at play maintains a curiosity coincidental with knowledge that the approaching reality of integrating others into the scope of a maturing relationship will change the physical rules as previously defined.

As impertinent social responsibilities impinge on private encounters, and thinking about the future co-mingles with desire, the next phase of relativity enters the scene. There are still those wonderfully inviting evenings, like soaking in a hot tub on a cool night, where the pressures of the outside world melt away and the loving pressures of the inside world melt in. However, like a cold shower when your lover is out of town, a dualistic world of relativity makes one day's rules engender fun and games, while another day's rules tend to frustrate and obfuscate. The wonderment of intimacy, still in full bloom, overlays the power plays and expectations that create a starkness in the landscape.

The lovers' view of the universe changes again, as they integrate their new life together into the swirling primordial pool of the imploding and exploding of an ever expanding universe.

As the relationship becomes mature, it is possible to observe the bigger perspective of the true value you place on your lover. Through the metamorphosis, there are periods where time stops to enter a cocoon where the lover becomes a friend whose council is magnified by a shared intimacy. Through the relationship, the lovers now observe themselves with a clarity, that often leads to a comparison of the past together versus prior relations. As the dynamics explode, a universe could be opened that leads to commitment, or alternatively to the splitting of atoms which could be the over-analyzing that splits hairs. In this realm of atoms and sub-atomic particles, one leads to resolution and the other to dissolution. Here the waves of energy have been observed creating the fusion energy of lasting passion, or confusion energy is created, where distractions lead to interference and limp hypotheses.

Here the parallels leave off, but to continue the relationship, it is necessary to break into a new science. At the frequency that is resonating with unlimited potential, the emotional particle accelerator pushes the lust and the relationship to the speed of light. Only one force can hold the universe together, and bring climactic ecstasy - Love. With love, yes, a deep lovingness where compassion and integrity is blended with honest, wisdom-laced equality. Only love can cradle the volatile energy that could end in the dark powers of destruction or find boundless possibilities through eternity.

To reach this height of human interaction opens another realm. Metaphorically, if you dare, imagine horses, full of energy, stampeding from a corral and laughing at the thought that a harness could ever restrict their unbridled, passionate love. With a connection based on anything less than love, the horses representing humans, would be broken into useless fragments, and barely be able to function with the sensitivity required to relate to another. With love, the horses trust their focus. The wild, natural, and seemingly unpredictable animal instincts combine with a directed and balanced intelligence creating a dynamic oneness from two beings. The metaphor comes to mind of a rider on an Arabian stallion galloping around the Egyptian Pyramids melding together the two separate beings into one fluid singularity.

The theories, and applications, of Chaos and Complexity also enters the field of love from a grand, overview perspective. Briefly, it is that many behaviors precipitated in the name of love, although appearing very much to the contrary, have the intention of love buried within. What looks complex and chaotic on the surface still represents love.

Love, however magnificent, is still but a foundation for the greatest imaginable aspect of life - Creation. Creation is what exists beyond the quantum realm of love, and gives love purpose.

To keep it simple initially, imagine creating a flower garden with love. Then imagine creating music or art with love. The imaginary sciences of virtual reality pale in comparison to what humans can and do create.

In respect to creating another human life; in the umbilical sense, as in "cutting the", creation in its most believable and unbelievable sense of willing into being is to know another life exists because of your part in creation. This act of creation transcends the simple physical birth, as though any woman would use simple and birth in the same sentence, but speaks to imparting knowledge and guidance to the little critter throughout its life. Our mandate to procreate is actually an expression of our willingness to create. The point is to realize, that as we do create a life for ourselves and everyone around us, the love we infuse into our lives will ripple throughout our universe. We expand the horizon to all we influence, and become guides to children of all ages, and the kids of our ever-expanding world of family, friends, community, state, country, earth and all included in and beyond our universe.

Finally, at least for this little philosophical expose', we can take another step to reach beyond time, the physical world or science, at least as one might commonly think. The ultimate personal relationship embraces the ultimate imaginable when you encounter your soulmate. Soulmates go beyond sharing, and actually blend together to become one in a holographic universe; together for eternity to teach and learn in the physical and beyond.

Cheers and final toasts were raised to Randi, followed by a profound and respectful silence for her "seat of the pants" genius. All the guests then headed for sofa beds, spare rooms or cars for a predawn ride home. Later that morning, when everyone reconvened for a late breakfast or early brunch, we shared some intriguing dreams apparently precipitated from Randi's thoughts. Other ideas were called in early the next evening from band members who sleep during the day, and work and play at night; what they affectionately call a "Dracula" schedule. The consensus was I should summarize it all and give Randi an honorary degree in life.

* * *

Sam and I agreed we may have bypassed some of Randi's categories or entered a few in just one day. However, since the month of July rarely found us under the same roof, we clearly landed on the separate side of "relativity."

Sam had enough on her mind with work. The demands of her two businesses were still expanding. Originally, when Sam had returned from her trip three years ago to see her uncle, every free minute had been spent with Randi and John putting together the art auctions. The pattern for the auction business was to completely arrange it in the spring and summer for the auctions in the fall, and run two or three a week staring in late September and going into early January.

Sam declared, "Had I been clearer in the details of what I desired, I might have integrated a more enjoyable home life into the original plan. Now that we're living together, I appreciate you even more and realize I love coming home to you. I know I'll find some way to readjust, even if every day is booked from September to New Years. It's funny, but I'm still fired up about the upcoming auctions and meetings this fall, even though my life has become like a magnet with opposite poles pushing and pulling on my life."

Sam sighed, "You do realize that if this fall is like last year I'll be busy or away almost every day."

"Now that I know what your schedule is like, I truly appreciate how often we did, and do, see each other." I consoled, "Hey, you're really doing great with it all. You know the combination of creating a loving relationship and running a business could send someone less committed cascading over a falls and splintered in the crash."

Sam smiled acceptance, "The balancing of this instant karma is giving me an equilibrium imbalance. That is, I'm getting what I asked for, but in floods. You know, 'too much of a good thing, and'

"Yeah," I finished her thought, "even a relaxing bath done to excess turns fingers to prunes; not to mention a room with spilled water to clean up."

"Really, we can joke, but everything is as good as most people could imagine. I guess the key is to forge ahead, and apply what got me this far to the next step."

To reaffirm Sam's thought I added, "This probably is beyond what you imagined in your wildest dreams initially, but look at you now. In a socially responsible and respectful way you've achieved a lifetime of goals already. You've taken your artistic talent and through it connected with lots of people. Then you combined the ability to give the same opportunity to others, while funneling a sizable amount of money to charities in the process. Whatever it took to make those achievements understandably took some toll on you, but you did it and the results stand for anyone to see."

Sam agreed, "It's amazing in perspective how events of a few days and a series of interrelated decisions shaped the nature of my life and the lives of all those connected to me.

"Our new home here sets a place of balance where we can create the basis for a family. Phil, thank you for sharing this dream with me, and thank you in advance for your patience while it all comes together."

"Well, maybe we can find one day out of each week just for us, but no matter what, we'll make it work."

"Yes," Sam affirmed, "I'll make some adjustments. I know the pieces will fall into place."

For June and half of July, Sam, Randi and all, as always, were in the fray of planning. The good news was that by the middle of July, 85% of all the arrangements were made for the entire series of auctions, and any work remaining was only possible in the weeks immediately preceding the events. They were confidently prepared for complete success to be the only possible outcome, as it had been since the first season.

With all of the business activities under control, Randi took off the last two and a half weeks in July. The first few weeks in August were Sam's to get away. The summer lull had mercifully brought the hectic pace of traveling and meetings to a halt; not to mention we were still settling in and unpacking.

At some point I had agreed to visit Sam's family in Washington that summer, and Sam had promised her family that all of us would come out for a long visit. Within two days Sam made all of the travel arrangements, and two weeks later, on the first of August we were off for nearly three weeks of rest and relaxation; finishing the unpacking would wait until we returned.

* * *

During our trip, Sam handled a few minor emergencies from the west coast, and I met a number of times with Wil, a colleague who shared my research interests at Evergreen State College in Olympia. But, most of the month was like stepping into a timeless paradise. The simple pleasures worked deeply into our minds and bodies like a much-needed massage. It felt as though we were adding the years back to our lives that the stresses and strains of life drain away. Unless required to acknowledge the outside world, we often did not even know what day it was.

Anna and I quickly felt at home as I knew Sam and Alex had at my mother's place. There were always people around and something to do, and it felt like being away at summer camp. Every day we chose from among a variety of activities on or near the farm. On walks just minutes away we could step into the forest and the peaceful presence of cedars, hemlocks, fir and nature's 'friends.' Anna and I even joined in the morning Aikido workouts, and made it part of our daily routine.

I overheard Anna on the phone with a friend on the east

coast describing some of our travels.

"We took a trip around the peninsula to the Pacific coast and stayed in cabins on the cliff over the beach. It was so cool. The beaches had whole tree trunks, like a giant threw a pile of sticks by the bottom of the cliff, and I climbed up and walked like I was on big balance beams and then jumped from log to log. It was great. The next day we hiked on a trail into the Quinault rain forest where there was moss and ferns and waterfalls and huge trees, and it was sunny. We stayed at a lodge that night by a lake and it was amazing, we saw humming birds at the window during dinner. The next day we hiked on a two mile trail to natural hot springs fed by water warmed by volcanic heat. It used to be a spa and they made six or seven small pools with wood and rocks along the hillside. The top one was the warmest and had a break in the stone wall where the water poured like a fountain from just above my head. Later the same afternoon we swam at a lake that was so clear it was a perfect mirror of the green and blue of the trees and sky.

"Hold on." Anna turned to me. "Dad what did we do the day after the mirror lake?"

"We saw the quartet from Philadelphia at the barn, before taking the ferry from Port Townsend to Whidbey Island where we spent the night."

"Oh, right." Anna returned to the phone and either skipped what I had said or assumed her friend heard. "The next morning we got up at dawn and took the ferry to Orcas Island in the San Juan Islands. We were sailing between islands covered with mist when the sun rose and made the water glow. The best part of the whole trip was when we went whale watching and saw the Orcas; they're really dolphins. There was a whale lady on that boat who identified each one by name from the white patch called a saddle behind their fins. And, we saw the baby ones with their mothers really clearly when they jumped out of the water playing. And, we could hear them talking when a microphone was put in the water. You should come out here and see them. My dad said I could adopt one through some program. Right dad?"

"Yes. We'll have to call the group that studies them to get the papers."

"Anyway. We went to the top of the mountain on Orcas at sunset and we could see forever. There were islands for miles and way in the distance snow-capped mountains in almost all directions. It's really beautiful."

I loved hearing Anna so excited about the trip. She hardly seemed to take a breath while describing everything. I stayed in the room to hear her relate our last stop on Vancouver Island, British Columbia.

"The next day we took the ferry to Vancouver and went to the most incredible gardens called Butchart with the biggest rose garden I've ever seen and a Japanese garden that Sam explained to me. Then we stopped at a butterfly museum where we watched one come out of its cocoon. The museum is a hot house filled with tropical plants to make the butterflies feel like it's always summer.

"The next day we went kayaking from Gabriola Island. It was cloudy and cool out on the water, but they told us that was the perfect and much better than being hot. I was in one with my dad, and we learned to paddle together. It was incredible. We saw seals and bald eagles, and at night we stayed in a house right on the beach with windows so we could see out over the water. It's a bed and breakfast and Trudy and Gottfried who own the place were really nice. My dad and Sam loved the food and became friends with them. They have a platform and let us lay on it to watch stars and listen to the waves."

As much as Anna told her friend, she still only related the highlights. Everywhere we looked on the trip, we saw vistas and views that were the most beautiful I'd ever seen. There were golden and bald eagles soaring over placid waters in inlets where seals and otters rested or played, and all surrounded by views of snow-capped mountains that on clear days extended from Mt. Baker to the northeast, Mt. Olympic to the west and to the southeast even Mt. Rainier. Anna didn't even tell about our trip to Mt. Rainier and the walk from Paradise with wild flowers for acres leading up to the snow fields where we hiked in shorts and tee shirts. Looking up we could see the glaciers which hung from the fourteen thousand plus foot summit and looking out we could see the peaks and valleys of the Cascade Range. Even on hikes to a few waterfalls we could see the summit through the trees and it looked close enough to touch.

Back by the orchard whole days were spent picnicking in high meadows or by the water. We were painting, reading, writing or playing songs and becoming acquainted as a family.

Sam's family came alive from my imagination once I put faces with names. Anna and I were received like long lost kin finally returning home. Sam's mother, as mothers probably do everywhere, asked about our plans for marriage. The bluntness of the question was less of a surprise than the simple fact the question had not yet come up. I replied, "Ask Sam."

After her mother asked, Sam and I discussed the idea, but agreed we had done enough for one year. We decided to make a commitment to each other that was the equivalent of an engagement and leave it at that.

Whenever possible Sam and I found privacy to share. Making love was energized, and the leisurely pursuit of sensual pleasures were expanded by an intimacy in which we connected in mind, body and soul like our first times together.

The day we were returning home we went to lay in the hammock strung between two apple trees at the edge of the orchard. We sunk into the meshed rope that was big enough to hold three people, and snuggled together. As the summer sun warmed the morning, and us, we took stock of where we were.

Sam said, "Vacations in any paradise give perspective. This

one will be a constant reminder contrasting the pace of life here with our 'real life'. We'll have to find a way to balance this timelessness with our daily pressures when we return."

I agreed, "We've stepped into another world on this trip. I feel any limitations we had has melted away and now we can create anything. But you're right. the trick is going to be integrating the happiness into the whole process and not just one concentrated period. Since we're really still just coming together, our choices are open for us to create a 'new and improved' life with whatever we decide."

I suggested, "We can make our new home a retreat from the day to day grind. The key will be to start by merging some of the feelings from the trip into every day and then add, and then create a transition to an even greater dream."

"That sounds simple. I guess we start with the concept and go from there."

"Considering how well the trip went, we've passed a significant reality check on compatibility."

"Yes," Sam agreed. "We can do anything if we can travel together and be with family for an extended period."

Sam added, "Anna and Alex are even more like the sisters and seem to have accepted our little family."

"I know. It's almost like we have our daughters' blessings, and now we're free to explore the next part together."

Chapter 12

When we returned home, Sam's schedule resumed the same basic pace as before. The sense of relaxation made a quick exit from Sam's short term memory, but the trip gave a spark of perspective which began to flicker with an air toward change. Our getaway lingered like a favorite song. Whenever the vacation would come to mind, a smile from within lightened any day with the knowledge that happiness was always accessible.

One day when Sam was spurred by thoughts of the trip, she began reviewing the nature of some turning points in her life. The visit to the farm this time and when her uncle had his "accident," reminded Sam how she valued a more open, interactive life with neighbors and community. The first visit is when she decided to begin visiting her family more regularly. The attack and the meetings had provided the wake-up call and the means to leave the city for a home in a setting more conducive to her desire to live closer to nature. From the brain-storming on the plane she had initiated the auction business, and Present Works took off to a new level of success.

Ever since Sam met the two contacts, Jack and Lou, over the breakfast meetings Randi had arranged, they flew off to Europe and all over America to wine and dine prospective art buyers. The new wealthier clients seemed to have an unquenchable thirst for the new American and international artists as well as the initial ones in the Philadelphia area.

While Sam and Randi ran the original business Sam's friend

and pseudo partner, Jean Pierre, practically ran the auction business. Now that she had raised more than a few hundred thousand dollars each for art students and charities, she could see the ever-expanding rings, like a pond sending ripples from the center, through the lives of everyone she knew and at least thousands more.

Her life had opened to the rewards justly deserved by a person willing to take control of destiny and create her own life. But, achievements are always fraught with challenges. Even with everyone who helped, there was not quite enough time in a week. Sam was living a life she might have dreamed, however, adding another key ingredient, a loving relationship, she was now questioning all of it.

Sam was putting so much energy into her businesses, it was as though she was having an affair with a secret lover, who demanded endless attention. Even when she was not at work, Sam was thinking about work, or dreaming about how to work less. Either way, she was inexorably and passionately tied to the work she had always loved. When she was away, she let go, but once she returned, it quickly went to the other extreme of being all-consuming. The switch from one side to the other was like day to night. Something needed to change.

While Sam worked through her reformulating, I realized her challenge was my opportunity. The conflict reminded me of my schedule when I overworked, and the toll my absence from my family took on my life. Sam's situation, with me switched to the receiving side, stood out like a nightmare from my past coming back to haunt me, or give me a chance to fix it. It was my turn to learn what it was like to be in a relationship where I lovingly supported my partner. The symmetry was wonderful, but eerie like a lucid dream where I could make choices with an awareness of the scene.

Fortunately, recognizing this, and having already evaluated my life from a similar perspective, there was a place for my input to help vault us out of the repetitive karmic cycle. I knew Sam was very open to my thoughts, but she also knew she was the one who had to make the decisions that would change it for her. As we became more aware our actions through review and observation of ourselves and each other, I had a sense we were moving toward balance rather than more extreme "lessons" to learn.

An awareness creates an opportunity. It was my mission, and Sam's, to collect the clues, analyze the ways we might find ourselves in a quagmire and figure a way to turn it around. Though the testing process might not appear easy on the surface, with the foundation we had already laid, I believed even the struggle would somehow continue to foster love. I was beginning to see that once short-term problems were overcome, the outcome could propel life toward sweeter rewards.

It appeared lessons were equally well learned through pain as through love. As Sam and I became aware of the process, we also became aware we could turn what could have been painful lessons into loving decisions. Truly either way was constantly available, but we were catching on enough to choose to learn through love.

* * *

One way we recognized the choices, whether good or bad, was to look at our children. They are emotional sponges that soak in and reflect the emotional states being projected to one's universe. I knew this was true for me, as Anna was always a catalyst to spur me through lessons in my life, especially by mirroring unconditional love. I also knew in Sam's case, Alex was her teacher. Through the mirroring process Alex showed Sam that the basis of an underlying love and respect would even unite a family with separate schedules and activities.

The transition to the country went well for Anna and Alex, but in different ways, but in all cases offered an almost immediate, representative example of our decisions.

Alex was seventeen and in twelfth grade and her life revolved around school and her friends. She had a fair amount of freedom most of the time since she would drive Sam to the train station, and then have the car to herself for a few days while Sam was traveling. By most standards, Alex was trustworthy and responsible, and considering the added task of getting to school in the city. It was clear she studied because she maintained excellent grades. She particularly excelled in writing and wrote for the school newspaper, worked on the school yearbook and was also involved in all the school plays.

On the other hand she could be impossible. Alex always had an independent streak and was self-righteous about how her own decisions were correct, no matter what others might suggest, unless unequivocally proven wrong. Then she would become withdrawn and moody. I was told these were some of the typical characteristics of teenagers.

Then there was the opposite behavior which was absolutely loving, cuddling and the wonderful stuff her family loved in her as a child. Even when she demanded to be treated as an independent adult, her openness, caring and respect were straight from her heart, and were anything but contrived.

Alex's activities were her primary reasons for being home infrequently. When she was in rehearsals for a play, she worked into the evenings helping with the sets and rehearsing her part with her friends. Those school nights she would often sleep at her friends' homes. Even some weekends Alex would go right to a friend's house from school on Friday and go to school from there on Monday. It was common not to see her for days at a time. Normally she would call to check in, and if Sam was out of town she would sometimes just drive directly from where she was to pick up Sam at the airport or train.

Alex was never a problem, she just was out of touch with us. Sam knew Alex loved her even though on the surface there was less or varying modes of communication. Even Anna, who looked up to her, had a hard time getting through to her. When Alex was home, she was often locked away in her room, or on the phone. Part of me wanted to connect with her since in a year she would be away at college, but my well-intentioned attempts just did not fit her schedule.

Having grown up with the demands of Sam's schedule, Alex was familiar with the need to be flexible and understanding, and now seemed to expect the same in return. The process pushed Sam into explorations of her own strengths and weaknesses. Alex, by her actions and attitude, effectively demanded to be treated as an adult. Whether it was due to Sam's absence or not, it dove-tailed into our life as an effective reminder of the ramifications of our choices and actions.

Sam would say, "I'm consistent with Alex and my trust and faith underscore my love for her, but I allow her a reasonably wide latitude so she will make decisions and become responsible for her actions.

"In other words, I give Alex a long enough length of rope for her to become her own person, but not long enough to injure herself."

In Sam's childhood her parents were always home, whereas Alex had to adjust to her mother's absence. The poignant part is that independence and self-reliance were dominant characteristics in Sam and Alex; opposite approaches, but similar results. Also, even though Sam was wrapped-up in her work, as I had been while I was married, but we were growing closer; similar situations, and opposite results.

Perhaps all approaches work out reasonably well if the decisions are based in loving intentions and actions. I trusted in Sam's beliefs and allowed myself to watch and learn. Sam always reassured me, "Alex will only learn if we let go of trying to control her, otherwise she'll only resist more."

The words from her mouth sounded like advice to me, "Give Sam as much room as she needs, with love, and she'll work through her stuff as well."

* * *

Anna and I were also busy, but many of our activities were based around the house. I arranged my schedule to be home in the evening so I could make dinner for Anna. In this way we shared some part of every day together, and I still thought the connection we had developed since she first came to live with me made us a "pair".

Anna started ninth grade at her new school when we returned from our vacation. I arranged private voice and piano lessons for her, and Anna also took horseback riding lessons. She always had plenty to do, especially since she made friends with everyone at the horse farm next door.

At night when Anna and I were home we would always take a break from whatever we were doing to play and sing the old jazz standards. Anna had learned them from an early age and loved to sing them while I played the piano. I was in heaven when we sang and made music together.

But, Anna began baby sitting to contribute to the never-ending expenses associated with horses. Once in a while Anna slept overnight where she was baby sitting, and sometimes she would spend a night at a friend's before a horse show so they could leave early the next day.

When I was alone in the house the peacefulness opened an inner self contentment. I simultaneously became more understanding and accepting of others. Greater patience had been required with Sam and Alex. With the added intensity of all the energy they were focusing into various projects, I found myself being a grounding force and stabilizing, balancing center where they could be secure. It seemed the crazier everything became around me the calmer I stayed.

Part of the way I maintained my balance was by taking classes in T'ai Chi combined with Taoist meditation practices. I walked on the tow path between the canal and the river every morning, and encouraged whoever was home to join me. The additional freedom also afforded me the ability to put my energy into music again, but this time in a healthy, balanced way. It offered me the chance to overcome the stigma of my overindulgence which had been an element in my failure with Marcy.

I decided to look into performing in the area, and talked to the manager of a restaurant/inn nearby in Yardley. After hearing me, he was immediately willing to have me play whenever possible. We started with a schedule for Friday nights since that was a night Anna and Alex were usually away from home.

The connection was a resounding success. Playing was like being reacquainted with an old friend, and the atmosphere there was relaxed, the patrons friendly and everyone quite receptive. The inn was filled to capacity every Friday. When Sam was home, she would join me or dinner and stay to listen. The nights she was away I would go home afterward, and with my creative juices still flowing, I would play the piano for myself late into the night.

Anna was unexpectedly at home one Friday night I was scheduled to play. I decided she could come with me to the job. When I was warming up, and only one or two people were there, Anna sang along when I started playing her favorite song, Skylark by Hoagie Carmichael. The manager and a couple of others there immediately begged us to do another. So we played few more before I insisted that she sit at the small table where I sat during my breaks. She had brought some school work, and some light reading if it was to difficult to concentrate. However, we had opened Pandora's box.

The owner came over to our table, and offered to double my already generous pay if Anna would sing just six or so songs a night.

Anna's face lit up. She pleaded, "It's what we do at home

anyway, and I love singing with you more than anything."

She was also quick to point out, "I'm already beginning to dread the thought of baby sitting, and the extra money can go toward saving for college."

Anna was a natural performer and her enthusiasm shone like a star within her. My main objection was that she was too young, but she was clearly as mature as a young woman twice her age. If my nature was to be overly protective, I might have put my foot down and said no, but that was not me.

I agreed, "We'll give it a trial period."

Anna was all over me with hugs. Then, she immediately wanted to decide what songs we should play. There was at least an attempt on my part to retain a calm demeanor, but in truth I was as excited as she was. Playing music with my daughter was a dream come true.

I could not conceal my joy of sharing music with Anna. I felt a connection running through my family to my daughter. It was more than genetics. Music connected our hearts. Playing at home was an outward expression of the love, and I sensed it transformed the music when we performed. Like when you cook with love everything tastes better, when Anna sang with love, she was radiant and the audience beamed.

Her voice was a mixture of sweet and innocent while also sassy and bluesy. Perhaps I was biased, but she had the best voice I had ever heard, and my playing was imbued with a new passion. To say the place was filled to capacity the nights she sang would be understating how people responded.

What appeared to be a treat for Anna, actually opened a new world to me.

Another night while performing with Anna, it was as though I floated over the scene watching and listening to us play. I must have entered a hypnotic, trance-like state. The feeling was similar to the one reached years ago that special night at Zanzibar Blue. However, the sense of observing myself was new and excited me; not to mention how it tied into my research. I entered another dimension it appeared I could access through music. The feeling of being an observer was the closest to what had always been my motivation to do the research that combined music and science.

I reflected when I was home later that night how Anna was the catalyst for entering a new level of music, and another world. My curiosity was peaked by the realization. It resembled what I was proposing to begin as the next step in my research, and there I was experiencing the state of mind I thought my hypothesis would lead. I had recently written a proposal for a grant to explore meditative states and music during my sabbatical the coming fall.

But, the excitement about my research was secondary to the priceless meaning of reaching that level with Anna. Playing music together for strangers opened my relationship with Anna to being peers and friends, augmenting our special ability to understand each other. Sharing the grieving process, and maturing through it together, created an interdependency beyond a typical father-daughter interaction. Then, just when I thought she would grow away from me, we found a new way to connect in which she also developed self-confidence and appreciation for her individuality. As if we were ritually shedding an old skin, I sensed a rebirth that would infuse new life into all we knew.

Our daughters were truly awesome mirrors for Sam and I to see ourselves. They not only taught us to respect the ways they were choosing to discover the world and themselves, but drew Sam and I together through the mutual wisdom gained.

I was still awake at dawn's first light. My mind remained alert all night, still being so energized I felt I could function at peak levels for days. I decided to take a walk along the tow path, and watch the sunrise over the river. Before I left the house, I finished writing the various thoughts flowing through my mind in the form of a philosophical, poetic essay called:

Earth/Air

Do you have a tree that you can picture clearly in your mind? Can you trace the outline of the branches reaching into the sky? Can you memorize the shape of the leaves, or whatever grows on your tree? Then look closely at the trunk. Can you recreate the complexion of the curves and ruts, or if there is some moss, lichen or ivy, or honeysuckle vines that hide the scars or initials of I love you with a heart around it carved into the side? If you looked closer, what would be the texture of the bark that runs up to the sky and down to the tops of the roots where they meet the ground.

Then, after you have studied everything you can see, touch, smell, taste or hear, let your teacher know when to pass out your exam questions about the tree you have studied and know best. The first question, like many tests in school, asks the one question for which you did not prepare. Please describe the roots.

Perhaps you saw through the trick question. As much as many people are aware of their families' roots, very little consideration is given to the invisible root systems of even a tree you know quite well.

Are the roots the brain? How does the helix coding the existence that holds the genetic foundation support the pushing, reaching and letting go? How will nature, human nature, adapt or change the nature of generations to come?

Perhaps heredity is intertwined with knowledge, and teaches through role models and stories of ancestors how to break new ground, or remain in the same old mold. The ground is carefully groomed with the style and dreams of generations whose seeds were planted. Everyone was fed on harvested grains of truth tracing back to the parents of parents. The mixing produced the hybrids of seed stock coursing through our veins.

Just as the germinating seed pushes its roots into the soil of the land from which it came, the early sprout pushes with an inborn strength to choose life while striving toward the light. The roots suckle the rich earth and receive nourishment as if a baby at her mother's breast. The nutrients flow through the bloodstream to support the new life.

And not only physical because the essence is connected in spirit, soul, and the balance of all that is, just like those before, preparing now to spread into the future too. The subatomic particles of photons and electrons circle the nucleus to make the foundation for the cells of budding life. Each bud clearly understands the deep workings of the planet earth, and its connection to everything from the cosmos to quarks. The light reaches the new leaf beginning the first experiment of photosynthesis for this new shoot, just as a baby thrust from the womb takes a breath and processes the first image when light enters the pupil.

The air breathing life into life, and the minerals providing a steady diet that is perfectly balanced for the internal and external worlds. Darkness opens into light, and returns to darkness. Unknown becomes known, but creates the next unknown, fundamental basis for life.

Each unknown raises questions that start the travails from fears and doubts to unquestioning acceptance. The quest will be negotiated on the best terms one can. For there is no possibility of returning to the womb. So bon voyage! Let the youngster ask some questions, and face a challenge or two. The back drop has been provided. The root stock is immutable now. Societies' paradigms surround the next victim, or support the newly initiated life.

When would I start, and then stop, giving advice before realizing a child must eventually survive on its own; the answers I would like to give to questions unasked. Then, I'm more surprised by the strange ones they do ask. Sometimes I can barely watch as their uncharted, unfathomable course leads them to the edge of a chasm. I imagine I can run and save them, but once there, they have already turned around excited to tell the story.

Already the impact of the story has changed their view on life forever. The exact experience I was all too ready to protect them from, finally opens a blossom from a pod that appeared would never open. Now flourishing, the next series of questions begin, and the next. So they ask, but even if one tells all he knows, each individual will only truly learn from first-hand experience. Even if I began to try explaining, I must realize, in silence, not telling is the answer. Allow the young one to take the best of what she can from the wealth of knowledge available that everyone from me to the sun and back again can offer. The next step is for them to make. To take all that is available, and use the foundation to find new adventures that will expand the knowledge base for the next generation. These dynamics of the inevitable evolution make every decision a means to explore the process.

Everyone's life always has new seeds being planted. Some of the prior ones are now shoots, and some already mature trees. The process is continual. New life begins at any age, and is dependent only upon a continuous thirst to ask the next series of questions. Moving forward, evolving, gives clarity to the meaning of the family roots as they extend into the vibrancy of an awakened life. Taking the most that could be gleaned, consider what new possibilities to dive into next. Then take that knowledge to the boundary of what it will offer, and do a swan dive over the cliff together diving deep into the crystal water below. Once floating on your backs, before swimming to the shore, look up to see the dive was not as risky as it appeared from the top. What seemed like an insurmountable challenge that would send anyone flying off in different directions, actually closes the gap through sharing the process.

Chapter 13

Sam was returning home from a business trip the day I received the news that my proposal for a grant to fund additional research had been approved. In addition, Wil, my colleague and close friend at Evergreen State College, had agreed to collaborate on the project. He called to say he had been able to arrange access to the facilities of a research lab that could handle the medical and sound equipment required for the study. We had been corresponding regularly to initiate the ground-work, and these were the final pieces to give us a green light. The best part of sharing the research with him was his enthusiasm, coupled with his previous experience in doing studies similar to mine.

Wil had done research on a parallel study exploring human physiology during T'ai Chi movement. Our collaboration intended to explore the physiological parallels between how the feeling when Chi, or life energy, was created through meditative movement, and the tingling feeling singers experience from the resonating of the voice in the body. It would be a continuation of our previous work, but would extend the approach for an understanding of cumulative effects. By running two groups and a control group continuously for as long as a year, we believed we could uncover more sustained "beneficial" changes in their physiology.

Since singing and the meditative states each produce a high alpha-wave state in the brain, my interest was piqued for drawing a measurable connection between brain activity and lowering stress. Other studies had shown that both the right and left hemisphere of the brain pulsed at sixteen cycles per second during normal activities indicative of a beta-wave state. The measurable difference exhibited while singing was that the right hemisphere continued at sixteen cycles per second, while the left hemisphere dropped to twelve cycles per second which is associated with a high alpha-wave state. We wondered how long afterward the effects would last, and how long after regular singing or T'ai Chi practice the results could be sustained.

These areas were tangential to more esoteric concepts. Once our imaginations got started, we even questioned philosophically how music might bridge the brain hemispheres the Tao precept of Yin and Yang merging. But, we agreed to focus on something identifiable for our project, and leave the rest for pontificating. Needless to say we were outrageously excited, and wanted to begin the year immediately. So many pieces were falling into place it literally made me jump for joy.

Sam knew of my hopes, and had been intrigued at the possibility of joining me in Washington and being near her family for six months. We had even discussed how she could fly back and forth for a week or so each month, and handle other aspects of business by phone. I knew she shared my enthusiasm for the research, and would do anything possible to support me, but I wondered how she could make it happen for a whole year.

The one thing I believed with all my heart was that our relationship could handle anything we chose to do and always find a way to be stronger for the process. I was excited to share my news, but also apprehensive. The possibility that our work would take us farther apart than we already were was not something I wanted to consider. Even when Sam was away from home, the bond between us ran deep and was always renewed when she was home. If my research was going to take me to the

Seattle area, and near her family of all places, I wanted Sam to be with me instead of thousands of miles away. Again, I knew our relationship could withstand the distance, but it was not my choice for "how" to live.

I had told Alex I would pick up Sam at the train station. She had been away all week, and had flown directly into Philadelphia to meet with Randi and John, who, like Sam, I now called Jean Pierre. As usual the meeting went late into the night so Sam had stayed at Randi's place for the night.

On the way to meet Sam at the train station, I ran through the guidelines for bridging communications in our relationship that had been etched in my mind. My thoughts were clear about what I wanted, and I knew how my ideas could be beneficial to all of us. I simply had to tell Sam directly, with love, that I intended to spend the whole sabbatical in Washington and work with Wil. The big part was that I wanted Sam to be with Anna and me.

Sam was excitedly waiting to see me, and tell me all her news. When I arrived, she met me with an exceptionally exuberant embrace. Even though we were eager to share our news, we were happy for a moment to linger in the embrace. Then neither of us could wait any longer, and we started talking at the same time. We stopped, and I gestured for Sam to continue.

Sam dove in, "I've been with Randi all morning discussing how to completely redesign the structure of the businesses. Last night Randi left the dinner meeting with Jean Pierre early, rather than stay to tell or hear travel stories, but back at her place we stayed up most of the night.

"I had considered leaving the restaurant early with Randi because I was almost too tired to think, but there was something in the air that evening. I sensed something had reached a critical turning point, and stayed. Somehow without Randi there, a door swung open and a solution was on the other side, just waiting for someone to look. It was Jean Pierre who finally found the courage to say something.

"Jean Pierre took all of his daydreams, and took the chance that the time was right.

"He swore, 'In reality I've been rehearsing this proposition for most of the year, but my fear to take a risk and change my life, even when a change might have appeared obvious or simple to everyone else, is my greatest challenge.'

"Through all of his apparent successes, he lacked the entrepreneurial spirit that propelled many people he knew toward success. He even admitted, 'Most people would consider my life quite successful, but I've always felt more unsure of myself than I could ever let on to anyone.'

"He then confessed, 'From the first day you presented the idea for the auctions, I've considered leaving the school to work full time with you, but I was afraid to give up the security and prestige of my position at the school. However, now that Larry, my youngest, graduated from college, and my financial concerns are mitigated, I decided it was finally time to act. I've considered different approaches to broach the change, but in actuality the process of building a successful business with you over the last three years gradually started the steps to bridge careers.'

"At that point I was re-energized, and Jean Pierre was ecstatic. I had secretly wanted him to take over the auction business, but had not found the time to think through how to convince him to leave his position at the school. As soon as he made the suggestion, my mind was in full gear figuring out how to make the transition. It was evident to me, he should be made a full partner in the auction business, and then I had the further thought of handing the whole business over to him and Randi for a reasonable percentage of the profits. The more I thought about it, the more I realized how much I wanted a break so I could return to doing my own art.

"Once Jean Pierre opened his mouth and started, we talked

for almost two hours going over the hows, whats, whys and whens. I was almost dumbstruck, but mostly I was relieved. As we were leaving, so I could go talk with Randi, I practically jumped into his arms with delight."

* * *

From the beginning, Sam and Randi had been dependent on Jean Pierre to see to most aspects of the auction business. Much of the success of the business was due to his enthusiasm. He had made most of the contacts for the charitable organizations, he had organized the collecting of the student's art work and had also prepared the show in order of the quality of work being shown. However, since Sam had created the dream, it was still her baby to nurture. Even though Jean Pierre was the surrogate father, and Randi the ever-present nursemaid, Sam felt the overriding responsibility to make the dream a reality. Fortunately, once she initiated the process, he was there to guide it into and through life.

Jean Pierre had originally jumped at the idea to help in all aspects of the auctions as he saw the benefits to all parties concerned exactly as Sam had outlined on her plane ride to Seattle. The charities were able to participate in raising significant amounts of money, and that created a positive image in the community. He was serving the art school's purposes by promoting the its visibility which helped in recruiting new students and aiding existing students. Of course the sales of the students' art helped to cover the increasing costs of tuition and art supplies. Another aspect was the benefit of giving the students an opportunity to gain exposure for their work while still in school, and then possibly open more doors toward being able to make a living from their art work when they graduated.

Jean Pierre would have asked to be a partner in the business earlier, but he also questioned if it would be a conflict of interest to his position as dean of the school. Besides, in the beginning he could facilitate the process more efficiently from his position as dean. And even without a personal, financial incentive, he had been happy to put a spark of excitement back into his job with a new project. The cinching synergy was to finally relieve Sam, and subsequently Randi too, so they could create art again, while he took the reins from them.

* * *

Sam dove into the rest of the night's events, "Jean Pierre explained to me how he would present the change to the school, since of course maintaining access to the students' art work was a key component to sustaining the business.

"He said, 'I'll set the stage for the trustees meeting next week, and make a proposal to the board. I've already been recognized numerous times for adding to the school's level of excellence, the additional financial contributions the auctions created, and my allegiance to the school. I've discussed the idea with most of the board members to prepare for this discussion, and they have given me their personal approval to create a position as a paid trustee. That will allow me to dedicate my full energies to the business.'

Sam said, "Of course I agreed to support him a thousand percent, and assured him Randi would love the idea too.

"When I got back to Randi's, we stayed up the entire night laying out the new plan.

"Randi's response was, 'It was all inevitable. I only wish it happened sooner. You've had this planned all along, haven't you?'

"As we were setting the wheels in motion to shift the auction business to Jean Pierre, we both realized it was time to consider shifting the original business to him as well. After all, Jean Pierre's group of art students were already well trained, and with input from Randi and me through the transition, the business would continue to function like the well oiled machine it already was.

"For years the two of us had been making an income that surprised us, and the balance was always reinvested back into running the businesses. Of course as our revenues grew, so did the travel and food bills, but it was evident from the year-end accounting reports that through the expansion the income was consistently out-distancing the expenses.

"The question was 'How could we ever step back from the business without walking away from the value that had been built from our years of effort.' In the morning the second piece fell into place.

"First Randi and I confirmed that Jean Pierre was willing to take on both businesses, and be willing to work with Lou and Jack if they bought in. He agreed to as long as we worked through the transition with him and he also became a partner. With Jean Pierre we then initiated a conference call with Lou and Jack, who had gone from setting the expansion wheels in motion to being involved in many daily aspects, and offered them partial ownership in the businesses. Over the preceding three years the two of them had become very close to us, and each had joked more than once about buying the businesses if we ever wanted to sell. The chance to actually do just that, after it was already running so successfully, had them practically yelling at each other to make lunch reservations, and start discussing details before Randi or I had a change of heart."

As Sam was relating the details of the meeting, there was almost a visible burden melting away from her, and from me as well. The change was in motion, and a resolution in sight for finding closure to the full cycle which started when Sam chose her work as the "relationship" to pour her energy into. Sam's true desire was never driven by money, but she had found a way to be financially successful. She and Randi had wanted to make a living in the field they loved, and contribute to others in the process. Now that the dream had come to fruition, it was time to pass the baton and infuse new life by letting go of control.

There is a humility, as in raising a child, where you plant the seed, nurture with all your heart, give guidance, and realize the essence of giving, which is the process of allowing those receiving to have pride in themselves without feeling indebted or obligated to the giver. In this way the child is set free, and opened to developing in a direction you could not have imagined. This is the true gift of self-empowerment, but with a foundation that supports and encourages continued success. To give up control is to find freedom.

Sam was sensing the experience of finding equilibrium by balancing extremes. There was a simple efficiency to her life and she could return to her initial passion of painting. The business would be in good hands and sustained with the original integrity.

Sam accomplished what she had set out to do, and the reward was that she could now step back from the pressures of working to re-enter life, be with her family and loved ones and have time for her own creative pursuits. Best of all she had opened the way to be with me in Washington.

There was a tremendous amount of work and negotiating for her so she could go out in June, and have the summer with Alex before she headed off to college in the fall.

My news about the extension from six months to a year seemed anti-climactic after Sam's news, but as I related my news to Sam, she realized how the pieces were falling into place all around. It was only March, but having made it through our second winter together, we felt the coming of spring was a beautiful parallel to the miraculous sensation of rebirth in our lives. We would have, and definitely needed, at least a few months to get everything in order, but it could wait one day. We stopped on the way home to pick up food for a quiet celebration dinner.

Chapter 14

At the end of June, even though we had only moved to our new home a year before and loved the countryside of Bucks County, Anna, Sam and I filled suitcases and boxes to ship our things to Washington for a year. Alex joined us for the summer, but planned to leave in late August to attend Columbia University in New York. There was plenty of room in Uncle J's farm house for us, and he insisted he would be happiest with us there.

We planned less traveling than the previous summer and quickly settled into life on the farm. It was easy to find privacy, or join in as many of the activities on the farm as we pleased. Sam and I went for long walks or hikes in the area most days. Anna and I continued our work arranging songs, and some evenings we performed or led sing-a-longs for the community. I found plenty of opportunities to talk with Wil about the preparations for our work in the fall, and periodically drove to Evergreen State College to meet with him. There was a mix of activities for everyone which worked well for me since Anna, and Alex also, made friends and found plenty to do on their own.

We all started off the day together as the four of us joined the others on the farm for Aikido and meditation every morning. Emile, a young man from the community, had returned for the summer to give Aikido lessons and work on the farm. He was between his freshman and sophomore years at the University of Washington, and was a biology major with a concentration in environmental studies. On the farm, though, he was much more than a student or helper, he was like a grandson to Uncle J.

Emile's bright blue eyes, sandy brown hair and broad smile were the highlights of his otherwise average height and build. His "hidden" strength as a black belt in Aikido almost matched Sam's ability, and he had taken over most of the lessons from Uncle J the year before.

In the early mornings on the farm everyone taking Aikido came for Emile's instruction, which was usually under the watchful and approving eye of Uncle J.

The days were filled with general activities to keep a working farm, orchard and now greenhouse operating. Sam's mother and father were still considered the managers of the place, but Emile was almost an equal in decisions regarding more and more areas. The three of them were always around working with or checking on the army of Aikido students and workers, who willingly worked hard and labored lovingly as many had over the years. Uncle J walked around giving encouragement, pitching in whenever an extra hand was needed, and contributing an infectious smile and laugh.

Sam visited with her family, which often meant she worked along side them, but she also went off to paint by herself each day or with her father when he could.

For a few hours in the middle of the day Sam worked on business. Randi had agreed to work full time through the transition, and the plan was for Sam to travel back to the east coast only if necessary. We had made arrangements to maintain the house at home so she would have a place to stay, but she believed most of the transition could be handled by phone.

However, turning over the reins was more complicated than had she expected.

Through the summer I wrote many observations in my journal in an attempt to gain some perspective on Sam's situation. This was especially pertinent since my "unbiased" input was occasionally requested.

* * *

In general Randi and Jean Pierre did a magnificent job. But, they had not realized just how fundamental Sam's knowledge of clients had been for handling details efficiently "before" complications occurred. In her absence subtle aspects were increasingly being overlooked while everyone thought things were okay.

Sam had had a system for making sure everything got done when it was needed, and the continuity was broken by her absence. As she thought she was simplifying and finding peace, she was actually creating an imbalance. More and more when Sam returned from painting or walks, she had to clean up problems and smooth ruffled feathers. Then, there was the added complication of attempting to explain to Randi and Jean Pierre what they missed and how to fix it.

To compound matters, much of the "quality" time spent with me became crowded with complaints or questions about how to remedy the situation. I was willing to be a sounding board, and I was, but I could not understand the nuances of what they were missing any more than they could.

After awhile when Sam set up for painting, thoughts of business bounced around in her mind so much, that what seemed like a vacation to others was a debilitating and artistically uninspiring brain-twister.

We were in Washington living our dreams, but Sam was finding it increasingly difficult to enjoy herself. The ridiculous part was that I was the only one Sam could complain to, since on the surface our lives appeared fabulous, at least to everyone else. In truth they were probably happier merely having fantasies of time off from work and living in beautiful places, instead of having to make it fit with the rest of the world.

* * *

While functioning day to day in the "real" world, one accepts the tasks at hand and works at the grindstone to get through the days, weeks and years. Changing the flow of life from the "norm", is like suddenly turning a kayak around after just descending raging white-water rapids and trying to take it back upstream. That may seem absurd initially, unless from the perspective of a helicopter one observes that even though the kayak is past what appeared to be the toughest part, it is headed for a huge waterfall. And the kayaker, as she fights for her life, suddenly questions, "Why did I have to take this risk anyway? Why didn't I stay in the smooth flowing part of the river?"

Sam had already done the tough part of the river by successfully creating her dream businesses. She was now in what appeared to be the calm placid water of a well deserved respite. But, in fact, the placid surface was covering the fastest under-current yet.

That is the still moment when one thinks the worst is over and it's time to relax just before all hell breaks loose. Almost immediately the realization hits that there is a humongous water fall ahead, and it takes some fast thinking while scrambling for all your worth. There she is, paddling with every ounce of energy to fix what was not supposed to go wrong, but just standing still.

This is the time someone else might plead, "Mother come and hold me, fix everything, kiss me and make it all right"; or, go to the freezer and get the private stash of frozen chocolate bars and a pint of the most expensive ice cream God ever concocted; or to go out and run five miles, or ten miles or a marathon or whatever it takes to find a large enough distraction to forget the looming dilemma. Another option is to throw up your hands and say, "You win, all come in free", and start another round of hide and go seek with your playmates.

I could picture Sam sitting at the head of the board of directors meeting going on in her mind. She opens the floor for suggestions. The first thought registering is that in everyone else's mind, "It's not that bad," or "It's nothing that can't be handled," or "I've seen her fix bigger problems than this." She realizes the difference this time is, it was a series of small steps that got her out near the ledge, with each step taken willingly and proudly, and, having come so far, she can only go forward. Others may be sympathetic to her predicament, but it is clear that even with their understanding and faith, she must find her own answer.

* * *

Sam had only been away a short time, but a handful of clients from the biggest to the smallest began to stop doing business. It was probably coincidence. There were logical reasons like a shift in approach or they were retiring. Only one expressed appreciation for how she handled everything in the past, but wanted to work with someone new who would give them greater attention. Through it all, rationalizations could initially pacify the doubts and challenges of the new direction, but Sam had a feeling of responsibility to fill the expectation that it was possible to continue to keep everyone happy and solve everyone else's problems.

The situation was analogous to being a head of a household or the head of a religious organization. Everybody loves the top person, but expects that one person to have all of the answers. They respect their privacy, sort of, and know they have their own personal life to deal with, sort of, but since they accepted the weight of handling everything before and were so good at it, everyone maintains confidence that they will step in and do it again.

* * *

Even the money Sam made, which seemed like a lot based on her lifestyle, all went back into the business, to buy the home in the country, which then stood empty. And, beginning in the fall she would start paying thirty thousand dollars a year after taxes to send Alex to college. So, after the three years of exceptional growth, there was just enough money left to do what she thought would make her happy, but the solution was now the source of the problems. And, the arrangement for an ongoing percentage of the profits to provide Sam income had already started to deteriorate, and was creating doubts about the whole transition.

* * *

Sam spent only two weeks in this state of purgatory, neither enjoying her work or her semi-retirement, before she decided to go back to the business and resolve the outstanding matters. She knew she had to devise a way to move forward rather than retreat to a paradise filled with doubt, since it was unrealistic to hope the ever-mounting problems would just go away.

There were times in my life when I thought escaping to an island in the South Pacific might be the perfect solution to social drudgery. However, Sam realized, as I suppose I must have, that as long as she took her mind with her, she would always be haunted, even in paradise, by nagging, unresolved issues.

There was only one choice left. Sam returned to the house in Bucks County, and began to focus on how to give proper closure to a great chapter in her life. She realized that so many possibilities and decisions in giving birth and nurturing the life of the business needed to be set free into life by a proportionate effort on the closure side. Years of energy into anything would leave an imbalance if closed in a short period of time. She had gotten herself into the situation and she had to find her way out.

It had taken Sam two weeks of not being able to relax, paint, or feel like herself, before she came to that realization. Once she did, she saw that jettisoning her overwork too quickly had created a new imbalance. In her present state she was of little use to me, her family or Alex, so she began to make plans to return to find a balance between the two extremes. I could listen to Sam's dilemma or try to make her happy, but really the only thing to do was drive her to the airport.

Alex decided to stay on the farm for the summer, and Sam went off alone. She promised to make her trips to visit us at least as often as her trips for business. Every business trip had to be balanced with a family trip. That was the first decision in balancing her lives. Her original decision to handle everything from the west coast had to be put in a bigger perspective. After making the diagnosis, her course was to stabilize the patient's vital signs and make adjustments so the healing process would take its natural course.

* * *

From daily phone conversations with Sam I pieced together the crowning part of her transformation.

* * *

Once Sam returned home, a sense of peace came over her. For the first time in her entire life she was alone. All the years raising Alex, all the years living with Randi, all the years growing up with her family and finally for the first time in her life she was alone in her own place.

There was much to be done, but it turned out with measured attention it was simpler and not nearly as overwhelming as she, and everyone else had made it sound. Since people and clients needing attention thought she was gone from the main picture, they accepted her back without insisting on receiving attention from her in person. It was enough knowing she was nearby, able to handle any minor emergency. Jean Pierre and Randi had prepared for her to be out of the picture, so even with a few hours of input a day, they felt like she was contributing at a life-saving, and business-saving, level of participation. Almost immediately everything was running smoothly again.

Sam woke up early each morning and painted for hours before the rest of the world might want her, and she painted again in the evening. Many evenings she had dinner at the restaurant where I had played jazz. The owner would join her for awhile over dinner, and then leave her to listen to my replacement.

Sam also worked in the garden a little each day, read some of the books piling up on her reading list, and even visited the neighbors next door who talked her into learning to ride the horses. Sam surprised herself and became proficient fairly quickly. She became friends with another woman who kept a horse at the barn and began riding with her.

As her friends began to come and visit her at the house, for a mix of business and pleasure, she really settled in. Randi and Albere came for an overnight visit, and they actually only spent two hours of the visit on business. Even when Randi came back with Jean Pierre, Jack, and Lou another day, ninety percent of the time was devoted to conversation, eating and laughing.

* * *

She stayed four straight weeks before she decided to fly out to visit us for a week. When she arrived, I could see an new light in her eyes. She had released her tension, and the clearest evidence was in the slides of her most recent paintings.

They were just slides, but the work had a life to it that jumped out at me. She had given them to Randi to show people before leaving. The day of her arrival she received a call from Randi exclaiming she thought she had buyers lined up and others asking for more new work.

Once everyone was happier to have Sam painting so they could own her latest works, she knew that the other pieces of the transition would fall into place over the course of another six months or so. That was the turning point, and we could both feel it right away.

* * *

Anna and I planned a small welcome back party. Alex joined in the festivities, but she was with Emile all evening. Sam was clearly disappointed and realized another assumption needed to be rethought.

Sam told me she had hoped to squeeze a whole summer of being with Alex into the following week before they flew home to pack and drive to school. Sam had realized one of the next steps in her life was to connect with Alex. The more she saw how Anna and I nurtured our loving connection, the more she wanted to make up for how busy she had been the past couple of years, or so.

As Sam was finding a happy balance in her business, it dawned on her that she could raise tons of money for others, but she could not buy a year with her daughter Alex had spent the last few years silently, or sometimes not so silently, rebelling, and was now was about to leave for Columbia in New York City. Irrespective of how she had related to Sam, she had maintained excellent grades and had been accepted at her first choice with the intention of pursuing a degree in journalism and writing. This decision had been well thought out and had our support, although it was ironic that while we were moving away from cities and spending time on the west coast, Alex was headed to the city and remaining on the east coast. And, just as Sam finally had time to be with Alex, she was about to disappear for four years or more.

Sam decided she had to start somewhere, but she could see it would be hard to find time with Alex since she was otherwise occupied. Even though I had mentioned Alex and Emile often when we talked, only upon seeing them did it register that they would spend most of their time together before leaving. Now Alex wanted to stay in Washington, but not to visit with Sam, she wanted to be near Emile.

* * *

It started with the planning for the fall Shakespeare play started during the summer. Alex's experience working on high school productions and stage managing made her a natural to assist the other two women from the community who directed and stage-managed. They had worked on plays at the farm since they were Alex's age. She helped and learned, and was accepted and accepting, and, even though they had separate titles, there was an open sharing of ideas, and on any given day they could have exchanged hats.

The planning, auditions and set design meetings started in the evenings and then the rehearsals and other details progressed as the summer-long project took shape. Alex began working closely with Emile, who helped with designing and building the props, and they started to get to know each other better.

Emile was also naturally talented with plants, and invited Alex to see the beginnings of a biosphere he had created in the greenhouse Uncle J had erected for him. He was studying, testing and applying his knowledge, in what was effectively his own one hundred-foot by twenty-five foot laboratory. Twenty feet on one end had been finished, and served as a combination office and living space complete with a small kitchen, plumbing and a wood stove which was installed in the wall adjoining his living quarters and the greenhouse to heat them when necessary. Alex offered to lend a hand with the plants, and Emile happily agreed.

Alex seemed to really enjoy working in the greenhouse, but they both knew it was primarily to be together. Alex only had a few boyfriends during high school, and had gone through an awkward looking stage, but she was now a lovely, quick-witted young lady. Alex, like Sam, had sleek black hair, although Alex wore her hair shorter to show her non-conformity. Alex also had the strength of spirit that ran through her family from her years of Aikido training. Her eyes varied between green, hazel and gray depending on her demeanor and the sunlight. Her eyes and smile lit up her face, but especially so when Emile was around

Whatever the change was in Alex since our visit the prior

year, caught Emile's attention and he quickly reciprocated her interest. But, he, they, had the will power to let it develop slowly since she was the "boss's grand niece."

Emile and Alex seemed to be everywhere together, and she was drawn into the activities at the farm like a woman with a purpose. The two were inseparable and, for the first month we were at the farm, there was a courtship dance that was progressing in a well-mannered fashion. Under the watchful eyes of everyone at the farm, patient steps and discretion were appropriately considered. The game of appearances tied in with creating a bit of mystery and anticipation which seemed to add to their mutual attraction.

By the end of the summer, Alex and Emile were openly coming and going together. She was as happy as I had ever seen her, but as the time neared for her to leave, I occasionally noticed her eyes were red from crying. She had been so single minded that Columbia was the only choice she would consider, but now it was like she was going to prison. Feeling convicted, she prepared to go, but they agreed to write and talk on the phone everyday, and then see each other during school breaks.

* * *

Alex flew back to Philadelphia a day after Sam so she could postpone leaving every day possible. A friend of Alex's met her at the airport who was supposed to drive her home so she could pack during the weekend. Instead, though, she convinced Alex to go directly to her parent's beach house for a last get-together of all their friends before they headed off to college.

Sam was more disappointed that she would not be able to visit with Alex than annoyed that Alex was going to wait until the last minute to pack. Alex promised she would be back on Sunday, pack and be ready to go Monday as planned.

As it turned out Alex arrived late on Sunday and spent the whole night packing. By the time they got in the car to leave, Alex was exhausted and fell asleep for the hour it took to get to

New York. The two hours after they arrived were the closest they came to interacting as they crowded into elevators along with a flood of other parents and students all moving suitcases and boxes into the dorm rooms.

Before Sam knew it she was back in the car and driving across town to see visit a friend for the night. She had decided to stay in the city in case Alex needed her the next day, but the following evening she drove home assuming Alex was okay. Sam still planned to travel back and forth from the Washington to the east coast, and decided she would visit Alex another time after she settled into school.

* * *

I pieced together Alex's roller-coaster that fall from Sam as the events transpired:

The first time Alex and Emile had a chance to see each other after the summer was the first week in October. Although there was no break from school, Alex's grandparents sent her a plane ticket so she could come and join in the festivities for the farm's harvest festival, and stay for a long weekend. Alex immediately changed the return flight so she could stay for the entire week, and fly back at the end of the subsequent weekend.

The first weekend was busy, but it was no secret Alex and Emile had become an item during the summer, and the family "looked the other way" when seeing them together too early in the morning to have met for a morning workout.

They were in heaven and hell. They were simultaneously thrilled to be together and already in agony at the thought of being separate again. The only redeeming part was that they were both engrossed in their respective school work, and realized they would have to be away from each other to get any real work done. Of course, that was being too rational for the feelings they had for each other, but as smart as they were, they knew it was true.

Alex attempted to concentrate on her studies when she

returned to school, but by the end of November when she had planned to fly back for Thanksgiving, she canceled the trip until the winter break. In part she was playing catch up for the week she skipped and had fallen behind in her work, but the real reason was she was sick almost every morning and was afraid to face what she already knew.

Alex had considered the reason she missed her period in October was stress related to starting school or something. Even before it should have come in November though, she went for a test to confirm what was already obvious.

Upon this discovery, a progression of thoughts and emotions ruled her as she fought to understand what to do. Initially she was afraid but hopeful. She felt dumb, but an inner resiliency told her she could face anything. She would be sullen, then buoyant. She hated Emile and loved him more than ever. She wanted to end the pregnancy and she wanted to keep the baby. She cried frequently and doubled her energies toward her school work. She ate enormous amounts of food, or couldn't eat at all. She wanted to tell her mother but couldn't quite find the words yet. She was scared and she was scared. She wanted to tell Emile, but she wanted to know what she wanted first. She wanted to get married and run away with Emile, and she wanted to avoid having to tell anyone and run away by herself for the next twenty years. She wanted to have the baby and put it up for adoption. She wanted to have the baby and raise it herself as her mother had done with her. She decided the baby must have a father and know him. She could not even begin to imagine having a baby at all, let alone keeping one. She wanted Emile to marry her and support her while she raised the child. She didn't want to rely on any one, and she wanted an angel to come and tell her what to do.

She wanted Sam's input, but every time she called, she hung up before the second ring. She knew her mother would understand, but realized she was not sure how to talk with her mother.

Alex felt like the weight of the world was a yoke on her shoulders. She was growing up faster than she wanted. After years of wanting to thrust into adult responsibilities and to be respected for her outlook on life, this was unbelievable. She had always wanted to make her own decisions, but after this, she turned to wanting only to be a child without any responsibilities. Things had taken a wrong turn, and like her mother with only a business gone awry, she was determined to set it right without hurting anyone in the process.

She wanted help deciding, but knew no one could give the answer but herself.

Alex finally called Randi the day before Thanksgiving. Randi drove to New York the minute she got off the phone, packed Alex and some stuff into the car and drove her back to Philadelphia to spend the long holiday weekend with her and Albere. Between shared tears and occasional laughter at the absurdity of the situation they talked like daughter and combination mother, father, sister, aunt and friend that Randi had always been to her.

Telling Randi made clear to her that no one could have a suggestion that could change anything, or really know exactly how she felt. She appreciated the premise that no one can ever really know what another feels, but suddenly she seemed to have answers to questions she had had all her life. Alex realized she was living what her mother and grandmother had experienced in the only way she could come close to understanding their turmoil. She knew that she was an accident and conceived while Sam was in college. She also assumed from the stories she knew of her grandmother that Sam had not been planned, either. And, their decisions to keep their babies and not tell the fathers, or see them again, were the same.

The sense of understanding was awesome, but Alex swore

the pattern of repetition would stop with her. She did want the father, and she wanted the the baby and the father more than anything else in her life. Just telling Randi and having an understanding friend gave her a sense of self-confidence. There was no right or wrong any more, she just needed to make a decision, just a decision.

She did. Alex decided to have the baby whether Emile agreed to be in the picture or not. But, she wanted him to share the experience and together find the joy in it, and not because he felt forced. She would wait to call Emile until two days before she planned to fly there for winter break and tell him so he could have some time to himself to explore his own heart and mind just before meeting face to face.

She asked Randi to call Sam and tell her to fly into Philadelphia the next day, Sunday, to meet with her, that there was a "minor" emergency, but to wait to ask questions until she arrived. Alex realized Randi was the one confidant she had, and resented herself and Sam for not being closer. Although she could not imagine talking to Sam yet and felt a great distance from her, still, she needed to tell her mother.

Once she was clear about what she wanted, she knew the day to day decisions would have perspective and could be taken one at a time. In that way she let go of worrying about how, and focussed on the present.

* * *

The next morning Alex convinced Randi to tell Sam about the pregnancy for her, rather than have Sam fly in early. Alex wanted to be mature and tell her mother herself, and Randi encouraged her to, but Randi finally acquiesced.

The phone rang exactly as Sam reached to call Randi to explain that complying with her request was simply impossible, that she already had a return ticket for Monday, and absolutely had to know what could be so important, or wrong.

Randi started by telling her she had a reprieve and to stay

with her original flight on Monday, and Alex would met her at the airport Monday.

Sam sounded shocked, "Alex, why Alex?"

I was in the room when Sam answered the phone and watched as Sam went fairly quickly from being her normal, calm self, to being agitated and then subdued. Simultaneously, her expression grew pained and sorrowful.

I moved toward her to see what was wrong. She gave me a look that froze me, but as I turned to leave her alone, she motioned for me to stay. From hearing half of the conversation I understood volumes.

Within a second of hanging up, after an hour on the phone, she began to cry harder than anyone I had ever seen. She was obviously distraught about Alex, but she was inconsolable about herself. She was afraid to face her own daughter, and needed someone to receive the words in person, "Did I fail as a mother?" It was clear it was not because of the pregnancy, but that was the event that uncorked the bottle of self-questioning she had held within. Her biggest doubt was if she could be Alex's friend and how to talk with her.

She told me it was as though someone found her weakest point and was tearing apart how she viewed herself. I just listened as she poured her heart out to me. As she spoke, I felt like she was counting on me to be a closer friend than at any time before.

I held her and decided my best advice was an understanding presence and offered thoughts only when requested.

The day after talking with Alex on the way home from the airport in Philadelphia, Sam repeated a similar scene with Randi as she had with me, and, then again with me on the phone that night. It was evident Sam's talk with Alex did not go very well.

Sam had started by assuring Alex of her support whatever she decided, but it was more a strained conveyance of information than an understanding heart to heart. Afterward, each of them felt more alone than comforted. They communicated reasonably well, which was a start, but, neither found that satisfying sense of achievement from reaching a resolution together. The missing elements were probably due to the lack of clarity in each of them, and the dialogue remained as muddy as Alex's feelings about what to do with her life and much like Sam's uncertainty of how to dissolve the unspoken separation between parents and teenagers. They were speaking about the same topic, side by side, but on slightly different frequencies.

Alex had returned to school that same Monday night. She did not require an interpreter to understand there was a crush of school work that would require all the attention she could muster.

The work was a welcome chore. She attempted to force her heart into silence and embraced the temporary distraction as a substitute. She put her energy into studying, but the futility of avoiding her heart's attention could be seen in her tear-stained lecture notes.

The end of the first week in December, while finishing papers and preparing for finals, everything changed. Perhaps it was her nerves, her wishing that the problem would disappear or the tendency of women in their first pregnancy to have miscarriages, but that was the result.

With the miscarriage the physical decision had vanished, but the emotional ones remained.

This time she called Sam first, who rushed to the hospital from Bucks County the second she hung up the phone.

The reality had changed their willfulness into humility, and the episode that had elicited the self-evaluation of a lifetime, had in the process, created a bridge to a new relationship between them. It awakened a strength from knowing they had been weak together.

The string connecting them had worn thin, representing their distance and separateness, but it was now being woven into the fabric of a new understanding. Through her emotions, Alex discovered a new respect for the decision Sam had made to keep her, and the decision to give up freedoms in life for her, an unknown child. No matter how much or how little attention her mother paid her, Alex now knew her mother in a new light, and, just how much she wanted a connection with her.

Sam found resolution to many of her doubts about raising Alex and to the awful feeling of resistance between two people who loved each other but found communicating difficult. She thought, especially with the perspective of having resolved the business, that she had traded her chance to know Alex, which was priceless and irreplaceable, for her own drive to be successful. Now there was the basis for anything, together or apart, because each knew how to offer what really mattered, the ability to accept each other and know the other would always be there.

* * *

Alex decided the only way to tell Emile was in person, but, she would spend the first week at the farm with him before saying anything. Finally, on the last day of December Alex found the courage to tell Emile.

Emile realized why Alex had treated him so tenderly that prior week. Although he had been spared the prolonged questions that Alex bore for him, the emotions, questions and beliefs of what his actions would have been hit him all at once. He vowed he would be forever aware of the precious meaning within each kiss and act of physical love, and, how each contains a lifetime of decisions.

Although purposely excused, she forgave him for being absent through her crisis. He appreciated Alex's integrity and felt honored by her continued love for him. The awakened wisdom from the impact of the experience seeped into the marrow of his bones. Even though the seed was lost from her womb, a seed was planted in their minds that separately they could survive and rebound, but there was the potential to create a new life by joining together. Their thoughts and emotions had lived an unborn lifetime in a brief eternity.

Chapter 15

What brings some people together sends others flying apart. What creates disillusions for many may be a catalyst for others to unite. What sounds like unbelievable tales of dubious exaggeration are another's day to day existence. What brings a misery of bad luck from disbelief and doubts is laughed at as amusing, once absurdity is given perspective. What is a mountain to survive another day is impossibility conquered by the imaginative. What is chaos to the uninitiated is chaos to the faithful as well, but a step closer to clarity. What is adversity but a process that may bring together those that share it? And, what people perceive as fanciful characterization is at most two steps removed from personal experience.

*   *   *

I looked at Sam that rainy, first evening of January as we lay in bed together and asked her, "How do we do it?"

She looked at me questioningly, "What's going on in your mind that makes you ask?"

"Well, considering we've gone through more transitions in the short time we've known each other than the Italian government, there must be a key to the process."

Sam smiled, "Maybe its because you have a sense of humor and you're willing to share in dreams and day to day stuff. Just keep finding ways to keep me laughing through everything. With all the continuous changes I go through by myself or with you, or anyone else who takes a number on a given day, you find something funny in it."

"Really, I always thought I was too serious with my philosophies or schemes to find a way through the dilemmas. You mean all this time you thought I was being funny?"

"Well, the way I get through life is finding something to appreciate every day and something special in the people I meet. Whenever I find maintaining that approach challenging, you have a knack for seeing it from a different perspective, or as you say, 'How can we turn this around, inside out or upside down?' and by then we're both throwing out ideas from the mundane to the ridiculous. After a few that range from silly to serious, I tend to have a fresh perspective. Even if I don't use any of your suggestions, once I've been able to laugh a little, even at the toughest problems, it takes the edge off and I find some door that will get me through.

"What about you, and what brings up the question now?"

I shook my head. "Well, maybe you haven't noticed but we lead somewhat unusual lives. We've stayed together through work schedules that defy the nature of the word schedule, we co-habitate but rarely in the same city or state before we move or your life makes it necessary for you to be elsewhere, and your daughter, all right my daughter too, as I suppose kids are meant to do, find something to fill in the less dramatic moments."

I paused thinking Sam was going to interject a comment, but she prompted me to continue.

"Do we continue at this pace forever, or do we settle into some routine for more than a day?"

I could see Sam was considering my question even as she bantered, "Was there a day that had a routine? I can't remember one. You're the one who is more predictable, well maybe not predictable, but you have patterns to what you do each week. Truly though, maybe it's that we each take turns supporting the one who is pushing the other. Then, when we are both accelerating into a creative period, we keep a tandem or trapeze passing act going to spur the dynamics even more. It's probably that by doing these occasional reality checks and realizing everything is still working, we can be present in each day's drama. And, by knowing ourselves and what matters to us, all our choices fit within the perspective of our values."

Sam pulled me closer. "Last time I checked our connection was still working. How about you?"

"Yes," I replied looking into her eyes, "that's exactly the point. No matter how much we push the limits of what I knew about relating, we are able to push right through. What I didn't imagine was possible before, becomes something I take for granted. Then I feel closer to you, and the next day or situation seems to find a way for us to question how to turn something else around."

"All right, so what's the question?"

"The question is, do we continue like this forever, or will there be some period when we're bored with each other? You do realize, if we weren't always focused on what we're doing next, it's possible we wouldn't be as happy as we keep being. This is the longest I've been with anyone since my marriage, and I feel like every few months we become reacquainted as if I have a new partner."

Sam grinned broadly, "Ah, so what you're saying is you'll discard me like all the others when my entertainment ratings fall?"

Sam stopped me as instinct had me beginning to defend and explain myself, and she kept continued.

"Phil, I know what you mean. Half the time I'm amazed I keep up with myself and the other half I wonder how you put up with me, and then you completely bewilder me with your steadfast patience and kindness."

Sam's tone became very gentle. "Look, sometimes I'm afraid if I doubt myself for even a moment, I'll find that my life is a house of cards that will collapse. It's like the only way to keep it stable is by actually adding cards. When I stop to admire or feel comfortable, a couple of cards fall off making me scramble just to get back to where I was. I feel like what works best is to add a card into a new space, while somehow knowing that something I've already started will support it; even if it is not apparent at the time."

"So I'm just another one of your cards?" I asked.

"Touche'," she replied but ignored my jibe, "I know neither of us will discard the other, even if we wanted to. We're linked. We're connected deeper than our thoughts. I know when you're thinking of me." Then she joshed, "You do think of me, right?"

I nodded and smiled my obvious agreement, but looked intently beyond the comment for her to continue her thought.

"We're linked beyond the physical in a way that gives me confidence that you will always reach into my life like overlaying ripples in a pond. But, rather than going off in different directions we return to the same center to ripple outward again, together."

I just listened as Sam spoke to the essence of my questions.

"I always thought my connection with Randi might be the ultimate friendship I would ever know. But, intuitively I know you too are a kindred soul. By knowing that aspect of Randi, I could recognize it in you."

I was speechless, and looked into her eyes for more. My heart and soul felt as though they were receiving the nourishment they had always sought.

She continued, "The miracle is that there is a multiplying effect. When Randi and I met, it was like four instead of two. When you came into the picture, I felt a shift to three multiplied by three. It's like looking into the night sky and seeing the prominent constellations when I'm around you, Randi and of course, Alex. And, when my family and other friends, who are always in my heart, are added the brilliance of the whole Milky Way comes alive. It was always there, but a newness is instilled into the picture to magnify it all."

I considered Sam's imagery and the parallel of people I knew to stars.

The silence was comfortable, but I felt compelled to ask, "So where do we go from here?"

Sam laughed out loud, "You ask such simple questions."

Her laugh was contagious. I said, "It's funny how a little question like, 'How do we do it?' has led to a significant expression and understanding of how our connected relationship had been self-sustaining. While apparently built on air, we have a solid foundation of love, respect, and emotional and intellectual understanding that feels quite down-to-earth in our daily life.

"As I listen to your insights and contemplate the wisdom in your words, I realize how typically unanswerable that question can be in a relationship. Perhaps it's especially well hidden when everything is great, and easier when presented with hurdles to overcome. We've gone through both, so the question remains, 'What is that nebulous glue making us a whole?"

"For me it is to see the big picture and listening intuitively to what meaning each person and experience means to me. I acknowledge the elusive nature of understanding objectively what is being done while actively participating. With persistence something like my miscommunicating with Alex breaks into the light of day."

I pondered out loud, "So you are aware of your actions while involved, you make plans for the future and take life one question at a time?"

"Precisely, except when I can't. I do know, though, that the answer is always somewhere inside me. If I ask myself each step of the way and listen to my heart, the answer for that moment will come to me."

Sam sat up in bed and reached for her sapphire necklace, "For instance, my business was but a thought initially. It would have been impossible to have everything magically appear the next morning. And, even if it did, there wouldn't have been the foundation of my experience to support the knowledge without living the process. By setting the dream in place, as I learned to do with all my goals in life from the simple to the grand, the learning process seems to be eternally continuous. I created an awareness to recognize what questions to ask and how to make each step correspond to making the dream a reality. In that manner I appreciated and truly lived my dream."

"Can you give me an example of what you mean?" I asked.

Sam thought for a moment before continuing with an example, "In a way it's like having a magic genie inside. You make a wish or focus on a dream, and then turn it over to the magic genie. The genie is wise though, and knows that the way you'll appreciate the gift the most is by participating in the creation of it. Sure, initially it would be fun to just have it show up, but there are two problems that would soon occur.

"First is what I implied a moment ago. If you were suddenly given a powerful computer without an instruction manual or without having participated in the process of learning on smaller computers, you would be overwhelmed trying to use it and not understand the steps necessary for the purpose you have in mind.

"You could say, 'Well I'd ask the genie for the knowledge to use the computer and then use it.'

"That doesn't work either. As you continually ask the genie for the answer, you become dependent on the genie, since you have relied on someone or something besides yourself every step. You do not have the experience to do it yourself, and you missed all the real fun which was in the doing.

"The real fun is in experiencing the wonder and amazement of seeing each step of your creation magically appear with your own hands. It's like art, and why I love art so much. I certainly would enjoy being given a painting of a beautiful scene, but imagine the real joy of spending a day in that scene and envisioning every aspect that nature offered my senses as the picture unfolded upon my canvas. Then the joy of sharing the creation becomes magnified ten-fold when I share the art with others because I did it myself. Then a friend, who is sharing in my experience, would also come alive as I express, and he personally receives, the passion that I felt while doing it."

Sam paused, but continued, "If I only purchased the painting, or if the genie just gave it to me, my friend observing the work might acknowledge the beauty, but then either just want the phone number of my genie, who would be lavished with the true appreciation that only the creator of the art work can actually receive, or I would become insatiable and always want something more. I would never have the experience myself no matter how much of the genie's artwork I collected. At some point I would become jealous of the genie's ability and spend my life wishing to be given another talent or object; but even those would all become boring if I never did it myself.

"If someone got so far away from the ability to create and was always dependent on another for happiness, the worst wish the person could ask the genie for would be eternal life. Once that was given, the boredom would be complete. The person would have forever to realize that he could always ask for one more trinket or dream but never do it himself."

"Your best wishes to ask the genie would be: 'Help me learn to do it myself. Teach me so that I may appreciate the wonders of creating something myself. Guide me so that each step of the process so I can learn how to do it.' Then someday you might even reach the true joy of being able to teach and guide another child or person to share the joy of creating.'

"The highest level of learning takes place when you become so competent in your knowledge and self ability to create, that in showing someone else, you learn even more by seeing the process anew through their eyes. In this way, you would always have the joy and even the reason to live, not only forever, but more importantly another moment of another day.

"Of course you might ask the genie how to reach it so, when you reach an impasse and cannot find another teacher, you can call on the genie to appear, but only as a guide and never to just give you the end result. For as anyone knows who is dissatisfied when they reach what was once a seemingly unattainable goal, that in the process another more far-reaching dream develops, making the first one only a means to the new dream."

I was awed by her answer, especially since she could put into words the credo that she practiced in her life. I did not realize at that moment that it was the first time she had ever put those thoughts into words. The essence of her motto was evident as the skeleton that supported her decisions in every day with her family, friends and all.

Words finally came to me, but slowly and with a reverence for my friend's willingness to share her wisdom with me that seemed to spring like a fountain from her soul, "How did you learn to do, and integrate that theory into your daily life? And, can you teach me how to do it?"

"Since you've asked, I'll tell you who instilled these precepts into my life, and even teach you what I know so that you will know how to do it yourself, but you must promise, as I did, to offer these thoughts freely, but only to someone who asks. Once someone asks, they are ready to appreciate the answer. It is like the saying that the answer lies in being able to ask the question, and being able to ask the question means someone is ready for the answer. Also remember, if there is such a thing as an answer, it is only a means to asking another question that broadens the scope infinitely."

I nodded as though I was agreeing to some sacred ritual, and the secret password was only to ask.

"Only to ask," I thought shaking my head.

The answer that Sam expressed in a few moments of this

one evening already sounded like a lifetime of doing, before I could ask another question.

Sam continued, "Like your question, the answer is easy to give, and then the fun, or tough part, depending on how you choose to do it, is how you decide to do it yourself. There is no one way, and actually, the various possible ways are countless. The only limitation is what you believe or if you have somehow been taught that you cannot do something. But, even the limitations can be overcome once you're aware and choose to change.

"Few break beyond what society will accept as possible, and all of them are initially ridiculed and laughed at, often until long after they are dead. However those same unaccepted thoughts become accepted facts generations later, and anyone disbelieving them then would be ridiculed and laughed at; very much like how scientists once believed the sun revolved around the earth.

"The answer lies in asking yourself whatever question you have, and listening for the answer in your heart. Let the initial gut reactions go, and feel a tingling or pulsing in your chest. Let go of any fear that the sensations are an ailment, and feel, sometimes for the first time, what resonates within you regarding the question in each case.

"My Uncle J was my teacher in this, and he says he learned from masters he studied with in Japan who traveled from the west. This sapphire stone in my necklace has no meaning in and of itself. It is a reminder that I wear over my heart to ask and bring an awareness to my heart of everything I do, think and say. As the saying so wisely goes, I truly take it all to heart, and in so doing I become a master of myself."

Sam asked, "Would you like me to lead you through a simple exercise I was taught?"

"I'm in your hands. How do we begin?"

Sam suggested, "If you're ready to begin, first lay back, relax and take a few deep breaths."

For the next few moments there was a stillness, and the only sound I was aware of was my own breath. My body became relaxed as Sam told me to feel the weight of my body like a rock on the ground. Her voice guided me to feel the connection of each part of my body to the earth, until I felt the ground under me.

I was pleasantly surprised to realize my rarely acknowledged back existed, and feel a tingling there as I imagined the cool earth next to my skin.

Sam whispered, "As you feel the earth, pose a question to yourself you wish to know and ask to know an answer."

The first thought that came to my mind was the question, "What is the purpose of all of this?"

Without me saying anything or having the chance to think if I had even asked myself a question, Sam began again. She directed me to briefly open my eyes, take a close look at the blue stone, and then to close my eyes while holding the picture in my mind.

I stared at the stone until I was able to clearly remember the shape and color of it with my eyes closed. I had seen the stone hundreds of times before, but by studying closely I could see gradations from the darker blue center of the sphere shape to the many faceted sides. The small stone seemed to be floating in the center of the gold star where it was set. It was small and almost unnoticeable until looked at closely. As I looked and pictured the stone, my mind became filled with the blue as though the entire sky had condensed into a small sphere-shaped earth within my mind, but without boundaries. Sam's voice softly returned, but seemed distant even though she was still next to me.

Sam began, "Now imagine that the front of your body is blue like the stone. Imagine the dark blue center being your heart, and lighter shades of blue are radiating out in pulses from the center. Feel yourself become the blue as you sense the life flowing from the blue light flowing out and beyond the edge of your body."

Sam continued after pausing, "Feel the stone become liquid light, and picture yourself in crystal blue water. You are now floating as pulsing blue that continues into the surrounding water."

Although I had a vague recollection of the sky in my mind, those were the last words I remember consciously hearing before entering another world. When I opened my eyes next, I was in a strange, but somehow familiar, one-room cottage. I was alone in my bed, and curious as to why I was there. I called for Sam, but knew she would not answer even before the words left my mouth. I looked out the window to see the light of dawn coming through the trees that separated my yard from the neighboring cottages. I had an odd sensation as I wondered what the purpose of this all was.

An energy within propelled me to greet the sunrise. With the thought, I was at the door, dressed and looking out at a hillside that would give me a vantage point of the sun rising over the town where I awoke. I picked up a small pack from the table by the door, and headed toward a well-traveled path from my door toward the hill. The way was lush with ferns and wildflowers as the path wandered through meadows and into the cool, mist-laden trees on what I already knew was the base of a higher mountain. The path ended at an outcropping of rocks that opened to an expansive view of an oceanside town with fields and woods bordered by cliffs reaching up to the surrounding mountains tops. I drank in the smell of the sea air and the fragrance of the woods.

The awesome scene was mixed with melancholy as I remembered I was captive there with no way to leave. I recollected that I had arrived there unconscious after deciding to begin an adventure, but had effectively become a prisoner in a friendly and lovely community when it was explained to me that no one had found a safe passage out.

Many generations lived in this idyllic wonderland of abundance, and chose willingly to stay. There were stories of their forefathers arriving with the underlying essence similar to my experience. However, through retelling and interpretation, the legends of the origin of life beyond this town became allegories and metaphors that comforted and pacified everyone, and almost all were content to stay in their little heaven. As more memories of my situation came to mind, I remembered the townspeople were accepting of my initial attempts to return to my place of origin. When I had only recently arrived, my ventures to scale the cliffs to leave through a mountain pass, or to sail a boat away by sea had been abandoned as being impossible as they all told me it would be.

As the sun began to warm the day, I changed into a pair of white cotton shorts and a shirt I found in my knapsack. In my sack was some water and fruit for breakfast, and a wooden flute which I realized I knew how to play. While in this state between remembering and settling into the contentment of the moment, I played a melody.

I played a while, but stopped when the scent of jasmine drew my attention. I looked behind me for the source of the perfume, and a girl or very young woman appeared from behind a tree. She wore a loose fitting cotton sun dress that showed her shoulders when her reddish-gold hair was not covering them. As she came toward me I could see a tear sparkling in her green eyes that turned to rainbows in the sunlight. She asked me to continue playing, and as I did she sang words to the tune which I had not remembered.

I wondered were she came from, why I had never seen her before and how she knew a song that I was uncertain I knew before that playing. But, before I could ask her, she encouraged me to join her on the flute on another song. Our duet blended exquisitely and the words of her song brought tears to my eyes and filled me with emotion. She expressed feelings of love that united people as I remembered in the land of my origin.

When she finished singing, she spoke with such sweetness, "Thank you for adding such a passionate expression to my song. I felt the song was as fresh and vibrant as the first time I learned it." Then looking behind her at the setting sun, she excused herself saying, "I'm on my way to meet my family," and she turned toward the woods to leave. I called to her, "Wait, please tell me where you've been and where you're going!"

She looked surprised, and said, "Over the mountain, of course." She said "The song you played piqued my interest because it's from the land on the other side." She explained, "I was sunning myself above here after playing by the waterfall and pool by the top. I followed the sound of your flute until I found you."

"After all," she continued, "the song you were playing is an old ballad from the other side of the mountain, so I assumed you were also from there." She added, "Usually I stay near the top, but I followed the sound of your music."

I was astounded by her casual talk of the other side, and asked her, "Will you show me the spot you described?"

She agreed, saying, "Meet me in this same spot for the sunrise tomorrow morning," and then she disappeared into the trees.

The walk back to my cottage was not a walk, for I literally floated back, and the path was always lit even in the forest. The melodies stayed with me throughout the whole evening. I prepared my knapsack for the climb in the morning, and went to sleep early.

That night I had the most unusual dream. I dreamed that I was floating on a lake looking up into the royal blue sky. I felt lightheaded from the heat, but I was certain that as I watched the sun set in the east that another sun was rising in the north.

As the second sun climbed into the cloudless sky, the mercury rose making the lake steam around me. Then I saw a mirror image of myself in the sky above me. My mirror called me to join the water in its exodus, and come into the sky. There was no question really of staying anyway, for the lake was evaporating quickly. With my eyes wide open I committed to the sky, but asked "How?" My reflection answered for me to know within myself that I was as light as the air.

Soon I began to fly. I realized there were air currents just like in the water in which I had initially been floating. As I soared above the earth, I felt the stars like a blanket. Venus was the brightest in the sky and shone like a guide.

I was jolted awake suddenly, and checked to make sure it was still dark for I wanted to be prompt to meet the young woman who was to show me the way over the mountain. I sprang out of bed with anticipation for the day ahead, and decided to get an especially early start. The thoughts of the dream stayed with me as I hiked into the hills to meet the person I intuitively thought of as my new friend.

As I approached she was there waiting, and waved for me to follow her before I could reach her. The climb was steep and arduous, but I gained strength and covered great distance in no time. Whenever we approached spots that appeared to be certain dead ends, a small jump or narrow crevice would lead to a path so we could continue up the mountain.

At one point I stopped and looked down for a moment. The town was miles away and looked like a tiny dot on the blue water. I could tell that the water was actually a huge lake, and that a hundred miles out was another side with hills and mountains too. When I turned to say something, I realized my friend had disappeared from sight. I took a few steps, and then happily heard her voice singing, and what sounded like running water.

Chapter 16

I woke up to the sound of Anna's singing. The sun was coming in the window, and I looked around to see where I was. In a moment I knew I was at the farm in Washington and realized I was hearing Anna outside.

I threw on a robe and wandered into the kitchen to look for Sam.

Sam was sitting at the table writing what appeared to be an outline for something. She got up and greeted me with a big hug.

"What are you working on? It looks like you've been at it for a while."

"Yes. While you were sleeping there have been a lot of changes in the works."

"I feel that way too. I want to tell you my dream while it is still fresh in my mind. I especially want your insight into the dream I had within my dream."

Sam said, "Go in the other room, and write down all you can remember. Do not mention the dream to anyone yet, not even me. Only when you know what it means to you, and how it answered your question will it be appropriate to share the dream.

"And, when you come out, I'll fill you in on my and every one else's stuff."

"You're a wise soul," I said turning right around to do as Sam instructed.

I went back to our bedroom and sat down with my journal. The soft morning light filled the room as I sat to write my thoughts. I started a new entry:

I believe my journal is one reason I am able to observe and appreciate the richness Sam brings to my life. By processing the information as it is happening, I become conscious of the ramifications of the majority of my choices. I know my acknowledgement of who and what is in my life, and why, is an opportunity showing me the value and nature of all presented to me. And, in so doing I have gradually become able to comprehend the significance of the decision tree process and proactively realize the impact of my words, thoughts, and actions. In that way we mirror our learning experiences to each other.

I realize from my dream that every morning I wake up on my mountain top, if that's what I choose. Some years I climb and reclimb the same summit albeit from different approaches. Other years I remain at the base camp, or process what I've already learned. Every once in a while I begin to go over the top.

I love the thought of beginning the game anew, and renewing the process by accepting what each day offers. The amazing realization that every summit of the mountains in my life, no matter how high or great the challenge, is only a foothill to the next mountain.

Truly there is only going ahead. Even if any of us think we have stopped or stayed in the same place, the mountain is always changing. We are shaken just to keep the foothold we already have in life.

The good news is this: going up is actually easier than going down anyway. The key is to have left a smooth and honorable path for any one who follows. Only then will it be possible to prevent the need for retracing steps to shore the foundation and strengthen the support already achieved.

Without support, moving forward on an already fragile branch creates imbalance and may dead end. In those cases pushing the pace, or the mountain itself, is not only futile, but may lead to falling down the side precipitating painful repercussions.

Placing one foot in front of the other allows me to appreciate myself and others daily. Then by reaffirming with praise for myself or my climbing partners, there is gratitude and understanding blazing the trail for other friends who select adjoining pathways. Occasionally someone will remark, 'Wow, look how high he made it!'

Simultaneously others are looking back questioning, 'Should we give him a hand up or let him find his own way?'

At the moment the farm in Washington is full of mountain tops. Everyone is making decisions, some more dramatic than others, on how to begin the next ascent. Some will vault into dynamic new changes while others of us are continuing one step at a time on the pathway we have already begun. All of us comprise a network which forms a whole from the parts.'

With each one of us focused on what matters in life, the morning air is alive with energy.

* * *

I returned to the kitchen to make one of my smoothies and Sam was still at the table writing notes.

"What's going on?"

"The farm is abuzz with news from Uncle J and Alex, but I have some of my own."

"Okay," I said. "Where do you want to start?"

"Alex announced that she was not going to return to Columbia, but has decided to stay and work on the farm with Emile. They are planning to learn who they are first as individuals, and then together. Alex did say she intended to attend the University of Washington beginning in the fall, and any further decisions would wait until she graduated.

"Prior to Alex's decision, Uncle J had met with Emile and my parents to inform them he was leaving on a trip of indeterminate length beginning in Japan, and that he was turning the farm over to them, and Alex if she stays."

"Those are some awesome decisions. What about you?

You've been working on notes all morning. Now tell me, Sam, what are you planning?"

"I've decided to begin organizing the camp for talented art students that was part of my initial dream. The part of my business idea still incomplete is to have some of the profits fund a summer arts program like the camps for music. The art students can come to paint and study with professional artists in a creative environment."

"At the farm?"

"Absolutely! Nowhere is as conducive for art as this place. We could set up bunk houses and cottages around a center on an acre at the other end of the orchards. I've even considered how the artist's families could join them to create a connection through sharing it together.

"Alex says the farm is a multi-generation camp anyway. And, my idea is to present a broader scope if Alex and Emile would consider offering programs on organic farming concepts, Aikido, and drama."

Sam paused and looked at me.

As if on cue I added, "And Anna and I could round it out with music workshops.

"It sounds so grandiose and simple all at once. I'm drawn to your enthusiasm. It brings together all the things we love to do, and opens a way to share it with others. I take it the dreamer in you has decided how to do it so you can continue with your recent changes. Is this your way of developing your relationship with Alex, the connection with your family and nature, and me?"

"Precisely! I'll have the rest of the next six months to plan, and this summer we can start small and do a trial run. We could start with about five students, and their families, picked from the schools already contributing art to the auction business."

"After this summer, the program can evolve in its own natural way?" I contributed.

"Indeed, and so can we!"

Epilogue

Picture walking through the temperate rain forest on the Olympic Peninsula in the Pacific Northwest. If you listen closely you can hear the wisdom from the web of ecological systems whispering subtle messages to the surrounding flora about the interdependency of life in nature. A hiker traipsing through, looking only to catch a glimpse of the gangly but graceful elk might not hear it. However, someone with a well-developed sense of curiosity, and a highly developed imagination would hear the plant life dancing to the sound of a New Orleans funeral band. The horns would be celebrating the new life, and anything but bewailing the decomposition of the last parade of plants. Playing for the memory of what were once the lush, vibrant colors of stamens with blossoms, spiraling leaves, and vines that are now decomposing into the earth, becoming nourishment, rich as mother's milk, for their offspring that grow where they once stood.

The old plants are gone, and the next generation lives. They live without judgment of good and bad. Reaching for the sunlight by day, and drinking toasts at night, the plants become inebriated on the water laced with intoxicating nutrients. The lists of ingredients filled with vitamins and minerals could fill a nutritionist's library and go off the charts of the recommended daily allotment from some government agency. Amazingly their world thrives without any government regulation, self-help books, or talk shows. Nature gives them a loving stamp of approval for the inherent wisdom that teaches about the foundation of life.

Each leaf holds secrets of the universe. Observe anything in nature, and a simple understanding will be found. Each does its job, and plays its role perfectly, in spite of being totally self-absorbed. If it didn't show up for work, the hole left would be noticeable, and knock out the balance of the web.

They are not workaholics though. Nor would they consider a life of solitude that a recluse or monk might retire to. And, not one of them is modest or celibate. In fact, the passion poured into their lives is represented by the ultimate in flagrant, sensuous delight to the extent that the birds and bees must work full-time to keep up. This is their responsibility to each other. Going all day at pollinating, being both the hand maiden and the mid-wife to bring life into an environment already teeming with life.

This is wisdom for life from which humans could take a lesson. No, it is not to spend an entire life pollinating everything. That is the job of nature. What nature is expressing, is for humans to learn about loving each other with the respectful wisdom exhibited in nature. Remember the goldenrod rule, "Love your neighbor as you love yourself."

The relationship these lovely creatures exhibit is a harmonious balance that only the Creator could have designed, but no matter how plentiful, they compete selfishly for light and nutrients to survive. Now, you may ask how this model for harmonious living could be based on such blatant egocentric behavior, or even why this seems so important at the moment. Well in a nutshell, humans have the ability to rise above this type of behavior by compassionately supporting each other by engaging in an evolving growth process including loving partnerships.

Just like the flora, many people are primarily driven by self-adventure, and compete on the backs of others. The alternative that humans can choose is to be balanced and to progress, or to choose disharmony and destructive natures. In selecting one of these paths, their intentions are reflected back to themselves, and experienced as either self-destructive behavior or self-love and respect. In a sense, respect nature and you will respect yourself.

People can and will wake up, and then make changes in their lives where respect and companionship, or even altruism are reintroduced into life's decisions. Then energy will be focused toward looking for where to contribute. Working together will replace profiting at other's expense. Humans could take some lessons from nature, and then make improvements.

As in nature, even the most selfish act of independence by people is simultaneously the most selfless act of compassion. The process creates the awareness that forces a decision as to how to proceed consciously to the next adventure in life. Only through the mirroring process of nature will humans understand the stimulus they encounter.

They will also realize their current place in life is the composite and culmination of every step and every thing ever done in one's own sweet life. Then, they will come face to face with the next magic moment, which coincidentally connects perfectly with the webs of others extending from the current point of interaction. And, even though almost everyone else was driven by a self-motivating decision process, it all comes together to intersect with others lives; to be the network that supports life from infanthood to and through maturity.

We were never alone, and although like nature, where each plant seems selfish in its fight to live by growing on another's back, each act of those supporting actors in our lives is truly selfless as it supports its role in the interdependent web of life we call our society. This is the essence of the challenge if we choose to accept. It is to take a step beyond the trillions of imperceptible hows and whys that produced a place for us in society's web of relationships. When we realize the desire to share life experiences with others, we wake up to what we can offer to the world.

About the Author

Ken Friedman is a synergy of Eastern and Western principles, right and left brain, east and west coast, and masculine and feminine awareness. He combines the logical business world with that of a sensitive, romantic philosopher. The words and images of his book give a compelling perspective of the characters as well as what they reveal about the author.

-Karen Seal

In keeping with my life philosophy of balance between Man and Nature The Decision Tree is printed on recycled paper and conservation of resources was considered in all aspects of the publishing process.